Moments

Heart's Desire...or Soul Destroyed

By

Angela Verdenius

(Sci-fi Romance)

Table of Contents

These stories are romances with action, set on distant worlds and in outer space, with a variety of heroes, heroines, and interesting side-characters (funny, good and bad) most of whom later feature in their own books. Not heavy on sci-fi technology, the stories are very much character driven, and so saying the intimacy between the couples range from sweet to hot, depending on the storyline and the characters. Like real people, they are all different.

Though it's a series, each book is a stand-alone story with a different couple.

Oh, and if you're not Australian, you will find some of the spelling different. I'm an Aussie, I spell the Aussie way, so if you think you've stumbled upon an error, it may not be!

Cheers
Angela

A Quick Word

*

Why a book of three short stories, you may ask? Well, basically, this is the book I wanted to do for a long time. This is meant to tie up some loose ends.

Firstly, for all those who have told me that Lysie has been pregnant *forever*, and those who have been dying to know how Marten is coping with his Felys wife's pregnancy and subsequent labour, here is their story in "Love: Marten & Lysie".

Secondly, in case no one has noticed, I accidentally forgot to do a story on a couple who have briefly been seen or heard in earlier books. Davan is a Daamen Head Peacekeeper, and there are obviously issues between him and Delias. Delias is Red's sister, and she was first mentioned in Heart of the Betrayed. She was briefly heard (not seen) in Soul of a Hunter. Davan, the Daamen Peacekeeper, appeared briefly in Soul of a Hunter. I always meant to do their story, but somehow, as the other characters spoke to me and I wrote their stories, Davan and Delias fell by the wayside...*sheepish face*...and then it was too far along the time line to actually have their own book, but I still wanted to do their story! This was my chance, and so their story takes place not long after Soul of a Hunter and is presented in "Heart: Davan & Delias".

Thirdly, Cam & Sabra have always held a special spot in my writing world. I've always wondered how they've managed, and while later books depict them as happily going about their business and lives, I never had the chance to follow them in the early stages of their marriage, to know what they're thinking, their issues, etc. I don't believe the intimacy would be so easy for Sabra. I always believed that Cam had a few hurdles yet to go over for his lass, and Sabra still had some issues of her own. And so I took this chance to delve into their lives a little more and see what's happening to them. Their story follows on from Davan & Delias in "Soul: Cam & Sabra".

This book has been a pleasure to write, even though short stories don't always come easily to me. It's way too easy to head out into space and go further! But these stories are tight, close, and they turned out better than I'd hoped. At least, I think so. I hope you do, too! Please enjoy this little insight into the lives of three couples of the Heart's Desire Soul Destroyed world.

Marten and Lysie

Love – is one ever really prepared for all it entails? Marten thinks so!

Chapter 1

*

Marten awoke to find his wife missing. Again. Propping himself up on one elbow, he sighed at the empty spot beside him. No little feline-type female was curled up purring in the big, comfortable bed. No tortoiseshell hair curled wildly over the pillow to rest against his face and tickle his nose. No cuddly body, now big with child - correction, five kits - was snuggled against him.

Lysie was once again on walkabout, restless and prowling. Since the latter part of her pregnancy, she had gone very nocturnal.

Throwing back the covers, Marten got out of bed and crossed to the big window to peer outside. Nope, no little Felys wench lurked in the flower-laden garden. The full moon shone down brightly to show it empty of all but plants, the graceful table and the big swing chair. That meant one thing, Lysie was prowling the palace or the grounds.

And that meant the other thing; once again he was going looking for her. Lysie prowling around on her own, especially this far advanced in her pregnancy, was something he didn't trust.

Marten pulled on his pants, stamped into boots, and strode from the bedroom while shoving his arms through his silk shirt sleeves, buttoning the front expertly and tucking the shirt tails in neatly. He walked through their apartment and out into the little corridor that led to the main palace corridor.

First he searched the areas he knew were his wife's particularly favourite spots. The kitchen with its sweet offerings was first, but no, the table was bare, though a little pile of crumbs on the clean surface at one end told of a midnight feast of cake. But that could very well have been Katina, too. His leader's equally pregnant wife had as sweet a tooth as Lysie.

The second place he went to was the big balcony overlooking the front of the palace. She wasn't sprawled in one of the big chairs. Nor was she in the main gardens, the library, or the game room.

He didn't pass her in the dimly lit corridors, the palace guards at the front and back entrances to the palace hadn't seen her, and Marten was really starting to get worried as time passed and Lysie was not to be found.

Worry turned to fear and he was ready to rouse every guard in the palace to organise a search party until he glanced through the doorway into the healers' quarters as he hurried past.

"There you are!" Relief steadied his knocking knees and he changed direction to enter the healers' quarters. "Stars, wench, you'll make me old with this wandering habit you've developed."

She didn't answer, just continued to gaze into the gloom beyond.

Coming up behind her, Marten laid his hands on her shoulders. "Lysie? What's wrong?"

Looking down at her, which wasn't hard to do considering the top of her head barely brushed his shoulders, Marten ran his fingers through the thick tortoiseshell hair, baring the tips of her little pointed ears to his gaze. Her ears flicked slightly, acknowledging his presence, but she didn't say anything.

"Lysie?" Concern filtering through him, Marten moved around to stand before her, bending so that he could study her face which was hidden in shadow. "Lykitten? Is something wrong? The babes? Do you need me to get Sarcan or - "

Lysie spat, and even in the gloom he could see the golden flash of her round eyes, the black swirls moving agitatedly through her irises.

"Easy, little lykitten." Slowly, so as not to startle her, Marten reached out to gently cup one rounded cheek, his thumb caressing the soft skin tenderly. Almost immediately Lysie closed her eyes and purred softly, rubbing her cheek against his palm. "Now tell me what's wrong."

Lysie shook her head.

"Something's bothering you." Marten glanced around. "Why are you here? I can get Sarcan - "

In one movement, Lysie's head jerked back and she spat again, her eyes narrowed, her ears flattening against the sides of her head.

Well, that exposed one problem. For some reason known only to his Felys wife, she didn't want the Argon healer around her. Marten couldn't even begin to fathom why. Until this moment she had gotten along quite well with Sarcan.

"I could call for Hanna - "

The growl that came up from his wife's big-bosomed chest would have alarmed a lesser man, but Marten was made of sterner stuff. He'd faced her in her heat, and having survived that dangerous and erotic episode, he figured he could face anything to do with Lysie.

"All right," he said soothingly. "None of the healers." *Yet.* "Are the kits coming? Are you in...?"

"Labour?" Lysie lifted one corner of her luscious lips in a silent snarl. "You can't even say the word."

"Of course I can. Labour. Are you in labour?"

"Don't be ridiculous. Why would I be in labour?"

Marten eyed her warily. *Mood swings. That was a sign of impending birth, wasn't it?* Suns knew, his little wench had been acting odd - odder - than normal lately. "Just a random thought."

"You get the strangest ideas, Marten."

"I'm not the one standing in the healers' quarters at two in the morn."

Lysie got the funniest look on her pretty feline-like face. Her round eyes, tilted slightly at the corners like a lycat's, blinked slowly, the oblong pupils narrowing to slits before enlarging again. The tips of her ears twitched and then those big eyes filled with tears.

It nearly broke Marten's normally sarcastic heart. Reaching out, he gathered her into his arms and cuddled her close. Or as close as he could with her big belly between them.

"It's all right, little lykitten." Trying to tamp down the alarm starting to surge through him, Marten dropped a kiss on top of her head. "Tell me what's wrong and I'll fix it."

"What if you can't?" Lysie sniffed, her voice muffled against his chest.

"I can."

"But what if you can't?"

Fear grabbed him and it took all Marten's will power to keep it from his voice. "Lysie, tell me what's wrong."

"Nothing."

"Nothing? You're standing in the healers' quarters at two in the morn and you're crying. I'd say that's something."

Lysie titled her head back to look up at him. The black swirls in her irises were undulating slowly and her smile was sweet. "I'm pregnant. That makes abnormal normal for me."

The tension seeped slowly from him, but he kept his gaze searching as he met hers. "Just tell me what's wrong."

Her smile faded and she started to pull back. Marten refused to relinquish her, keeping his hold gentle but firm.

A low growl rumbled in her throat.

"Hiss and spit all you want," he said in the reasonable tone that he realized too late was the same one he used to annoy her. He immediately changed tone but going by the scowl that creased her smooth brow, it was too late.

Lysie was annoyed.

Tough. The little chit was going to answer him.

Then that plump bottom lip started to tremble and he was lost. Almost. It was hard, but he managed to keep his compassion and love in control and take a firm stance.

A very shaky stance, but a stance nonetheless.

"Tell me," he pressed. "Tell me why you're standing here and spit every time I mention Sarcan or Hanna's - there, spitting like that. What is that about?"

A slow flush graced her cheeks. "Sorry."

Marten's brown arched up in surprise. "Sorry?"

With a sigh, Lysie laid her hands on his arms and looked up

at him, her expression so troubled it tugged at his heartstrings. Again. "I know they're your friends."

"They're your friends, too. Or so I thought."

"They are. I just..."

He waited, and when she simply continued to look troubled, he prodded gently, "You just...?"

"I don't..." She chewed her bottom lip. "Marten, I don't want to birth the kits here."

It took several seconds for the words to sink in, and then Marten blinked. "You don't want to birth them here?"

"No."

"But I thought you were happy here?" Disbelieving, he stared down at her.

"I'm not. I hate this place."

The words cut right into him. "You hate it?"

"Yes."

"Even though I'm here?"

"It makes no difference whether you're here or not. I hate this place."

Stunned, he could only stare at her. *She wasn't happy here? She hated the place?* "I don't understand, Lysie."

"See? You can't fix it. You can't fix everything!" And she burst into tears.

Part of him was still stunned, the other part already forming soothing words. Her statement rang through him even as he rubbed her back comfortingly. He didn't understand, couldn't even begin to fathom it. She'd seemed so happy, laughing and living here with him, planning for the future of their kits. Now she cried like her heart would break.

It was killing him. His first instinct was for her, even though he couldn't imagine leaving Argon. Letting her leave him.

"By God, no!" He whispered fiercely. "You're not going back to Scytha without me!"

"What?" Lysie sniffled.

"I said…nothing."

She lifted her head once more to look at him, her cheeks wet with tears. "What do you mean I'm not going back?"

"No, no, it's all right. You're going back, I'll see to it."

"What?"

"Back to Scytha. We'll go back to Scytha." Marten tried to smile reassuringly, even as his mind still battled to come to grips with the horrible turn of events.

"Back to Scytha?" She wiped her cheeks with the sides of her hands in a movement reminiscent of their pet lycats.

"I'll arrange it first thing in the morn. I'll have to tell Kiile... oh God, Kiile..." Marten shook his head. "He'll understand, he... I don't know... Lysie, I don't know if I can just leave him. I'm his bodyguard. But I... of course we'll go..." He was rambling and knew it, but couldn't stop himself.

"By Jocat, Marten, what are you on about?" Frowning, Lysie shoved back out of his arms.

"You hate it here."

"Yes."

"So I'll take you back to Scytha... only, I don't want... But I'll have to..." How was he going to tell Kiile?

"Why would I want to go back now?" Lysie rubbed her forehead. "You're giving me a headache, Marten."

Not as bad as the one she was giving him. "Where do you want to go, then? If you hate it here so much?"

"Our bedroom."

Marten blinked. "Pardon?"

"I want to go to our bedroom."

It was his turn to rub his forehead. "But you just said you hate the place."

"I never said I hated our bedroom." She gave him a bemused look. "My pregnancy is really weirding you out, isn't it? Maybe you should get Sarcan - " she spat once, "to give you a check up."

Marten flapped one hand. "Stop. Let's back up."

Folding her arms atop the mound of her belly, Lysie turned a concerned expression on him. "Of course. What troubles you?"

"Troubles me? I'm not troubled."

"You couldn't string two sentences together a minute ago."

"That's because you..." Seeing her pupils slit, Marten stopped, took a deep breath and said slowly, "Let's start again."

"That might be safer." She added just loud enough for him to hear, "For you."

He ignored the little dig. "Right. You said you hate it here."

"Yes."

"So you'd be happier in Scytha?"

"Why Scytha?"

"Why the bedroom?"

She stared at him. "I'd have thought that was obvious."

"Obviously not."

"This place is so cold and clinical."

Marten was astounded. "Cold and clinical? Argon is known for its sensual, sexual people, the heat of lovemaking, the burst of colour in the plants, the blueness of our skies, and the friendliness of our people towards each other. How could you think we're cold and clinical?"

Lysie started to grin.

Marten didn't think it was that funny, and annoyance started to creep through him. "Listen, wench - "

"You dill! I meant this place." Still grinning, Lysie swept her hand around to indicate the room. "The healers' quarters."

"The healers' quarters," Marten repeated.

"Yes! The healers' quarters are too cold and clinical." Leaning forward, Lysie reached up and patted his cheek lovingly. "Poor baby. Did you really think I didn't want to birth our kits on Argon?"

Relief was pouring through him. "I thought - "

"Well don't. You'll pull a muscle."

"I'm not surprised. With you I'm always working overtime."

"Just keeping you on your toes, sex god."

Leaning down until his forehead was resting against hers, Marten looked deeply into her eyes and said softly, "I haven't had a sane moment since I met you."

Lysie grinned widely.

It didn't take much manoeuvring to tilt his head and take her lips, swallowing the gurgle of merriment that was almost about to escape her. He swept in, his arms going around her to draw her closer as he took possession of her mouth, his amusement and relief turning quickly to ardour as her scent and taste filled his senses.

This was where she should be, in his arms, by his side, driving him insane. Right where she was now.

Heat swept through him as it always did when she filled his senses, but it was interrupted by something nudging him. Lifting his head, he looked down into Lysie's eyes, seeing the glow of heat within be replaced with a twinkle of merriment.

"Am I being kicked by a feisty Felys kit?" he asked.

"Half Felys, half Argon," she corrected him. "And it would be the Argon half kicking you."

Warmth of a different kind swept through him and he laid his palm gently upon her belly, his forehead once more coming to rest against hers. Beneath the nightgown he felt the ripple in her hard belly, the movement of a tiny foot or hand. His son or daughter.

"Here." Taking his hand, Lysie drew it to the other side of her belly. "Another one is awake." She started to purr, low and soft.

He could feel the kick and as he slid his palm further down, he felt something roll beneath his hand. Marten couldn't help but wonder at the miracle of it all.

Their miracles.

Soon their miracles would see the light of day, and it was both frightening and exhilarating.

"So..." Lysie looked him right in the eyes.

Still feeling the movement beneath his hand, Marten met her gaze and smiled. "So?"

"I want to birth the kits the way we do on Scytha."

"In our bed."

"Yes."

"With your own healers."

"Yes. Can I?"

Reaching up, he brushed her little chin with his thumb, a wave of tenderness going through him. "You're the boss."

A sparkle lit her eyes. "Really?"

"No, you're not the boss. Yes, our kits will be born in our bed."

"Huh. You sure I'm not the boss?"

"Positive."

"But you'd do whatever I asked."

"Within reason." He just knew she was going somewhere with this.

"Marten?"

"Yes?"

"Can we go for a walk outside?"

"What if I said no?"

"I'd just wait until you were asleep then I'd get up and go."

"I thought so." Taking her hand, Marten dropped a kiss onto her lips and gave her belly a gentle rub before straightening up. "Let's go, lykitten."

As they walked out the door, she snuggled against his arm and smiled whimsically up at him. "It must be good to be the boss."

"You'd know," he said dryly.

"You'll make a wonderful father."

"Never a doubt in my mind."

~ * ~

"I'd make a terrible father."

Kiile looked up from the viscomm screen. "What?"

Marten turned from the window where he'd been watching Lysie lying in the sun. Katina was sitting in the shade reading, one hand absently patting her rounded belly. "Or I would if I wasn't so prepared."

"Prepared?" Eulie asked from his prone position on the sofa.

"Prepared," Marten affirmed.

"What, did you study up on it?" Eulie opened one eye.

"Of course." Marten eyed him as his friend started to smirk. "I'm always prepared."

"Oh yes, you were well prepared when Lysie came along."

"Lysie was an unexpected... surprise."

"That's an understatement."

"But I got her in hand."

"And pregnant."

"One of my finer accomplishments." Marten sat down in one of the chairs. "And now I'm fully prepared for fatherhood."

"You don't say?" Leaning back in his chair, Kiile folded his arms and eyed him with amusement.

"You haven't studied any of that literature that Sarcan gave us, have you?"

"I had a cursory glance. I rather thought I'd just wing it."

Poor, deluded fool. "You can't just wing it, Kiile."

"Really?"

"Kiile probably can," Eulie said. "You, Marten, probably can't."

Kiile raised one brow. "What's the difference?"

"You're having a normal babe. Marten, on the other hand, is having half Felys, half Argon babes." Eulie opened one eye again and looked at his friend. "You've spent ages talking to Rilla and Marx both on the viscomm and when they've visited. I bet you saved the conversation and have read it many times, studying it up."

"I'm prepared." Taking up the mug of hot una, Marten took a sip and eyed his friend. "Being prepared is being one step ahead of anything."

"Ah, now, you see, babes and mothers don't come according to text."

Vastly entertained, Kiile pushed his chair back, kicked his booted feet up onto the desk, crossed his ankles, and put his linked hands behind his head. "Is that right?"

"Of course." Eulie gave a little yawn. "Any fool knows that."

Marten raised one brow coolly.

"See, I have many brothers and sisters," Eulie continued, blithely disregarding his friends' shared amused glances.

"You're number two in a family of four boys and three girls," Marten said. "So that makes you an expert?"

"I've seen my mother through five pregnancies. Trust me, that makes me expert enough to tell you that babes and mothers do not follow text completely."

Marten leapt on that statement. "Fine, I'll give you that. But they do follow text in most things."

"Pfft." Eulie flicked his fingers lazily. "Piddling details. The general birth is the same, but the reactions and the babies' behaviours are all different."

"I'm getting confused," Kiile said. "Are we talking the actual birth or after?"

"Mostly after, though the birth reactions can all be a bit different. For example..." Holding up his hand in the air, Eulie started to tick off his fingers with each point he made. "One: some wenches are controlled during birth, some are angry with their partners for putting them there, and some cry."

"Angry?" Marten echoed. "Ridiculous."

Eulie smirked knowingly.

"I didn't put her there alone," Marten continued. "Lysie is half to blame."

"Trust me, when she's trying to birth a babe and pain is rolling over her, someone is going to get the blame and it won't be her."

Marten scoffed.

Kiile grinned.

"You'll see." Eulie ticked off another finger. "After the birth, she'll be all loving and oohing and aahing over the new addition. New additions, in your case, Marten."

Marten smiled smugly and Kiile rolled his eyes.

"Three: now comes the sleepless nights and night feeds and things."

"Lysie's such a nocturnal creature right now, she'll be fine with that." Feeling very well done by, Marten leaned back and rested his ankle over his opposite knee.

Eulie just smiled knowingly. "And then those ankle biters start pooping and yelling, and the wenches will be tired and any sex you know of will go right out the window for awhile. Could be a long, long, looooong time."

"You just made that 'looooong time' up." Kiile grinned. "No Argon wench can go without love making that 'looooong'."

"True. But then," Eulie looked slyly at Marten, "You're wed to a Felys. It could be a looooong time before you ever have sex again."

That thought hadn't actually occurred to Marten. He frowned, trying to remember if Rilla had said anything about sex after the birth period. Oddly, he couldn't remember the Felys healer saying anything about sex.

Kiile started to laugh.

The mirth was dancing in Eulie's eyes.

"I have more on my mind than sex," Marten snapped.

"Such as trying to handle five energetic Felys kits." Eulie switched his gaze to Kiile. "And I don't know why you're looking so supremely happy. Katina isn't an Argon wench, in case you've forgotten. So you could be waiting a looooong time before you ever get into a cosy position with her again."

That wiped the smile off Kiile's face. He stared at Eulie, then gave a sudden laugh. "You're an arse."

"Just telling it like it is." Settling himself back into the soft cushions, Eulie closed his eyes and rested his linked hands on his chest. "Just telling it like it is. From experience."

"One day, Eulie," Marten said dryly, "You'll be sitting where we are now, and then we'll see who has the last laugh."

"Meanwhile, I'll be making love to comely wenches while you two reacquaint yourselves with your hands." A truly peaceful smile crossed Eulie's face. "And no wench has ever caught me, or is likely to. Would take a very special wench."

"Oh?"

"Refined, sweet, ready to run after me and fetch and carry, acknowledge me as her lord and master. Nothing less will do."

"Odd," said Kiile. "That's just what Marten thought."

"What? Me?" Marten glared at him. "What about you?"

"I never actually thought about what I wanted in a wife—"

"Snarch shit you didn't," Eulie said. "You once wrote down a list, remember?"

"When I was fifteen!"

"Beautiful, tall, slim, red hair, sweet tempered, and obedient. And what did you end up with?"

"Katina." Kiile smiled dreamily, his boyishly handsome face even more boyish, as though still an adolescent facing his first crush.

"Total opposite to your dream wench."

"Cute, round, soft, sweet - "

Marten snorted in disbelief.

"Kat is my dream wench." Kiile's smile got even sloppier, which Marten just couldn't fathom. The golden-haired sprite was an annoying little piece, of whom he had grown fond, admittedly, but…

"And as for you," Eulie grinned. "Marten, whatever happened to your tall, blonde, cool piece of wench-hood dream?"

"Lysie is all the wench I want or need."

"Definitely different to cool and calm."

"She's my life," Marten replied simply.

"See," said Eulie. "That will never happen to me. I know what I want and I go after it. I've seen how whipped you two have become."

Marten snorted.

Grinning, Eulie closed his eyes and resumed his relaxed position.

"The poor fool doesn't know what he's missing," Kiile remarked.

"No idea what he's talking about," Marten agreed. "When he experiences it himself, I'll be the first one laughing."

"Think what you will," Eulie said airily. "But I do know

pregnant wenches and new mothers and, my friends, that's what you two have. You should listen to me."

"I should stick my head in barrel and ask a Daamen trader to hit it," Kiile returned. "The day I listen to you, Eulie, will be the day it rains babies."

The smile on Eulie's face grew bigger, and he opened one eye and speared Marten with a knowing look. "It'll be raining babes for Marten very soon. What does that tell you, my friend?"

"That you're an idiot," Marten replied. But deep inside he was starting to think he better have another chat with the Felys' healers. It turned out he didn't know quite as much as he should know.

Chuckling to himself, Eulie closed his eyes.

"The man's an idiot." Kiile assured Marten while removing his feet from the desk and sitting upright. "And as much as I'd like to continue this lively debate, I have work to do. Unlike some." He cast his prone friend a glance.

"I'm here as always, guarding your arse." Eulie waved his hand.

Kiile rolled his eyes.

Marten was wondering how long before he could sneak away to contact the Felys' healers without Eulie knowing it.

Chapter 2
*

Lysie felt warm all over, all over and throughout her body. And it didn't have anything at all to do at the moment with the five kits inside her moving around, impatient to come out into the world.

It had everything to do with Marten.

"She's my life." Those three simple words she'd overheard while passing Kiile's office just made her go all gooey inside. She felt like jumping Marten's bones right then and there, but two things prevented her. One, she was heavily pregnant and just getting around some days was a challenge. Two, she wasn't into voyeurism. But boy, was Marten in for a erotic surprise once she'd recovered from her pregnancy. Had the silly boy forgotten she came from a highly sexual breed?

Laughing to herself, she wiggled her toes in the sunshine and contemplated the view outside the bedroom window. Their private garden was bursting with flowers and colours, day fliers and butterflies flitting amongst the tree trunk of the big tree in the corner. It was a garden that would soon know the scurrying of tiny, furred feet.

The laughter died from her lips but a small smile remained. A slightly troubled smile. She smoothed her hand over her rounded belly and contemplated it thoughtfully.

She loved her kits. Once they came out, she was going to love them to pieces, nuzzling them and rubbing her cheek against their little furry heads. Kissing them. Feeding them, seeing to their needs. Sharing them with Marten. But one thing troubled her...

"Lysie?"

Looking around, she smiled as Marten entered the bedroom. Here came her own sex god, his cool grey eyes warming at the sight of her, his calm face exuding a little worry as he crossed the room, his black boots sinking into the luxurious carpet. His grey jacket with the silver epaulettes and grey pants hugged a tall, muscular body that made her mouth water just thinking about it. The man was sex on two legs, testosterone plus, hair as black as ink, eyes as cool as winter, and a face so sinfully handsome it made her heart skip a beat every time she saw him. Knowing she was the only one who could run her fingers through that neat hair and muss it up, touch that warm skin and feel it grow hot under her fingertips, hear his heartbeat fasten up when he touched her, made her feel loved.

Powerful, true, and loved. She grinned.

"I'm not sure if I should be relieved or worried when you smile like that." Marten sat down on the window seat.

As usual, not one crease marred his perfectly fitting uniform. She nudged his thigh with her toe.

Those firm, very masculine lips curved into a smile, his whole countenance relaxing as he took her foot into his lap, settling himself back against the wall and proceeding to gently massage her arch.

Involuntarily, a purr burst from Lysie and she arched back against the wall, her fingers digging once into the cushion before she proceeded to knead the silk in bliss as Marten stroked her foot.

"So, little lykitten." He ran his thumb firmly along the top of her little foot, "What are you up to today?"

"Sunning myself. Lazing about." She purred.

"So I see."

"Want to join me?"

"I would but duty calls. I'm going out shortly with Kiile to walk through the settlement, check in with the people."

"He's so dedicated for a leader."

"Argons are like that." Marten ran his palm under her calf, trailing his hand higher, making her senses spin as his eyes grew a little hot. "Dedicated."

"Oh boy."

"Very dedicated."

He raked his nails lightly around the back of her knee.

"By Jocat!" Lysie nearly went boneless.

Marten laughed, coming up on his knee to lean over and drop a kiss onto her lips. She would have gladly turned it into something longer and a lot hotter, but he drew back before she could do so. Looking into her eyes, he grew serious. "What troubles you, lykitten?"

"Huh?"

"I know." He touched his nose to hers. "Tell me." She didn't want to worry him, but as usual he was attuned to her feelings. "Share with me, Lysie." His smile was faint, but his gaze was steady. "We're in this together, remember?"

They were, thank Delcat. But still, he was so happy, so proud at the idea of becoming a father. Lysie glanced away, her happy mood dimming.

"Lysie." Her name was a warm breath puffed against her ear as Marten skimmed his cheek slowly along her own. "If its Sarcan and Hanna worrying you, don't be. They understand and will simply be within calling distance if your own healers need them. They're not offended."

"I know. I spoke to them." Lysie met his concerned gaze as he drew back to look at her again. "It's not that."

"Then what?"

"Marten, what if one of the kits is a runt? Like me?"

"We'll love it as much as the others. They're all our kits."

"What if... what if it doesn't make it?"

He framed her cheek with one big palm, rubbing his thumb tenderly along her cheek as his gaze softened even more. "He or she will have the best medical intervention in the universe. We will do what we can, and if the worse happens, then we'll just love him or her until the time comes."

She rubbed her cheek against his palm, drawing strength from his steady gaze. "And then..?"

"We'll be there for our kit right up until the end."

She couldn't stop the tear that spilled over her lashes and down her cheek.

Marten caught the tear on his thumb and brushed it away.

"And we'll cry and mourn and never forget it, it will forever be in our hearts, and we'll be together again one day. But Lysie..."

"Yes?" She sniffed.

He smiled faintly. "There may be no runt. Our kits all might very well be born strong and hearty. There has been nothing showing in the tests."

"But - "

"I understand your fears, and I share them."

That surprised her. "You do? You don't show it."

"Of course I worry. I worry about your health and those of our babes. But I refuse to worry about something that may not happen, and if it does, then we have a plan all ready. Meanwhile, my little lykitten, I'm enjoying my last hours alone with you."

The man took her breath away with his commonsense and love. "Oh, Marten..."

"Call me sex god."

She hiccupped a laugh. "Oh, sex god."

"That's it." He dropped another kiss lightly onto her lips. "Now shake those blues, Lysie, and concentrate on the positives. You have five of our babes inside you, and they'll have the best of care and the best of parents. They'll know love, and they'll know what it means to be a responsible Argon - "

"Felys."

"Argon/Felys. Maybe we should shorten that to ArFel?"

"Why not FelAr?"

"Because I'm the boss."

Lysie laughed outright.

His frown was anything but serious. "Which means some respect, wench."

"Or what?" She leaned closer to nibble at his chin. "You'll punish me?"

"You might think yourself safe from that, sex lykitten." His voice was a low growl. "But soon those kits will be born and when you've recovered enough... let's just say revenge is sweet."

"I'll hold you to that." She winked.

"You are so evil." He kissed her again, a little deeper, a lot more hungrily.

Lysie was more than willing to go with that flow of thought and sensations, but Marten broke away, standing up to run one hand through his normally neat hair, the only sign apart from his hot eyes that he was having a hard time reigning in his instincts.

Lysie simpered up at him and then licked her lips slowly.

Marten groaned and swung around. "I have to go. And I mean now!"

"Good thing you're the boss!" she called after him as he strode over to the door. "You can keep us on the straight and narrow, it being your responsibility and all!"

Right before he went from sight she heard his muttered, "Yes, good thing. Damn it."

Feeling vastly happier, Lysie leaned back in the window seat and resumed watching the day fliers and butterflies while she stroked her belly.

When one little foot or hand - she really wasn't sure which it was, heck, it might have even been a pert little behind - hit her hand, she laughed softly. Maybe one of the kits would be a runt, it was a possibility, but whatever happened, she and Marten together would ensure the kits would have all the care and love they could give them. The kits would be a part of herself and a part of Marten, and together these beloved kits bound them into a much larger family.

~ * ~

Entering the apartment to inform Lysie of the latest development, Marten eyed the bed in resignation.

The normally neat covers were scuffed into a rough circle, the covers fluffed up and, basically making a snug nest. It appeared that Lysie was well and truly into nesting mode. It certainly wasn't the first time he'd come in to find their neat bed fluffed into a 'nest'.

The first time he'd caught Lysie doing it, he'd asked her what she was doing, to which she'd looked askance at him and replied, "What?"

"What are you doing to our bed?"

"Nothing."

"You're messing it up."

Well, that sentence had produced a hurt look. "You don't think it looks cosy?"

Marten looked at the fluffed up cover. It looked messy. He looked back up and saw the tremble of her bottom lip. "I think it looks exceptionally cosy, little lykitten." Rounding the bed, he drew her gently into his side with one arm and kissed the top of her head. "I'm just a little confused."

Tilting her head back, Lysie smiled up at him. "I'm nesting."

"Nesting."

"Yes, nesting."

Ahhhh, nesting. Of course. Now he remembered Rilla, the Felys healer, telling him about the instinctual nesting of a Felys wench. The closer they got to the birthing time, the more they started nesting, trying to make their bed and home cosier.

Just another weird but interesting phase. He smiled down at her expectant face. "It looks extremely cosy, lykitten."

With a pleased little *mew*, she snuggled up to him, laying her head against his chest and purring softly as he rubbed her gently behind her pointy little ears.

Looking down at the once-neat bed, Marten sighed inwardly and then smiled. His neat, perfect apartment was definitely cosier. Having Lysie in it made it cosy. Her extra little touches made it cosier. Her nesting instinct made their bed messier, and he really did prefer it neat, but if it kept his lykitten happy...

He eyed the cover and his smile widened. The nesting instinct. How motherly it sounded, how domesticated. When he thought of his little feral Felys in her dangerous heat phase, he'd never have pictured her nesting like a little plump house lycat. It just intrigued him further.

Crossing to the window seat, he leaned his hands on the window sill and peered out to see his wife relaxing back on the swing chair, her arms flung back over her head and her legs inelegantly sprawled out as she used the toe of one slippered foot to rock the swing. A butterfly fluttered overhead and she lazily batted at it with one hand. The sun shone full on her, and even from where he stood he could hear her blissful purring.

"Lysie," he called.

Immediately she pushed to her feet and came over to the window, an impish light in her golden eyes. "Yes, sex god?"

"Glad you know your place."

"Under you, on top of you, kneeling before you. Lots of places." She winked.

Manfully ignoring the tightening of his loins, Marten chucked her under her chin, watching in amusement as she stretched her chin out and purred, her eyes going all dreamy as he gently ran his nails along the tender skin under her chin. "I'd gladly take this conversation further but duty calls."

The endearing little pout she gave made him want to kiss her senseless. Lysie moved her head, rubbing her cheek along his hand. "Duty."

"Yes, duty." He rubbed his thumb along her cheekbone. "I'm heading out with Eulie to a nearby settlement to deliver something for the settlement leader there from Kiile. I'll be gone about half a day."

Her eyes widened in dismay. "Half a day?"

"Only half a day." He assured her. "Unless you feel as though you're going into labour? If so, there's no way I'll go -"

Lysie placed her palm against his mouth. "Of course you have to go. You have your duties, Marten, I know that. I wouldn't interfere in it."

He nipped her fingertips and she withdrew them with a darkening of her eyes. Hoo boy, his little wench still ran hot.

—

Marten ran his hand down her sun-kissed arm. "Are you sure?"

"Yes. You've been so patient and good to me with this pregnancy and little things." She laughed suddenly, her eyes dancing. "I know the nesting threw you, and I know you nearly had a heart attack when you thought I wanted to go back to Scytha. You've put up with so many new things, and with such good grace that Jonette said she needs therapy just to get over it."

"Jonette is a malicious Reeka. She takes great pleasure in my learning curves."

"I think all your friends do."

"Ah, friends, what would we do without them?"

Her eye softened. "What would I do without you?"

He could feel his heart melt all over again. Suns, he'd never thought he'd ever get so sloppy, but Lysie brought out his tender side, something no one else ever had done. "You're mine, Lysie. There's nothing I wouldn't do for you."

"That's so sweet." She smiled up at him. "In that case, you won't object to me coming?"

He blinked. "What?"

"Can I come with you?"

This was unexpected. He knew she'd become a little clingier lately, staying near him when she could, but he never thought she'd want to leave the palace right now. "Is that wise?"

"Pooh. It's just half a day away."

Marten eyed her swollen belly.

"They need fresh air." Sweetly she smiled up at him. "Please, Marten? I promise to be good. Really."

"You, good?" Marten snorted and grew serious once more. "Lysie, I don't know if this is a good idea or not."

"Please?" Her thick lashes fell over her golden eyes, and when she raised them again the black swirls undulated briskly in the golden depths. "All I'm doing is sitting around sunning myself. I want to spend some time with you. An outing would be fun. Come on, Marten. Kiile won't mind."

No, Kiile wouldn't mind. He often took Katina on trips with him. Marten eyed her swollen belly again. That was his worry. She was so close to birthing.

"Marten," Lysie cooed in a wheedling tone. "I'm not due for days yet. Please?"

He was such a sucker where she was concerned. "All right. But - " He held up one hand when she let out a *merp* of joy. "One twinge of anything even distantly related to labour pains and you tell me. One little weird contraction thingy - "

"Contraction thingy?" Lysie started to laugh.

Ignoring her amusement, Marten continued, "One little thing that doesn't feel right, you tell me and I'll have you back here faster than you can blink. Deal?"

"Of course." She batted her eyes at him. "I'll reward you handsomely for this one day soon."

"You're notching up a lot of debts, lykitten." He winked. "I can't wait to collect."

"I can't wait to pay up." Her pupils dilated. "To the sex god."

"That's me, all right." He dropped a quick kiss onto the tip of her nose. "Sex god and major sucker." *Oops, had he said that aloud?*

"I like when you suck."

God above, his loins were going to catch on fire. Pushing himself back off the window seat, he growled, "Wench, unless you want to waste time with me having yet another cold shower, gather what you need and let's go."

Eyes bright, she replied pertly, "I have all I need... sex god."

"Suns, this trip should be one to remember." Especially if she kept up her teasing mood. *God bless the little sprite.*

He was still having doubts as he, Eulie and Lysie walked to the docking bay. Lysie held his hand and cuddled up to his arm, pressed almost fully against him as they walked. Lately she'd been pressing close against him whenever they stood near each other. She slept with her arms wrapped around him and her body against his. Lysie needed close contact, something Rilla and Marx had assured him was normal.

She wanted Marten close by but knowing he had duties, she tried not to impose upon his work time. Back on Scytha, a Felys couple were almost inseparable as the birthing time drew near.

Both Lysie and Marten had made concessions for each other, accepting the other's ideas and needs, and managed to incorporate them in a way that kept them both happy.

It provided Eulie, Wylin and Kiile with much amusement to see their stiff-necked, proper, regimented friend running around in circles to keep his little Felys wife happy.

Marten didn't care what they thought, just as he didn't care when he saw the amusement in the eyes of many of the Argons they passed, when they saw how Lysie was cuddled up to his arm.

It was a true fact that when it came to Lysie, he was soft. But only with Lysie. With Lysie... he sighed fondly. He was putty in the hands of his little lykitten.

~ * ~

The trip had been fun, seeing a new settlement and meeting new people. But on the flight back home, Lysie became restless. Marten couldn't believe it when she asked him to stop near the river so they could walk for awhile.

"Walk?" He looked askance at her.

"You know, what you do on two legs?"

"Lysie, we'll be home in about four hours."

"Please? Just a small walk?"

Eulie grinned from his chair at the control console.

"Don't say a word," Marten warned him before turning back to Lysie. "Are you having contractions?"

"You think I'd want to walk if I had contractions?"

"Just checking."

"You know, Marten, sometimes you say the strangest things."

"It comes from living with you."

Lysie smiled whimsically up at him while snuggling close,

her hands wrapped around his arm. "Just a little walk? Please?"

Marten rolled his eyes.

"Whipped," Eulie said just loud enough for him to hear.

Marten frowned at him.

"Eulie won't mind." Lysie peeked around his arm at their friend. "Will you?"

"Not at all," he returned cheerfully.

"See?" She rubbed her cheek against Marten's arm. "The river is so beautiful, and it's such a wonderful day. It'll be lovely walking along it."

"Very well."

"Whipped." Eulie chuckled.

"Just get us down to the river." Marten turned back to Lysie. "Now remember, you tell me when you have anything unusual happen."

"When? Shouldn't that be 'if'?"

"Lykitten, with you it's always when, never if."

Eulie laughed outright.

Within minutes the ship had landed a little way from the river and they all disembarked.

It really was a beautiful day. Lysie looked up at the sun speckling through the treetops and then across to the river that swirled lazily by. Several fish jumped out of the water and dived right back in. Day fliers flitted about and chirped.

Holding Marten's hand, she pressed close against his side as they walked. Good bodyguard that he was, he had adjusted early to her clingy ways that made her seek the security of his closeness. As her birthing time grew near, she instinctively wanted him around, close to her, and she sought him out whenever he wasn't busy. It had taken a lot to fight her natural instinct to seek him out at all times but she managed.

Her Argon had given in a lot to her in so many ways. She knew he liked his life orderly, his home neat and tidy, and everything in its place. She kept things neat, too, but lately... well, her maternal instincts were making her do things that weren't so neat, such as nesting. But her beloved sex god, after first being taken aback, was taking it all in stride.

She looked up at him, her gaze lingering on his strong jaw and clean-cut, sinfully handsome features. She loved him so much. Sometimes she still marvelled that he had wed her. That he'd actually fallen in love with her after caring for her through that dark period after Redivac had kidnapped her... She shivered.

Sensitive as always to her moods, Marten looked down at her. "All right, lykitten?"

"Yes." She snuggled a little closer. "Oh, yes."

His expression was tender, his eyes so full of love that... well, yes, she would have jumped his bones then and there if Eulie hadn't been ambling along beside them and she wasn't heavily pregnant. Ah well, there was always later. What a tantalizing thought!

Time passed as Eulie, Marten and Lysie ambled along, chatting and enjoying the surroundings.

Gradually Lysie fell silent and Marten and Eulie continued to talk. Something wasn't quite right. She wasn't sure what, but something... she felt a little tug inside her and rubbed her belly. The kits were active today. Had been active last night, too. She felt a slow roll inside her, a pressure down low.

By Jocat, she'd be glad when these kits were born. For several days now she'd had niggles, and while she revelled in her pregnancy, absolutely loved it, in fact, she was getting tired of being so big.

And then she felt another pressure, a cramping like sensation, and almost involuntarily she pushed with a little grunt.

And felt a little gush of fluid suddenly saturate her panties beneath her long gown. Oops. It didn't take a genius to figure out what just happened.

Chapter 3

*

Lysie came to a halt.

Marten smiled down at her, only to falter when he caught her odd expression. She was biting her bottom lip, her brow furrowed in concentration. "Lysie? Everything all right?"

"Depends what you mean by that," she hedged.

"The babes playing up in there?" Gently, his hand came to rest on her belly. He frowned. She normally felt quite firm lately, but now... now she felt rather tight.

He felt the ripple cross her abdomen under his palm. This ripple wasn't like anything he'd felt before, and then he heard her give a little grunt, she bent over slightly and... *Oh shit!*

"Eulie," Marten said frantically. "How far are we from the ship?"

"We've walked for about an hour or so now." His friend was eyeing Lysie worriedly. "Don't tell me she's in..."

"I think she is." Squatting down so he could look up into her eyes from where she was bent over, her hands now braced on her knees as she panted, he felt panic start to rise. "Lysie? Are you birthing?"

"Not yet," she panted. "But soon."

Damn, damn, damn! Snapping upright, he reached for her. "I'll carry you."

"Too late for that!" She grabbed his hand. "You pick me up now, Marten, and those kits will pop out like fizz from a bottle. They're coming."

"What? Now?"

"They're coming." Lysie's hold on Marten's hand tightened.

He went a shade paler. "Then we have to hurry and - "

"I can't go anywhere."

"Of course you can. Now - "

"I *said*," Lysie growled, "I *can't*."

"You have to," Eulie said.

Lysie snarled at him, her pupils slitting.

"Or not," he added hastily.

"She has to," Marten objected. "Now, Lysie, you need to hold on."

"Hold on?" she glared at him. "I can't just cross my legs to stop them coming!"

"Of course not," he said soothingly. "You just sort of... stop them."

Even Eulie raised his brows at that one.

"Stop them?"

"Yes."

"Just like that?"

"Yes."

"That's going to be a little hard, Marten."

He glanced around, his hand still holding hers tightly. "Eulie, you have to run ahead and - "

"We might need him."

"Of course we don't need him. Eulie - "

"My water just broke."

They all stopped and stared at each other. Marten in shock, Eulie in dismay, Lysie looking mightily pissed off.

Marten rallied first. "It can't have. It's too soon."

"Well, I certainly didn't wet my pants through lack of a toilet." With one hand Lysie lifted her skirts to her knees to show the watery blood on her calves. "Going by the pressure accompanying this little 'accident', I- *ahhhh*!"

Both Marten and Eulie jumped.

"Oh my God!" Marten grabbed her shoulders. "Lysie? Lysie!"

"Contraction," she panted. "Again."

"Again?" Marten looked wildly at Eulie. "Run!"

Eulie hadn't even gone a step before Lysie's hand shot out and grabbed his jacket. "Stay!"

"Lysie, we need help!" Marten must have heard his desperation, because he took a deep, not-quite-calming breath, and said a little calmer, "We need the healers here."

"Then call them on the communicator," she said reasonably.

Mental head slap. "Of course. Stars. Eulie, call them." *Stay calm. Remember what you read. It was... Oh my God, I don't remember what I read.*

"Marten," Lysie started to pant. "I think... I think the first kit is coming."

"Eulie!" Marten roared. "Tell Rilla and Marx to hurry!"

Eulie was practically babbling into his communicator.

"They won't be in time," Lysie informed them both. "Now calm down, both of you."

Eulie shoved the communicator into his pocket. "They're coming."

Lysie gave a low, guttural sound. "I need to lie down." She started to lower herself to the ground.

Panicked, Marten grabbed her elbow. "No! You can't! Lysie, I forbid you to have our kits out here in the forest!"

"Let me go or I'll bite you. Let me- *owwwww*!"

Now they were all on their knees, Marten and Eulie one each side of Lysie while she half reclined back on her elbows and panted her way through the contraction. Marten almost wrung her hand to death while he bit his lip and silently went through his own imaginary contraction with her, the pain on her face making him break out in a sweat of his own.

"First time I've seen that," Eulie managed to say.

"A wench in pain?" Marten gritted his teeth.

"No. A man apparently giving birth as well."

Marten glared at him.

Eulie grinned sheepishly.

"It's coming." Lysie gave another low, guttural growl and started to push.

Marten glanced around wildly then looked at Eulie. Relief spilled over him. "Eulie."

"Yes?" Eulie lifted his partly fascinated, partly horrified gaze from Lysie's face to meet Marten's gaze.

"Help her."

"What?"

"You know about births."

"I what?"

"You told me - " Marten's voice choked off when a small hand knotted in his jacket and yanked him down to Lysie's level.

"Someone," Lysie panted, "has to go down there."

"Where?" Eulie asked, sounding almost scared.

"Down there."

"Oh my God."

Marten looked at him. "What are you hanging around for? Go down!"

Eulie looked really startled.

"I mean, go down there!"

Eulie went tomato red then snow white. He looked down at her. "Lysie, no offense, but if you were single and not about to give birth, I'd happily go down there, but you're married to my best friend and down there isn't one of those places I'd go to with you now."

A small hand shot out, fisted into his jacket and jerked him down nose to nose with Lysie. Sweat ran down her temple as she glared from one man to the other. "Listen to me, Argons. These kits are coming and I can't do this alone. Now someone go down there and start giving bloody directions! Now, damn *iiiiiiit!*" The last ended on a hiss that dropped into another guttural grunt.

Eulie looked desperately at Marten. "I don't know what to do."

"What?"

"I don't know what to do."

Marten stared disbelievingly at him. "You've been through the births of your siblings. You must know."

"I didn't say I was at the actual births." Eulie was trying a reasoning tone but it wasn't working.

Marten didn't feel reasonable or calm. "What the hell are we going to do?"

"You're the one who read all the literature."

Of which he couldn't remember a bloody thing. Bloody

literature.

Lysie snarled, bringing their attention back to her. She glared up at Marten. "If Eulie doesn't know anything about birthing, then you're going down there."

"Pardon?"

"You've seen what's down there, he hasn't."

Well, that was true, but -

"And it's staying that way."

Marten swallowed, feeling as though a huge log was lodged in his throat. Panic threatened to overwhelm him. Then he caught sight of her face. She might have been snarling, but the pain and fear in her eyes were very real.

Around them sounded the day flyers, the river lazily swirling past not far off. The ship was an hour's walk away, the healers were on their way, but even in a fleet craft they would take an hour at least to arrive.

Lysie, Marten and Eulie were on their own.

Marten looked at Eulie. His friend nodded slowly. Marten transferred his gaze down to Lysie. She gazed up at him, anger and fear both warring for supremacy in her eyes. He smiled slowly, trying to look reassuring. Leaning down, he kissed her brow. "We'll do it, lykitten. Don't fear."

He was shit scared enough for the both of them. Eulie didn't look much better, his face was still pale.

Trying to gather his thoughts together, Marten concentrated on taking charge - *huh!* - and shifted from his position at her shoulders, relinquishing her into the arms of Eulie who had shifted behind her. Once he was assured that she was resting comfortably back against Eulie's chest, Marten moved to her feet.

Sweet mother mercy, don't let me faint. Taking a deep breath, he lifted the hem of her skirt and carefully pushed it back to cover her pelvis region. With equal care he removed the ruined panties. Automatically, she bent her knees, her legs parting as she suddenly grunted and pushed, pressing back against Eulie who had his arms around her.

Oh shit! Marten could feel all the blood rush from his head to his feet when he saw something small ballooning at the opening to her body. *It's the... the what? What's it called? Oh God! It's a — a —* "It's a balloon!"

"What?" Both Lysie and Eulie stared at him, Eulie in astonishment, Lysie from a pink-tinged face.

"Nothing. I mean, it's a sac. I see the sac!" He pointed.

"Gosh, you mean down there?" Lysie managed to sound sardonic even when she was panting.

"Sac?" Eulie queried.

Marten nodded. "Yes. Sac. The kits are born in individual sacs, like our pet lycats when they give birth."

"Really?" Eulie's brows rose.

"I read the literature."

"Maybe I need to read it."

"Bit late for that now."

Eulie was about to reply when Lysie stiffened, closed her eyes and started pushing again.

Marten looked between her thighs again. The little sac bulged out more before retreating again. Sitting back on his heels, he glanced at Lysie's face. A trickle of sweat slid down her temple. She opened her eyes and gazed straight into his eyes. He felt love swell through him, as it always did when she looked to him for reassurance. He smiled at her, trying to maintain a calm façade.

In that moment she looked so small and fragile, in pain and straining to give life to their babes. She looked so beautiful, even rumpled and pink-cheeked. Her expression was scared, determined and slightly annoyed all at once.

Eulie looked plain scared. That quickly changed to a pained look when Lysie grabbed his hand and squeezed hard, pushing back against him as another contraction rippled through her.

Give the man credit, he tried to hide his own fear to give her encouragement. "Come on, Lysie, you can do it. Push. Puuush. *Puuuuuuuuuush!*"

If Marten wasn't so frantically ready to play catcher to one of his babes, he would have found it funny. Eulie's expression was almost as pained as Lysie's.

The sac burst suddenly, and the babe slid out into his waiting hands. It lay quietly. Panic burst through him at its stillness, but through his panic he remembered Rilla's words. *If you forget anything, treat the kit like you would a lycat's lykittens.*

Vaguely aware of Lysie's anxious gaze, he placed the babe on his knees and yanked his jacket off. Picking up the tiny babe, he proceeded to rub its nose and mouth briskly, clearing away the mucous. Suddenly it let out a tiny squawk and arched its head back.

Lysie started to purr and Marten made to lay the babe on her belly, but suddenly he stopped.

His babe was lying in his hands. So tiny, so fragile... so wet. He gave it a brisk rub with the jacket, watching as it arched and curled in his hands. Now he could see its little face, so sweet, little eyes shut, little pink mouth opening as it started to mew. It was a third of the size of any baby he'd ever seen, and a fine, fur coat covered it, the colour midnight black.

The little head turned, the face tipping back as it mewled and searched for something. Warmth filtered through him and he lowered his head. The little mouth bunted against his cheek and it was the most natural thing in the world to rub his cheek against the little fuzzy head. The babe mewed and bunted him again.

Love burst through Marten, his heart swelling as he held his babe, and he opened his eyes to meet Lysie's gaze. She smiled up at him, relief on her face, and it didn't take a genius to know what she'd been thinking. Fuzzy babes weren't the norm on Argon. But he'd expected fuzzy babes, and these babes, their kits, were his. His and Lysie's. No one was ever going to harm a hair on their cute, fuzzy, little heads.

Gently he laid the babe on Lysie's tummy, watching as she covered it with one hand, stroking it lovingly. Her expression was so loving and tender, it made a lump swell in his throat.

When she gave a small grunt, the afterbirth slid out and he retrieved the dagger from his belt and cut through it deftly, tying off the end near the babe.

Immediately Lysie picked up the babe - *good God, by the scruff? That wasn't in the literature* - and undoing the buttons of her bodice, she snuggled the babe to one breast. It nuzzled around and latched on.

Feeling Eulie's gaze on him, Marten looked up and smiled in relief. Eulie's colour was a little better and he grinned and held up the communicator. "We're doing everything right."

"What?"

"Rilla is on the other end of the communicator."

He could have done to know that awhile ago. Scowling at Eulie, Marten reached forward and grabbed it from him. Placing it to his ear, he queried, "Rilla?"

"You're doing just fine," Rilla assured him. "We've been listening to everything."

Thank God for that.

A breeze sprang up and Lysie looked worriedly at him. "The kits will get cold. We don't have a box or blankets."

"No problem. Eulie - "

"Sure," Eulie said. "They can have my jacket and shirt."

"No," Rilla said. "Tell him to put the kits down his shirt front, against his skin to keep them warm."

Oh, Marten enjoyed telling his friend that. Eulie, to his credit, looked shocked but meekly did as bidden, especially when Lysie's sharp nails dug into his hand.

No sooner had the protesting babe been slid down the inside of his jacket than Lysie started straining again. It wasn't long before the little sac appeared.

"Balloon?" Eulie guessed when Marten swiped a hand across his damp brow.

The next babe to slide from the shelter of its mother's body was a little cream-furred babe, and it quickly started mewing. Marten couldn't help it. As each babe slid into his trembling, waiting hands and he cleaned them, he nuzzled each and every one, delighting in them, before placing them on Lysie's tummy. Each babe was fed and then placed inside Eulie's shirt against his skin when Lysie felt another contraction.

Everything seemed to happen so quickly, and it wasn't long before all the babes were born, fed, and snuggled warmly against Eulie's body. He moved back to sit beside Lysie, his hands carefully cradling the precious cargo inside his shirt.

Marten took his place behind Lysie, easing her back against his chest. Sliding his arms around her, he looked down to find that she had tipped her head back against his chest and was looking up at him. Smiling down at her, Marten took her hand and leaned down to kiss her brow. Her smile was both exhausted and loving.

The love between them had never been stronger.

"We did it," she whispered.

"We did. And I'm so proud of you, little lykitten."

"We birthed the kits. Together."

"We did." The moment was so tender, he actually had to blink a tear back.

"We sure did," Eulie commented. "And someone forgot to mention that your babes have sharp nails."

Lysie laughed tiredly, and reaching out, she laid her hand against the bulge in his shirt.

That was how Wylin, Kiile, Rilla, Marx, Tera and Sarcan found them when their ship landed nearby mere minutes later.

While Rilla and Marx took charge of the babes, placing them carefully in a heated crib, Marten lifted Lysie carefully into his arms and carried her into the waiting craft.

Arms around his neck, she rubbed her cheek tiredly against his chest and purred. "I love you."

"I love you, too, lykitten."

It was all that needed to be said in that moment.

—

44

While Lysie and the babes were being attended to, Kiile and Wylin studied Eulie.

"You look a little shell-shocked," Kiile commented.

"Pshaw," Eulie replied. "Nothing to it."

"Really?" One of Kiile's brows rose.

"A few instructions and I had Marten on the right track."

"Do tell?" Hands clasped behind his back, Wylin rocked back and forward on his heels, his eyes bright with interest and something else.

"You know me." Eulie shrugged modestly. "Always cool and calm."

"Oh yes. Cool and calm." Kiile nodded thoughtfully.

"Dependable in a crisis," Wylin added.

"Really, it was nothing." Eulie took his shirt off and slipped the jacket back on. "Shirt's ruined by those little mites and their…er…sticky bodies."

"What would they have done without you?" Kiile continued.

"Just lucky I was here, I guess."

"Yes." Wylin grinned widely. "Lucky you didn't have to go *down there.*"

Eulie stilled.

"After all," Kiile said conversationally to Wylin, though his amused gaze remained on Eulie. "It was so considerate of him not to go down there."

Eulie's eyes narrowed suspiciously.

"And he makes such a good birth coach." Wylin shook his head in mock admiration. "Push. Puuush. *Puuuuuuuuuush.*"

"How the hell -?" Eulie began.

Kiile tapped Eulie's jacket pocket. "You left your communicator on."

Eulie was stunned, then he grinned sheepishly.

"Jonette and Katina can hardly wait for your return," Wylin informed him almost gleefully.

That wiped Eulie's grin off. "Just how many heard what

happened?"

"Only those that count. Me. Kiile. The Argon and Felys healers. And Jonette and Katina."

"My life won't be worth living."

"But it made the journey all the more entertaining for us." Laughing, Wylin strode back towards the ship.

Kiile clapped Eulie comfortingly on the shoulder. "Never fear, old friend. I won't be calling you to help with Katina's birthing."

"Thank the stars for that," Eulie replied with feeling.

Once on the ship, Lysie and the babes were settled comfortably at the back, and Eulie relaxed into one of the spare seats near the front. Laying his head back against the headrest, he closed his eyes and blew out a relieved sigh. It was over. The babes were born, Lysie was fine, and thank God his hand was regaining its feeling after being wrung out like a washcloth by Lysie's grip during the contractions.

"Eulie."

At his name being spoken quietly, he opened his eyes to find Marten sitting beside him, his expression serious.

Alarmed, Eulie started to get up. "Lysie?"

"She's fine. They're all fine."

Relaxing back against the seat again, Eulie smiled. "Good. So, how are you feeling… Dad?"

"Scared to death."

"Bit late for that now."

Marten laughed, Eulie joining in, but then his friend grew serious again.

"Eulie, I want to thank you. We both want to thank you."

Uncomfortably, Eulie shifted. "I didn't do anything."

"You did. You were there for us."

"I didn't know a thing, Marten. I was just there."

The normally cool grey eyes studying him grew warmer. "Yes, you were there. You supported my lykitten while she birthed our babes. You were with me. You sheltered my babes against your own body. Eulie - "

"If this is going to get any sloppier - "

"Eulie, you were there for us." Marten smiled at him. "Nothing sloppy about it. I know you, you don't like people to thank you for anything you did that you believe was right."

"It wasn't like we had much choice," Eulie pointed out.

Marten gave a bark of laughter. "Lysie never leaves anyone with much choice."

"She did catch us by surprise."

"Anyway..." Marten met his gaze intently. "Together we got through it, Eulie."

Eulie smiled slightly. "We did."

"I won't ever forget it, nor will Lysie."

"That's what friends are for." Eulie waved his hand nonchalantly. "And being my friend, you know I hate this kind of thing. Gratitude and such, especially when we both know I wasn't a huge amount of help."

"Without you we'd have had a harder time." A tiny mewling sound filtered through the cabin and Marten stood abruptly. "That's one of the babes. I have to go. But Eulie..." He looked down at his friend. "I won't ever forget what you did for us."

The mewling got louder and Eulie grinned. "You better go...Dad."

Marten looked a little scared for several seconds, which made Eulie grin widely, and then his expression changed to one of pride when the mewling reached a full scale squeal. "I better go see what the kit wants."

"Whipped," Eulie said to himself as his friend walked to the back of the ship. "And loving it." Chuckling to himself, he leaned back in the seat and closed his eyes.

Birthing babes was a tiring business.

~ * ~

Two weeks later...

*

It was late when Marten entered his apartment. He moved quietly, knowing that Lysie would be in bed and the kits would be asleep. Unbuttoning his jacket, he moved almost silently down the corridor, heading for his bedroom, but as he passed the room just before it, he automatically turned into it and entered the room.

A soft light shone dimly in the corner and he crossed to the big cot that stood on the floor of the room. It was on the floor because it appeared that Felys kits started moving around a lot earlier than Argon babes, and going by how these half Felys, half Argon babes of his were doing, they would be following the Felys trait in that particular area.

Standing by the cot, he gazed down at his slumbering babes, feeling the familiar warmth and love well up at the sight of them. They cuddled in a little pile, and he didn't attempt to untangle them, knowing they slept that way. Another Felys trait.

Sort of like the way their mother cuddled up to him.

Resting his arms on the top rail of the cot, he studied his babes. Five wee wenches. God save him, he was going to have his hands full later on. They were so beautiful now, he couldn't even begin to imagine what they'd be like when they grew old enough to capture the attention of the young Argon and Felys men.

Well, by God, those men had better not come sniffing around his little wenches when he wasn't in the vicinity. Or Eulie, their godfather.

Poor Eulie, Marten thought he'd pass out when he'd been informed that he'd been chosen to be the kits' godfather. The expression on his face had been a mixture of feelings — pride, happiness, and definitely terror. Mostly terror at the thought of being godfather to five wenches. It had given Wylin, Jonette and Kiile plenty of fodder to torment Eulie for the rest of his natural life.

Grinning to himself, Marten studied his babes. They were a fascinating little litter. Most of their fine fur had almost disappeared, that was obviously due to being half Argon, but they retained their little pointed ears. Their eyes were now open, and even though they weren't round with slight tilts at the end like his beloved Lysie and her species, they retained the black swirls that undulated swiftly as the babes took interest in everything. Three of them had the multi-coloured hair of a Felys, while two had one colour only. Their features were not-quite Felys, but nor were they quite Argon. They looked exotic. Heartbreakers, every single one of them.

Aisha was the firstborn, her hair the same black as her father's. Chiara was a tortoiseshell like her mother. Faine had tabby hair, taking after her Uncle Denyon. Katja had red hair, and that came from Marten's side of the family. And wee little Misty had cream hair shot through with patches of white and gold. Smaller than her sisters, she was the runt, but she was strong and insistent, her mewling and purring being the loudest of them all. It seemed that being half Argon had given her the strength she needed to survive and thrive.

Ah, his little wenches. His little lykittens. His nightmares in the years to come when they grew to eye-stunning teenagers and the over-sexed, hormone-ridden male youths came rushing to his door. Marten sighed. *Oh joy.* But for now…for now he could relax and simply enjoy his little wenches. Later, in the years to come, he could hone his young-men-tossing-out-the-door skills.

Leaving his babes, he went to his bedroom where his own little lykitten was a little warm bundle under the covers. Shucking his clothes by the light of the moon, he crossed to the bathroom and entered it quietly, shutting the door behind him so that the sound of water running wouldn't disturb his wife, who was no doubt exhausted after caring for the babes all day.

The water sluiced down, warm and fragrant, and he lathered up his hair, closing his eyes and tipping his face back to let the soap wash out. He was reaching for the washcloth with his eyes still closed when he felt a small hand smooth over his back and down over his buttocks.

He didn't have to guess to know immediately who was

behind him. Grinning, he queried, "Jonette?" He yelped when his buttock was pinched.

"Try again," Lysie said.

"Katina?"

A palm lightly smacked against his buttock. "Keep it up and I won't wash your back."

Whoo boy, he could feel the blood surging straight to his groin. "Tera?"

This time a soft, rounded arm slid around his hips and one small hand deftly wrapped itself around his already-swelling staff. "I know it's been awhile, Marten, but to really have forgotten me? Tsk-tsk. I can see I'll have to reacquaint you with me." That little palm slid knowingly, firmly, up his shaft, and heat flared to life.

In one quick move, Marten spun around, caught Lysie on each side of her naked waist and lifted her up to eye level. "Oh," he said in fake surprise. "It's... Lysie, right?"

Her golden eyes sparkled with mirth, but they also shone with passion. "Could be. How are you going to tell, sex god?"

"Taste test." Lifting her higher, he took one nipple into his mouth and tongued it, rewarded by her moan of desire. Releasing the pink nub, he licked his lips thoughtfully. "Tastes familiar."

Her eyes had gone all hot.

Oh yes!

Leaning forward, she wrapped her arms around his shoulders and her legs around his waist. Marten adjusted his hold so that one arm was snugged under her deliciously rounded bottom, while his other hand entangled in the thick, soft, tortoiseshell hair.

"Let's try another taste," she whispered, a hint of a growl in her words.

His lykitten was running hot. His staff swelled more, the engorged tip nudging the slickness of her perineum, taking her breath away. The feel of her slick heat was almost his undoing.

Almost, but not quite.

The water sluiced down both of them, and he moved so that their faces were free of water. Fragrant steam rose in the air, cocooning them in damp warmth.

Before he could ask anything, Lysie lowered her head to his neck, nipped the skin there, and laved it with rough little swipes of her tongue. She cuddled closer, and he felt her breasts press against the muscles of his chest. Always generous, those soft globes were now even more so with nourishing milk for their babes.

Her lips were hot on his skin, her body soft, her scent so fresh and clean and uniquely her. The soft down protecting her feminine secrets was flush against his abdomen, the heat from there moist. Her body was ready for him.

It had been awhile since they'd made love. Once she grew bigger with their babes, and after the birth, they'd done nothing but cuddle and kiss. He'd missed their closeness. Missed her heat, missed burying himself inside her snug sheath, missed hearing her moan and purr her pleasure.

Now she was here, offering herself, wanting him as much as he wanted her.

The knowledge was enough to make him move swiftly to brace her back against the wall, his hand going from her hair to slide beneath her bottom so that he could finger the hidden treasures bared so blatantly by her position.

Lysie arched back with a cry as his fingers slid along her perineum and found the opening to her body. When his finger slid unerringly inside, she tilted her head forward and he saw the ardour shining in her eyes, the redness of her lips right before she moved those last few inches and took his mouth in a kiss so ravenous and demanding that he nearly orgasmed on the spot.

Yes, it had been awhile.

Marten craved her like a thirsty man craved water. He kissed her back, ruthlessly plundering her mouth, feeling her little tongue lapping up his essence as they both strove to take what they wanted.

Each other.

His shaft throbbed hungrily, and he knew he had to have her now.

Sucking in a deep, harsh breath, he lifted his head to look at her. "Lysie..."

"Marten."

"Are you sure it's not too soon?"

"Any longer and I'll go mad." Her smile was all wicked, sexually aroused Felys. "Come on, sex god, show me what you've got."

Needing no further prompting, Marten bent his knees a little, then shoved upright, his shaft unerringly nudging through the slick entrance to bury deep inside her.

When Lysie gave a ragged cry and her nails dug into his shoulder, Marten stilled, concern warring with raging desire. Before he could say a word, she moaned, "Don't stop. By Delcat, Marten, don't stop!" She wriggled against him, and the sensation of her sheath gripping him tighter made his blood roar in his ears. "Take me!"

That was all he needed. Holding her with the wall pinning her back and his hips pinning her front, Marten pumped long, hard, and deep.

"Oh, stars, lykitten!" He kissed her hard, plundering the depths of her mouth as ruthlessly as he plundered the depths of her body.

Fire seared his veins, splintering through his nerves, pouring like molten lava to his shaft. His heart hammered in his chest as he thrust harder, more desperately, wanting everything that was Lysie.

He ate at her mouth, seeking her essence, taking it, her flavour bursting upon his tongue. His fingers cupped her soft bottom, holding her to him mercilessly as he thrust deep inside her.

The tension built quickly, the forced abstinence making his fire flare hotter and almost out of control. He felt the tightening of his scrotum, felt the coiling inside him. His shaft felt as though it was being gripped in a hard, hot, wet fist that fought to keep him deep inside her.

Dimly he heard her whimpers of pleasure, caught a flash of her golden eyes with the lazily swirling threads that came to an almost complete stop as desire threw her higher.

He pushed them both, higher and higher, relentless in his pursuit of that shattering orgasm he could feel inside them both. He felt her sheath spasm, felt the spasm along his shaft, heard her scream as she pitched over the edge.

Marten followed her, his seed bursting forth to coat her vaginal walls, spurting deep. He pumped harder, shuddering as stars burst before his eyes, pushing harder and deeper until all he was doing was staying deep inside her and pushing closer and closer.

A second orgasm burst through them both, hurtling them both out together, making them cling to each other as the erotic ride seemed to go on forever on a rich, carnal blaze of pure concupiscence.

They rode it, coming down slowly, their panting breaths filling the room.

When Marten finally floated back to reality, it was to find Lysie's head burrowed into his neck, her purring loud and contented, her arms wrapped around his neck and her legs still wrapped around his waist.

He was still inside her, his staff stiffening at the realization. He wanted her again. Now.

Reaching up, he flicked off the shower and stood easily, muscles moving strongly as he stood with her still in his arms.

Lysie lifted her head to regard him through sultry eyes. "My, my. Such strength, sex god."

He nuzzled her cheek. "You haven't seen anything yet."

"Are you going to show me?" She licked her lips, looking like a lycat that had gotten the cream.

"Oh yes, little sex lykitten." Marten nipped her ear, delighted as always when it twitched. Stepping out of the shower, he slid her down his length until her feet found the floor. "First, let's start with drying ourselves."

"Drying?" She gave a small moue of disappointment.

"I intend to make love to you until the wee hours of the morn." He chucked her under her chin, smiling when she purred blissfully and half closed her eyes. He continued to caress her under the chin. "And I don't want the bed linen wet."

"The great Argon bodyguard, afraid of wet linen." She danced back suddenly, eyes gleaming. "What if I ran in there right now and rubbed myself all over that fine linen? What then?"

That familiar spark skittered through his veins. "Punishment."

"I do believe I've heard that threat many times." She kicked open the bathroom door with her heel. "Let's see how you mean to keep that threat, sex god."

He was after her in a flash, catching her in the middle of the big bedroom and swinging her around and up into his arms. Her body was slick with water, warm and delicious.

Bugger wet linens. He wanted her now. Marten was just moving for the bed when the mewling broke through his lustful thoughts.

He froze.

The mewling sounded again.

Lysie peeked up at him. "That sounds like Misty."

"It's her hungry cry." Marten sighed.

"I'm impressed you know her cries." Lysie tapped his jaw. "You know all their mews and cries."

"That's because I'm the boss. I know all your cries as well, especially the pleasured ones." He leered before dropping one last, regretful kiss on the tip of her nose before lowering her to the floor. "Duty calls."

They both went back into the bathroom, Lysie wrapping a towel around herself and slipping away to attend to Misty while Marten dried himself.

He supposed they'd have to get used to interruptions now. The babes generally slept most of the night, but now and again one of them woke up and needed tending.

Such was fatherhood.

Marten grinned, wrapped the towel around his hips, and walked to the babes' room. He found Lysie sitting in a rocking chair, Misty at her breast. The other babes slept undisturbed in the cot.

Moving across to kneel beside the rocking chair, Marten tenderly ran his fingertip up and down Misty's cheek. Her tiny purrs came faster.

Lysie laughed. "She loves her father."

"And he loves her." He glanced at the cot. "And them." He raised his gaze to meet hers, and the heat turned to tenderness. "And you, my own little lykitten."

"Ah, you have such a way with words." Her expression soft, she leaned forward to kiss him gently. "My own sex god."

Marten rested his head against hers as they both watched their daughter nursing.

Life, Marten thought, was good. He had his six little wenches, and he'd never been more content in his life. Life was indeed good.

An hour later his gasps and pants filled the room as Lysie brought him to orgasm with her mouth, sending him soaring once again and shattering once more with her hands and tongue, touching and coaxing and sending him up in erotic flames.

When the moon was slowly disappearing and dawn touched the skyline, he lay curled around Lysie's back, her bottom snugged into his groin, her top hand in his, their fingers entwined. Her sleepy, soft purring filled the air as she drifted off to sleep.

Her hair tickled his chin and breathing deeply of her scent, Marten smiled. Life wasn't just good. It was excellent. Closing his eyes, he drifted off to sleep, his arms securely around his little Felys wife.

In the nursery, the babes stirred, shifted, tumbled over each other, and went back to sleep, their tiny purrs filling the room.

Davan & Delias

Heart – the pathway to true love was never meant to be easy. Davan knows all about that.

Chapter 1

*

Delias studied the cloth the visiting merchant had laid upon the counter. It was soft to the touch, neatly cut, and hid a flaw her sharp eyes spotted immediately. True, it was only a small flaw, but it was a flaw that would mean dinnos saved.

She looked up at the merchant and saw the small frown between his brows disappear as soon as her gaze met his. His face was politely interested.

Huh. As if. The man wasn't fooling her. He knew about the flaw and had hoped she wouldn't spot it. More fool him. She wasn't as brilliant a trader as her Mother, but she was shrewd, something her Mother had taught her in the game of trading.

Delias straightened. "'Tis flawed."

"What?" The merchant looked startled. "Flawed?"

"Aye. Flawed." Folding her arms, she gazed steadily at him.

"Oh, no. I assure you, it isn't flawed. Why, look." He stroked one hand along the rich length. "Perfect cloth."

"Perfect cloth except for this flaw."

"Where?" He peered down at it.

"There."

Squinty-eyed, he looked closer. "I don't see - "

Grabbing his hand, she slapped his palm down onto the faintly different pattern that swirled through the cloth. "There."

"Ah." He hemmed. "Hmmm. I think I see - "

"You see it all right. Five hundred dinnos."

The merchant snapped upright, his mouth dropping in outrage. "Five hundred? This is quality cloth! This - "

"Four hundred and fifty."

"Four hundred and fifty?"

"'Tis flawed. I'll not pay top dinno for flawed cloth."

"I hardly think - "

"Four hundred dinnos."

"Four hundred dinnos?" The merchant's mouth opened and

shut in shock. "The price cannot go down!"

"It can and it has. Four hundred dinnos, my last offer." Delias tapped the fingertips of one hand on the counter while eyeing him steadily.

"I can't possibly accept any less than the original price." The merchant gestured to the cloth. "Fine cloth - "

"With a fine flaw. Three fifty."

The merchant's eyes started to bulge and his cheeks redden. "Three hundred and fifty?"

"I know I said four hundred was my final offer, but I'm prepared to go lower after all."

He started to argue, but at the bored look on Delias's face, he stopped, shook his head and finally muttered, "Very well. I - "

"Done!" Briskly, Delias took out the handcomp, keyed in the family trading code and handed it to the merchant.

With a resigned sigh, he keyed in his own code. The credits automatically changed accounts and the trade was done.

"You Daamens will ruin me." Again, he sighed.

Delias grinned widely. He blinked, then smiled, shook his head and backed out of the trade building.

"'Tis a hard bargain you drive, Delias, my love." Melha, Delias's mother, tugged a blonde lock of her daughter's curly hair. "You make me proud."

"I learned from the best." Laughing, Delias rolled the cloth back up.

It was heavy and ungainly, and she pulled it towards her with a little grunt as she tried to lift it.

There was sudden warmth at her back. "Here, lass, let me help." Heavily muscled arms reached past her, big hands wrapping easily around the thick width of the cloth to lift it up and over top of her.

Delias didn't have to look to know who was behind her. The deep voice, the masculine scent that assailed her senses... bloody Davan.

Swinging around, her eyes narrowed on the big Daamen Head Peacekeeper. Like all the Daamen men, at seven foot tall and more, he towered over the visiting merchants. She was well used to her world men with their bulging muscles and dangerously good looks. Like all Daamen men, Davan had a small silver hoop in his left earlobe and his shaggy blonde hair, which reached his shoulder blades, was tied back with a strip of cloth. However, unlike the Daamen traders who wore a sleeveless, open vest with their long pants and boots, he wore the tunic and pants of a peacekeeper. The sleeveless tunic bared his arms, the massive muscles bunching and lengthening as he placed the roll of cloth on the hover tray beside the counter.

Frowning, she folded her arms. Bloody Davan, currying favour with her mother, who was smiling up at him and chattering. He smiled back down at her, answering her with laughter in his voice. His gaze lifted to mesh unerringly with Delias's, and the humour faded from his deep blue eyes.

With a slight toss of her head, Delias turned back to the counter, scrutinizing the handcomp in an attempt to add up the purchases so far. It was futile; she could almost feel that deep blue gaze studying her. His face, she knew, would be intent as he looked at her. She knew because she'd seen that expression on his handsome face before along with that other expression, disapproval.

That disapproving look had appeared when she was fourteen years old and somehow it had stayed. Disapproval along with... Delias squirmed, shoving back from the counter. She didn't want to think about it. For seven years she'd been trying not to think about it. But it was there, still.

Disgust. He'd looked at her with disgust and she had never forgotten it. And the disgust hadn't been just at that time either, it had lingered for several years, even though she knew he'd tried to hide it.

Bugger hiding things, she wasn't going to hide what she felt. If she disgusted him, he annoyed the hell out of her. He grated on her like rough stone against sensitive skin. And she didn't care that he knew it. In fact, she wanted him to know it.

In true fact, he did know it. She'd made no pretence of hiding it once she got older.

Davan, who'd always had the wenches falling at his feet since he'd been a callow youth. He hadn't stayed innocent for long, of that she was sure. He'd gained a reputation amongst the wenches and had happily pursued that for a long time. Now that he was Head Peacekeeper, his exploits didn't seem to come up in the gossip anymore. The great Davan appeared to have settled down into being a serious lawman, which also meant that every parent with an unmarried daughter was eyeing him off as a potential son-by-marriage.

Taking a deep breath, she turned around once more, steadfastly ignoring Davan as she addressed her mother. "I'm going out for a breath of fresh air. 'Tis kind of stuffy in here." She couldn't help the glance she cast at Davan as she added the 'stuffy' part. Aye, there 'twas again. The disapproving look.

"Of course, love." Melha smiled. "Have a break."

Fighting the immature urge to poke her tongue out at Davan, Delias left the counter to thread her way gracefully through the aisles of trading Daamen wenches and merchants. Outside, several Daamen traders were unloading hover trays, readying the items to take inside to the wenches.

Delias didn't think it odd that the men travelled off planet trading while the wenches stayed on Daamen and traded from the settlement Trade Building. 'Twas a known fact that the Daamen wenches were respected as much as the men when it came to trading, and the wenches ran the businesses on Daamen.

Trading was in the blood. Well, except for a few, such as those men who became soldiers, peacekeepers, medics and teachers. There were some things on Daamen that men could do apart from trading. But the wenches—ahhhh, the wenches loved sharpening their wits, skills and knowledge
on the visiting merchants.

"Del!"

She glanced around to see her brother Red striding towards her, a heavy barrel balanced on one broad shoulder. His grin was wide and infectious. "Mother's been expecting you."

"I'm coming." His green eyes sparkled with amusement as always. "Besides, she knows I'm picking out the best for her."

"Sucking up, eh?"

"'Tis not a nice thing to say to your brother."

"But true." Curiously, she eyed the barrel. "What do you have?"

"Wine from Vexna." He patted the barrel. "Mother should get top dinnos for it."

A fair-haired, bearded trader approached with a hover tray behind him. 'Twas stacked with trade goods. "Hello, lass."

"Shamon." Moving to his hover tray, she studied the cargo with interest. "What have you got?"

"Why? Want to do some trading?" He winked. "You'll have to see my Aunt for that."

"Huh." Reaching out, she touched a bolt of cloth. "Oh, 'tis nice. Where from?"

"Close to the Outlaw Sector." His gaze moved past her. "Davan! How goes it, friend?"

Immediately Delias scowled. Red saw her face and burst out laughing. Bloody brother. She'd be hearing about that little expression slip for the rest of his visit. Ignoring him, she nodded to Shamon, who was grinning widely, and strode away.

Behind her she heard the rise and fall of the men's voices and rather than soothe her, it made her irritable. Or rather, one voice made her irritable. Davan's voice.

She hated him. Moodily she continued onwards to her home. Nay, hate was too strong a word. She disliked him. She wished he'd leave peacekeeping and go off and trade, and that way she'd hardly ever have to set eyes on him.

Of course, she might miss him — *nay!* It would be a relief to walk around and not see him doing his rounds, checking on things, greeting his fellow Daamens, trading jests, attending to their concerns. Keeping vigilant when outsiders were present in his settlement. Being kind to animals and children. Charming the wenches, being all sweet, patting their hounds and lycats and smiling at them. Charming all the wenches except her. Every time he saw her, the humour melted from his eyes and he became serious.

For some reason Davan didn't like her, and not because she gave him the cold shoulder, either, because his weirdness had started long ago. What she didn't understand was why it had continued until she retaliated with the cold shoulder, and now they were at this point where he watched her with a faintly disapproving air, or a serious face, and she couldn't control her tongue around him or get away from him fast enough.

Hands in the pockets of her work tunic, she ambled along, lost in her own thoughts and memories.

~ * ~

Davan tried to keep his attention on what his friends were saying but he was well aware of Delias walking away. He could see her over Red's shoulder.

Delias of the white/blonde hair and brilliant green eyes. The work tunic she wore skimmed her slender shape, outlining her breasts and hips, the hem fluttering around trim knees. Her hair was up in an intricate braid of some kind, and he itched to bring all that shiny wealth down to tumble around her shoulders and into his hands.

If he tried it, he had no doubt she'd slap him silly. When it came to him, she had a temper and biting gaze. With others, she could be funny, caring and happy, but as soon as he came into sight a frown creased her smooth brow, or she simply looked right through him, or even more annoying, she had a smart, cutting remark for him. He wondered why. He got the cold shoulder from her so often, 'twas amazing he didn't have frostbite.

"Davan?" Red waved his hand in front of his face.

"What?" Davan jerked his gaze back to his friend. "Sorry. I missed that."

"You missed it because you were too busy ogling my sister."

"Nay, I was just…"

Red grinned widely. "That wench won't give you the time of day, Davan. I don't know what 'tis that ruffles her up the wrong way when you're around, but you get her into some doozy moods."

"Doozy moods?"

"Oh aye. But if you want to soften her up, you're going to have to try harder."

Davan raised his brows coolly. "Why would I want to soften her up?"

"Now that 'tis a question only you can answer." Red winked and walked past him, punching him lightly on the arm as he did so. "Just as only you can answer the question why your gaze so often wanders after her."

"Shouldn't you be protecting her?"

Red laughed. "Most men need protecting from Del, for when that sharp tongue starts, she can slice a man to ribbons with it. Besides," he added, walking backwards with the barrel balanced on his shoulder, "I trust you with her."

Davan wasn't sure whether to be impressed or disappointed.

"I know 'twill be no hanky panky going on between the two of you." Red winked again. "Not unless you want your manly parts frozen off." With another booming laugh, he turned and disappeared into the trade building.

Shaking his head, Davan strode back towards the main street of the settlement. That was the trouble with brothers, they didn't see their sisters as sexual beings. Red never noted the heat in Delias's eyes, that slow burn of embers that promised the fires of passion that Davan just knew lay smouldering inside her, waiting for the right man to spark it to life. Oh aye, he knew instinctively that Delias was a hot, passionate little wench, and the thought of some other man igniting that spark... Davan clenched his jaw and shook his head again. It wasn't his business.

Except, he reminded himself, her safety was his to pursue as a peacekeeper. She was his to protect.

Along with all the Daamens, of course.

Bounding up the steps of the Enforcement Building, he nodded to Moreb, his dark-haired peacekeeper. "All quiet?"

"As always." Moreb yawned and sipped at the hot cup of una he held in his big hands.

"Oh, aye, I can see how quiet 'tis in here."

"'Tis because I protect our office with my life."

"I am so grateful."

"I expect a pay rise for my dedication."

"The only raise you'll get is my boot up your arse."

"I'm hurt." Moreb sipped at his una and closed his eyes in blissful contemplation. "Ahhhh, the taste of hot sweetness in the morn."

Hot sweetness. Delias. Davan had no doubt she'd be a very hot sweetness in the morn. Nay, wait. He remembered that cold shoulder she always gave him. More like an ice block.

He wouldn't mind melting that frigid little ice block.

Stars above! He shook his head, pushing thoughts of her from his mind and forcing himself to concentrate on the task at hand.

Moreb sighed. "'Tis been awhile since we've seen any action."

"'Tis early yet. No doubt with the return of three of the trade ships, things will get boisterous tonight."

His friend brightened. "Mayhap a brawl or two?" He sounded hopeful.

Davan grinned. "You really are spoiling for a fight, aren't you?"

"Just need to work out a few kinks." Moreb rolled his shoulders. "Man gets lazy if he doesn't exercise."

Davan eyed Moreb's sprawled position in the chair. "Bit late to worry about that now."

"Just conserving my energy for the night ahead." Moreb took another sip of una.

Crossing to the desk, Davan checked the data base of the

Trade Building. "More merchants arrive this afternoon. We'll need to check their stock."

"I doubt any merchant would dare to try and trade illegal goods."

"Nay, they wouldn't, but they could still be carrying them onboard and I'll not have illegal goods on this planet." Transferring information from the viscomm to the handcomps, Davan straightened up. "Familiarize yourself with these; take note of what they're supposed to be carrying. Anything extra 'tis not on the listings they sent gets quarantined until investigated as normal."

Taking the handcomp that Davan handed to him, Moreb sighed. "Like I said, another quiet day."

~ * ~

"Damn it!" Manez snarled. "Where the hell is it?"

"I don't know." Czex threw down the metal container and looked around angrily. "It was here!"

"Well it's not now." Kicking the box aside, Manez glared around the warehouse. "And neither is the cargo it was concealed in."

"That can only mean the cargo has already left for..." He stopped and paled a little.

"Daamen." Manez swore and punched the wall. "Daamen, of all places! That idiot merchant wasn't supposed to leave until tomorrow!"

"What the hell are we going to do now?"

Striding across to the door, Manez gazed out at the night sky. Somewhere out there was the planet Daamen, and the cargo he needed to search through was on its way there, if it wasn't there already.

Czex joined him at the door and looked up into the night sky as well. "If we don't get it back, we're dead."

"And if we get caught on illegal business on Daamen, we'll be lucky to get away with all limbs intact."

"If we get away."

"Then we need to make sure we're not caught." Manez

stepped out into the street. "We've arrangements to make."

"Oh?"

"We're going trading."

~ * ~

The watcher in the shadows smiled slightly. *Game on.*

~ * ~

Ambling along in the moonlight, Delias hummed to herself. She'd just left her friend's home, her parents had left on a trading trip to Comll to deliver some goods to the Reeka settlement, and Red had left on a trading trip and wouldn't be back for several weeks. That meant she had the house to herself. Peace and quiet.

The river was a soft glisten of gently moving, clear water. Stopping under the shelter of a tree, she gazed at the water, knowing it would be warm and refreshing. Lifting her arms, she stretched, noting the little ache in the small of her back. She'd broken some rules today, lifting things too heavy and being a little careless in her handling of the smaller bundles. Her annoyance with Davan being around so much had made her reckless. Luckily her parents didn't know about her aches, or she'd have received a tongue lashing.

The water beckoned her and she nibbled her lower lip and eyed the glittering swirl. The merchants were all gone, and no Daamen man or boy who stumbled upon her would be a threat—they'd beat a retreat in a hurry. Any wench or child was perfectly safe on Daamen amongst their own kind.

Of course, going swimming alone was frowned upon for safety reasons, but who would know? Besides, the water was warm and would soothe her back. And there was no one to tattle on her.

Having made up her mind, Delias cast one more glance around before kicking off her sandals and whipping off her long gown. Her support garment and panties followed to lie discarded on the grass with the silk of her gown. Fastening her hair atop her head with a tie, she moved to the edge of the bank and waded into the water, sighing in satisfaction as the water slid up her body to encompass her waist.

Kicking off, she sliced through the water and proceeded to swim lazily, moving slowly, allowing the warmth of the water to lap at her body.

The night was so peaceful, the sound of night flyers in the forest nearby, the scent of the night blossoms filling the air, the splash of fish as they jumped out of the water and back down into the sparkling depths.

"Can anything be more perfect?" she murmured aloud.

Time slipped past and finally she started for the bank. Her feet found purchase on the ground and the water had just started to lap above her breasts when a deep voice growled angrily, "What the hell do you think you're doing?"

Delias froze. It couldn't be...

"Don't stop." Davan stepped out from the shadows, and even though she couldn't make out his features with the shadows cast from behind him, she could hear the anger in his voice.

Staying exactly where she was, Delias frowned. "What do you want?"

"I want you out of the water."

"Really? I don't think so."

"Now."

Coolly she looked him up and down. "Why don't you go and harass someone else, Davan?"

Big hands settled on lean hips, making his giant frame seem even more menacing. "You don't want me coming in after you, wench."

"Oh, I'm so scared." Scowling, she flicked her hand at him. "Go away. I'm not coming out until you're gone."

"'Tis too bad, wench. I'm not leaving until you're out."

"Oh, 'tis so?"

"Aye." The bite in his tone was sharp.

Delias tossed her head. "If you're hoping for a glimpse of flesh, Peacekeeper, I'm disappointed in you. You're supposed to be protecting me, not asking me to come out naked in full view."

Davan's hissing inhale from between his clenched teeth was audible. "Are you telling me that you're not just swimming alone, but you're also naked?"

"My, aren't you the quick-witted one." Delias raised one brow haughtily.

Those long, strong legs took one step closer and the air was suddenly tangible with threat. "Get out of the water now, Delias."

The shiver that went through her wasn't exactly fear, but it wasn't far from it. That and something else she wasn't going to examine too closely. Just as she wasn't going to take his orders. "Go away, Davan. I'm not interested in being bullied."

"If you don't get out right now, Delias, I'm coming in after you, and trust me, you don't want that."

She stared up at him, her thoughts starting to turn. It wasn't the normal tone Davan used, and his approach wasn't normal, either. Why was he in such a snit about her being naked in the water? "No Daamen man would touch me, so why the big performance?"

"The big performance, wench, is that there are visiting merchants here and any one of them could stumble across you. They wouldn't look the other way."

"'Tis no one here. They all left this afternoon."

"Which just goes to prove you don't know everything, doesn't it? A small group of merchants arrived this evening. Now get out of the damned water, for I'll not tell you again."

Now she could understand his concern, but still... "I'm not coming out with you standing there."

Without further hesitation, Davan strode to the edge of the bank.

He was coming in after her! A thrill of fear shot through her and Delias held up one dripping hand. "Stop! Wait! Davan, nay!"

The water was actually lapping at the toe of his boot when he halted. "'Tis your final chance, Delias."

"But I can't...you're there...I won't come out naked!" she finally burst out.

"I'm not leaving." Anger still threaded his voice.

"You can't possible expect me to come out of here naked? In front of you?"

There was silence for several seconds. "Why not? You put yourself on display for others who might pass."

Oh, 'twas unfair! The unexpected lash of the words stung. Delias could only gape up at him, stunned. She couldn't see his face, but she caught the glint of his eyes in the shadows. A slight breeze sprung up, stirring the loose tendrils of hair that escaped his ponytail. His very pose was almost a threat. Come out or I'm coming in. And she had no doubt that this time he meant it. For some strange reason, Davan was furious with her, and it wasn't the normal disapproval she would have expected.

Swallowing, she muttered, "At least turn away."

At first she didn't think he was even going to allow her that right, and she bit her lip and glanced around. Everything was quiet, there was no sight or sound of anyone else. They were alone. She was alone with a furious Daamen male, and that made her inwardly quake.

For about five seconds. The unfairness of it all, and a growing anger, propelled her into recklessness.

"Fine!" With a toss of her head, she moved forward. "Stare all you want, Davan! Get a bloody good eyeful, because I swear 'tis all you'll ever get! And I'll tell you this now," she continued to rage as she moved further up the bank, the water now lapping around her waist while she refused to contemplate how exposed she was, "When Red comes home, he'll thrash the living hell out of you!"

But for all her bravado, she couldn't look at him. The water fell to her hips, then to her knees, and finally she was standing on the bank before him. Totally humiliated, she looked up, almost ready to cry in furious embarrassment, only to find him looking the other way and holding up her delicate silk gown in his big hands.

"Get dressed," he ordered.

Relief washed through her at the realisation that he hadn't been watching her nakedness and snatching the gown from his hands, she yanked it over her head and tugged it into place.

It clung to her wet body and cursing under her breath, she knelt down and searched the shadows for her underwear.

"Looking for these?" A big hand was suddenly under her nose and the lacy scraps of her underwear looked ludicrously delicate in the big palm.

Cheeks burning, she snatched them out of his hand and jerked upright, narrowly missing hitting her head against his chin as he straightened quickly.

Balling the undergarments in her hand, she scowled up at him, her cheeks burning. "You're a bastard, Davan!"

Now she could see his face more clearly, the firm jaw-line, the dangerous handsomeness, and the fury in his eyes. At her words, a muscle ticked in his jaw.

"Nothing to say for yourself?" she goaded, pushed by her humiliation to rant at him. "No score for my body? Was it a ten or just a one? Maybe a five? Did you get a good look, Davan? 'Twas worth it?"

She swore she heard his teeth grind right before he answered, "I didn't look, wench, and well you know it. Now why were you out here alone?"

"Because I'm not on a damned leash!"

His glittering gaze swept her from head to toe and back up again. She could swear she felt it like a lick of fire. "Mayhap you need to be."

"Oh, you'd like that, wouldn't you?" Incensed, she stood toe to toe with him and glared up, having to tilt her head back to do so. "How about a muzzle as well? A little electric shock every time I open my mouth and say something you don't approve of? While you're at it, you could make me sleep in a hound's kennel!"

For a big man he moved fast. Davan gripped both her upper arms and jerked her up onto tip-toes so that she was flush against his body.

She could feel the heat of him, the hardness of his muscles against her softer curves, and his masculine, clean scent invaded her senses as she took in a deep breath. It was almost... disorientating. His nearness, his warmth, his -

"One day, wench, you're going to push me too far," he ground out between clenched teeth.

Her senses cleared in a flash. "Ooohhh, did I hit a nerve after all?" Delias tried to shrug out of his hold but the big hands clamped firmly around her upper arms didn't release her. "Let go."

Bending down, Davan was suddenly a lot closer than comfort dictated. Even in the dimness she could make out the hard set of his jaw and the glint of his eyes. The Head Peacekeeper was angry. Nay, furious. "One day, Delias..."

This was the first time she'd ever gotten a rise out of him and a smug feeling of satisfaction coursed through her. It went a long way to soothing her humiliated feelings.

"What? You intend to teach me some manners? Teach me to be all polite and nice to the big peacekeeper?"

The breath he sucked in was harsh. She could almost feel the danger in the air now. A zing of alarm speared through her. *Oops, mayhap I have finally gone a bit far.* No sooner had the thought occurred to her than she scoffed it away. She opened her mouth only to find one big hand clamped suddenly over it.

"Don't say one more word," Davan grated warningly.

As though she had much choice with his hand over her mouth. Reaching up, she wrenched his hand away and spat out, "Or you'll what? Throw me in the cells?"

"Keep this up, Delias, and I'll put you across my knee and give you the spanking your parents never saw to."

Delias's mouth fell open in outrage and shock. "You

wouldn't dare!"

"Don't ever dare me, wench. Not ever again." He loomed over her and now he was almost nose to nose with her, his very breadth and height blocking out the night sky.

Time seemed to stand still. The air was fraught with threat and something else, something she didn't quite understand but instinctively felt was a turning point to... something.

The night was hushed, as though every living creature waited for something to happen. The seconds ticked past as Delias and Davan glared furiously at each other. Delias had no idea what exactly would have happened if she hadn't suddenly shivered as the breeze across the river turned chill.

With a muttered curse, Davan released her and stepped back. "Get your sandals on, Delias. I'm taking you home."

Relieved to have some room between them, Delias shoved her feet into her sandals and stormed off.

Davan fell into step beside her.

"I can walk by myself!" She snapped.

"Don't," was all he replied grimly, but it was enough.

There was still something dark between them, something unchecked, untouched, and unknown. It lingered, and Delias was leery of facing whatever it was, because she knew she wasn't ready. And after his threat, which she instinctively knew he'd keep, she wasn't going to push anymore boundaries. At least not until her parents or brother were home to provide a buffer. She wasn't stupid.

Anger still burned through her and she said not a word to her equally silent companion as she strode out of the shelter of trees along the river, down the pathway and finally onto the street leading into the settlement. She was so angry she didn't take notice of the lights from several of the houses glowing dimly along the path, nor did she take delight as she

normally did in the scents of the night flowers that filled the gardens. The graceful, two story houses rose on each side of the wide, cobbled road, their white, thick posts entwined with flowering vines, weren't even glanced at as she stormed homeward.

Finally her gate appeared and she turned into it, storming up the pathway, stomping up the stairs and throwing the door open before her. She slammed it shut behind her without a glance at the man waiting at the gate for her to enter safely.

Running up the stairs, she entered her bathroom, stripped her clothes off and stepped into a warm shower, welcoming the fragrant, soapy water that poured down on top of her.

Furiously she soaped her hair and body, her thoughts racing with the exchange between herself and Davan. She rinsed with more vigour than normal, towelled off, and was still fuming by the time she was seated in the kitchen with a cup of hot una between her shaking hands.

Her shaking hands she ignored. Her jittery nerves she ignored. The something lurking in the back of her mind she ignored.

The dreams that made her awaken with a thundering heart and dampness between her thighs were something she couldn't ignore, but she tried her damnedest.

~ * ~

Manez looked around at the stalls in the Trade Building and grimaced inwardly. It teemed with women of every age from at least sixteen to seventy years of age. They came in all sizes and shapes, and every single one of them was mercenary when it came to trading. He'd thought the Daamen traders were hard bargainers, but their women were even more ruthless.

He smiled, he cajoled, and he searched, but that which he sought wasn't to be found. The small crate with the distinct marking was missing and that meant what it contained was missing. And that meant if he didn't find and produce it when needed, he was as good as dead.

Czex's expression across the big room wasn't promising. He looked gloomy. So he hadn't found it, either. They were so dead.

Manez resumed his search while discussing trade with the

women, making good on his pretence at working for the merchant he and Czex had hired on with to get access to Daamen.

He had to find it. He didn't care who he had to go through or over, but he would find it and get it back. Failure was not an option.

Glancing up, his gaze collided with eyes that seemed to weigh him and find him wanting. The Daamen Head Peacekeeper wasn't a man to cross, behind his affable Daamen nature was a sharp intelligence that Manez recognized. This was no man's fool. Manez gave the Peacekeeper a friendly nod, which was returned, though he wasn't idiot enough to think the giant Daamen was actually being friendly. Polite was the word.

Polite and watchful.

Manez would have to tread very carefully.

And he'd have to tread very carefully around a certain Daamen woman, too. He'd seen how the big Peacekeeper was monitoring the woman with the white/blonde hair, a pretty piece, to be sure, but with a sharp tongue and a mind like a steel trap.

He wondered what she meant to the man, but his expression was unreadable and he didn't approach her. Manez didn't care. All he wanted was the content of the crate.

He continued his search.

~ * ~

Unnoticed by him, cold eyes studied him shrewdly.

~ * ~

And from a second spot, the watcher observed it all. So, there was another spectator. How interesting. The game was getting more intriguing.

Chapter 2
*

Approaching the house, Davan looked up at the gracious pillars, the three wide steps with the roses that stood sentry on each side at the bottom, and finally at the big house. Double story, elegant, the usual for a Daamen home.

Except this was Delias's home, and she would probably scream at him to leave as soon as she saw his face.

But he wasn't going to go until he'd explained. Apologized. Well, not really apologized. Sort of apologized. Davan ran one hand over his face as he eased the gate open. He wasn't sorry for telling her off, but he had gone a little far. All right, a lot far. He just wanted to… well, first he'd find out if she'd even see him.

The afternoon sun was bright. A restless sleep and the draining of anger with the dawn had made him re-evaluate his actions of the previous night. He couldn't even begin to understand why Delias got under his skin so much. Why he let her get under his skin and affect him.

Wrong. The word resonated inside his head. You know why. He rolled his eyes. Aye, he knew why she disturbed him so much, but 'twasn't something he was going to proclaim to her, seeing as how she couldn't stand him, and after last night she'd probably slap his face as soon as she set eyes on him.

But still, he wanted to talk to her. Apologize for some of his actions and words. He didn't know what had come over him - *wrong!* All right, he did know…

Shaking his head, Davan squared his shoulders, bounded up the steps and knocked on the door. Silence greeted him and he knocked again with no result. He'd seen Delias walk to the house earlier, and her friend had told him that she was going to do some record keeping, so he knew she was home.

Mayhap she was resting. Or avoiding him. Since that was almost akin to the cold shoulder she gave him so frequently, it shouldn't surprise him, but he was still uncomfortable with the way he'd treated her the previous night. Not that she'd helped matters but his own actions were his responsibility.

Raising his hand, he knocked louder.

"Come in!" The frantic cry came faintly. "Please come in!"

Immediately his senses went on the alert and he opened the door and stepped in, glancing around as he did so, automatically looking for a source of danger. "Delias?"

"In here. Oh stars, hurry!" Pain resonated in her tone.

Concerned, Davan moved fast through the corridor, bypassing the lounge and an office, going under the stairs and further into the house. "Where are you?"

"The kitchen. Hurry!"

His gaze swept the room as he entered the kitchen fast. There was no danger but he saw Delias at a low counter near the wall. Bent at the waist, her forearms braced on the bench as she leaned down onto it, she looked up at him with tears shining her eyes. Beside the bench a small crate was overturned onto the floor.

"Lass! What happened?" Crossing to her, he reached out to touch her, only to have her jerk back slightly and cry out in pain at the movement.

"Don't touch me! Don't touch me!" she gasped.

Alarmed, Davan's gaze swept over her, looking for signs of injury. "Delias, what 'tis wrong?"

"My back!" she gasped. "I twisted the damn thing, pinched my nerve again. Damn it!" A tear slipped free and slid down her cheek.

"I'll help you to bed." He reached for her once more.

"Nay!"

He halted. "I'll get the medic."

"He can't help."

Davan felt helpless, a sensation he wasn't used to and certainly didn't like, especially in regards to her pain. "Lass, I can't leave you here like this."

"Don't you dare leave me!" Panicked, she reached out and grabbed his arm, biting her lip against the pain the sudden movement caused her.

Immediately he sought to soothe her, pushing a heavy curl back from her tear-stained cheek and tucking it behind her ear. "I won't. But you need to tell me what to do, how to help you."

"In my bathroom, in the drawer next to the sink, 'tis a jar of cream. I need you to rub it on my back." She looked up at him helplessly, the pain raw in her eyes and her pinched expression. "Please, Davan. Please."

Relief coursed through him. A plan of action. "Of course." Without hesitation, he left the kitchen, taking the stairs three at a time to the second floor.

It didn't take long to find her bathroom, and he located the jar of green cream and bounded down the stairs again, hurrying into the kitchen and coming to a stop beside her. When she looked at the jar and nodded, he moved behind her and looked at her gown. Long and silky, not the short tunic she'd worn earlier for work. It had no ties for him to undo. The straps were thin, the gown flowing.

Delias groaned with the pain, her knuckles white as she fisted her hands. "Hurry."

Decision made, Davan whipped the dagger from the sheath on his belt, unhesitatingly placed it at the neckline of her gown and sliced it down past her hips. The gown gaped open immediately, revealing her support garment and panties.

Normally he'd have taken time to enjoy such a view but right now his concern for Delias overrode all else. "Where does the pain start and finish, lass?"

"From the right-hand side of my waist." With a moan, Delias lowered her forehead to rest on her arms. "It runs down to my… my… oh God."

He glanced from her waist to her bowed head. "Where?"

"My…"

"Delias, 'tis no time for modesty. Where does the pain run to?"

"Oh God, oh God."

Suddenly he knew why she was getting even more upset. "Your bottom?"

"Aye. Nay! Not completely." Biting her lip, she glanced sideways at him, her pale cheeks filling with colour. "My right buttock. The pain ends just under it."

He studied the curve of her bottom beneath the gown. "Where your thigh finishes and your bottom begins?"

"Aye."

"Fine." He screwed off the lid of the jar, discarded it onto the bench, and reached for her panties. His fingers had just touched the waistband when she protested.

"Nay! Stop!" Delias jerked, gave a cry of agony, and slumped down again. "Do it! Just do it! God, the *pain*!"

He didn't want to wait, didn't want to waste time, but he couldn't in all good conscious not offer her a way out. "I can contact another wench, get someone to come over."

"I can't wait!" She was almost writhing on the bench, and he winced. "Just do it. Please!"

It was just fine by him. He couldn't even begin to understand the reason, but he wanted to be the one to tend to her. Scooping out some of the cream, he lightly touched it to the skin of her waist, using fingertips only to smear it across the right side of her waist. He could feel it, a little tingling followed by a cool rush that penetrated his skin, followed by heat and then a mingling of the two.

Delias groaned and pressed closer to the bench, only to whimper as even that small movement pained her.

"Hold still, lass." Davan rubbed a little firmer, just a touch more, and then gradually more as she didn't protest, until finally he was using sweeps of his palm.

Moving further down, he kept rubbing the cream lightly in until his palm brushed the top of her panties. Without hesitation, he hooked his fingers into the band and eased the lacy fabric down until her bottom was bared. Scooping more cream onto his fingers, he lightly smeared the cream over the shapely curve of her right buttock, firming each stroke until his whole palm was once again stroking her.

Delias quietened, and then slowly, so very slowly, she started to relax.

Davan noticed her hands relaxing first, the white knuckles easing as she spread her fingers. The stiffness of her spine relaxed and her shoulders slumped as she leaned more fully onto her forearms. He could feel the muscles in her back and bottom easing, the tension slipping away with each stroke of his hand.

He also noticed the curve of her bottom, the pale globe that fit his hand so easily. His skin was brown against the paleness, big against the trimness, hard against the softness. His fingers spread out over the soft flesh, skimming along the crease at the end of her thigh and beginning of her buttock, and he smoothed and ran his hand firmly over the silken flesh.

Heaviness settled in his groin, a fire sparked in his veins, and he was almost mesmerized by the sight of his hand gliding along her bottom. It wouldn't take much to slip his hand in the tempting crease between the soft globes, to trace it down to the hidden treasures beyond, to -

Delias sighed, and he felt her ease back into the stroke of his hand.

"That feels so good," she whispered.

For a minute he thought she meant his touch, and his blood heated a little more.

"The pain is gone." She stretched forward.

Of course! Giving himself a mental head slap, Davan firmed his palm up along her waist, reluctant to break the contact. "Better?" Hearing the huskiness of his voice, he cleared his throat.

"Much." She pushed a heavy fall of hair back from her face, flicking it back over her shoulder. She sounded tired.

"Do you need more?" He should shoot himself for feeling hopeful. The poor lass had been in pain and here he was wanting to rub her some more! And not just her sore back and bottom, either…

"Nay, 'tis fine. Thank you."

Damn. I mean, great. Reluctantly he withdrew his hand and eased her panties back up over that luscious curve of bottom, unable to help the slow glide of his palm over that luscious curve just one more time. Stars knew when he'd ever get another chance. *Davan, you are one sick bastard.*

Delias started to straighten and immediately Davan slipped an arm around her waist from behind, helping ease her up and back so that she leaned back against him. He looked down at her face and saw that her eyes were closed, dark shadows beneath, and his lust was pushed aside by concern. "Del?"

"I'm just tired." She barely opened her eyes. "The cream has relaxing qualities in it as well as healing properties. It makes me sleepy."

"I'll take you to bed."

"Mmmmm."

It said a lot for the wench that she simply allowed him to carefully swing her into his arms and cradle her to him. Her head rested on his shoulder, and he strode to the staircase, climbing it carefully. By the time he got to her bedroom, Delias was asleep. Obviously the sleeping properties of the cream were powerful.

Gently laying her down on the big bed, Davan covered her with a light, lacy cover, then he stood back to study her.

He couldn't help it. He didn't want to just walk away and get someone else to look after her. Not yet. Not now.

Arms folded across his chest, Davan looked down at Delias. Her thick lashes made half moons against her pale cheeks, and her soft, plump lips were paler than their natural pink.

Beneath the cover, her breasts rose and fell with each deep breath she took.

In sleep she looked defenceless, nothing like the sharp-tongued wench he knew she could be, nor did she look as though she was capable of giving anyone the cold shoulder.

He had the sudden desire to lie down beside her and gather

her close, to hold her against the warmth of his body and keep her safe as she slept a healing sleep.

Where had these sudden desires come from? This protectiveness? This over-protectiveness?

Spying a big armchair close by, Davan moved it where he could observe her, and he sat down to gaze at her thoughtfully. It was more than just protectiveness, he felt like that with all the Daamens under his care, be they men, wenches or children. Hell, he was even protective of animals. They all came under his care.

But what he felt for Delias was more than just protectiveness.

He wanted to hold her close, soothe her hurts, wipe away her tears and make her laugh. See her naked. Oh, aye, he wanted to see her fully naked. In his bed. Under him.

I'm in big trouble. Davan shifted in the armchair, hooking his ankle over the opposite knee and leaning back to stroke his jaw while regarding the sleeping lass more intently. *I can just imagine the look on her face if I told her I wanted to make love to her. Especially after threatening her with a spanking last night.* Davan actually cringed inwardly at the thought. *Oh aye, 'twill make her regard me fondly. Fool.*

He was a fool to think he hadn't felt something for her all these years, but time and circumstances hadn't provided an ideal situation for him to pursue her, and then she'd started giving him the cold shoulder and her dislike of him had made him bury any feelings that had started to surface way back in the past. Last night hadn't improved things. Now… now she probably hated his guts rather than just despising him. Or would when she awoke and realised he'd had his hand all over her naked bottom.

Broodingly, Davan rested his chin on his hand and contemplated the sleeping beauty. No doubt after his handling of her extremely delectable curves, she wasn't going to want to face him anytime soon, which was just too bad for her because he intended to pursue this further. A lot further.

His reaction to her last night, and then seeing her in pain and wanting to be the one to give her relief, had just reawakened feelings he'd thought long gone.

He wasn't sure how he was going to accomplish it, but Delias wasn't going to get away this time.

~ * ~

Czex sidled up beside Manez in the Trade Building. "I think I may have discovered who has the crate."

Manez glanced around to ensure they weren't being observed. "Who?"

"Some blonde woman, name of Delias. I overheard someone mention the crate."

Alarm filled Manez. "What was it about the crate that caught their attention?"

"Not what we fear, that's for sure. Apparently it was the symbol on the side of it." Czex pulled back his sleeve to bare the symbol on his arm to Manez. "It had this on it, remember?"

"Idiot!" Manez knocked his arm aside, then hurriedly glanced around again. No one seemed to have noticed his actions, and he turned back to Czex, his eyes hard. "Don't be showing that symbol around here, fool."

Annoyed, Czex jerked his sleeve back down. "The symbol was apparently on the crate."

"Bloody hell. Which fool did that?"

"The fool that wanted to ensure he knew the crate when he saw it. Apparently it had been drawn on quite crudely, so no one would probably recognize it."

"We hope."

"Anyway, I overheard someone talking about the blonde woman having the crate."

"Right." Manez looked around grimly. "We need to find out where this blonde called Delias lives."

"Asking will bring suspicion. These Daamens aren't very forthcoming with information that doesn't need to be known outside this Trade Building."

———

83

"So we need to spot her ourselves. Is she here now?"

Czex shook his head. "No. But she usually does trade from that area."

Manez followed his gaze and swore. Great. Just great. The blonde was the same one the giant Head Peacekeeper had been watching so broodingly. Bloody great. Taking a deep breath, he squared his shoulders. At least he knew what she looked like. Now all they had to do was wander around until they spotted her, and then follow her back to her home, get the crate and run.

A sudden chill went through him. Unless the damned woman had already opened the crate and found part of the contents. He glanced around again. He'd noticed nothing that indicated anything wrong in this Daamen settlement, which meant that in all likelihood the object hadn't been discovered. He hoped. He just had to ensure that he and Czex found the crate before the contents were inspected too closely.

He nudged Czex. "Let's go."

~*~

On the other side of the Trade Building, a pair of cold eyes watched them leave, and fingers touched the hilt of the sheathed dagger.

~*~

The watcher waited until Czex and Manez had left, and waited for the spectator to leave as well before following at a distance.

~ * ~

Delias stared at herself in the mirror. *Come on, you can go down there and face him. He helped you.* He'd had his hand all over her naked bum cheek. Davan had seen more than any man ever had of her.

A hot flush went straight through Delias to settle unnervingly low in her belly. The memory of his hand on her, the firm stroke of that big, calloused palm against her flesh… Hurriedly Delias splashed more cold water on her face, blinking and gasping as she groped for a towel with which to

---

dry her face.

He'd been so gentle, so caring, so concerned. His hands so sure, his big body reassuringly warm behind her… "Get a grip, Del!" Slinging the towel back across the rail, Delias gathered her hair up into a loose topknot. Curls slipped free to bob around her cheeks and she tucked them behind her ears.

Davan tucked my hair behind my ear, too. Right before he ran his hands over my body. "Oh, God, Del!" Delias scowled at her reflection. "He rubbed cream onto your sore arse and waist, he didn't make a lover's caress!" *Damn it.* "You are such a slut. You don't like him, remember?" Her scowl deepened. "Get a grip and just go down and thank him and see him out the door!" *I can always die of mortification after he leaves.* Squaring her shoulders, she took a deep breath and left the bathroom.

The smell of something delicious cooking wafted up the stairs to greet her, and she wondered where Davan had learned to cook. Refusing to shrink beneath her embarrassment, she entered the kitchen boldly, only to stare blankly at the tall, blonde, and very pregnant Reeka warrior wench stirring something in a pot on the stove. "Dana?"

Dana looked around, her blonde bob brushing her shoulders. "'Tis me."

"What are you doing here?" Delias moved further into the kitchen to see another warrior sitting at the table, a little boy on her knee playing with her long, golden braid. "Tenia?"

Tenia's beautiful face was concerned, her deep violet eyes studying Delias intently. "Davan asked us to check on you. Is your back better?"

"I'm fine. The cream fixed it, as always." Delias was relieved. The thought of facing the one man who'd seen her naked bottom was something she could put off for a little longer. *Gosh, what a shame.* But then, not seeing a concerned Davan waiting for her was a bit of a disappointment. *He did his duty, 'tis all.* She bit her lip.

"You don't look fine," Dana stated bluntly.

There was no hiding anything from the sharp-eyed Reeka.

"Just a little sleepy, an after affect from the cream."

Dana waved the wooden spoon in Tenia's direction. "Must be why Davan was so tired when he called you, cousin. The man couldn't stop yawning. I thought he was going to swallow the viscomm."

"You didn't have to wish it out loud in front of him."

"Hey, the man had the nerve to tell Garrett that I shouldn't be allowed to wander the forest in my condition."

Tenia grinned. "Garrett had no idea you were doing it."

"That's right, and Garrett nearly had a fit."

Delias peeked into the saucepan to discover a meaty stew whose fragrance made her mouth water. "Oh aye, I heard about that. Your husband tried to lay down the law."

"He tried." Dana smiled smugly. "I soon told him who was laying down the law."

"Oh aye, you told him all right." Tenia winked at Delias. "I noticed you don't walk the forest alone anymore."

"Garrett didn't win the argument," Dana said loftily. "I bloody told him I'd do as I wanted - "

"And now you only walk the forest if one of us is with you," Tenia finished.

"I still won the forest walking bit."

Tenia disentangled little Vulya's fingers from her golden braid. "If you say so."

Hands on hips, stew juice dripping unheeded onto the floor from the spoon, Dana scowled. "What's that supposed to mean?"

"It means, cousin, that we're only allowed to walk you within sight of the settlement."

"I still won the forest walking."

Tenia rolled her eyes. "Fine, fine. You won."

"Glad to see you agree." Dana turned back to the stove. "Hand me some bowls, Del, and I'll dish us up some food."

After mopping up the drops of stew on the floor, Delias handed the bowls one at a time to the Reeka and casually asked, "So Davan went home?"

"Aye." Sharp hazel eyes studied her. "Why, do you wish him back?"

"What? Nay! I mean, nay." Taking the now full bowl from Dana's hand, Delias placed it in front of Tenia.

"Because it can be easily arranged," Dana continued, expertly spooning stew into another bowl.

Delias kept her face calm, knowing from experience that Dana loved to tease and was like a hound with a bone if she thought she'd discovered a weak spot in a friend…or enemy, come to that. "No need. I'm fine now."

"It'd be my pleasure, seeing as how you two just love each other."

Delias nearly dropped the full bowl that Dana handed her. "I don't love him!"

Dana smirked.

"Uh-oh," Tenia said.

"What?" Delias carefully set the bowl on the table in front of an empty chair.

"You know what Dana's like when she gets started."

"I didn't start anything." Dana handed another bowl to Delias. "'Tis not my fault that she can't lie without fumbling."

"I do not fumble," Delias replied tartly. "And I don't lie."

Dana made a scoffing sound while picking up a bowl with a small amount of cooled stew in it. Handing it to Delias, she said, "Here, blow." She waited until Delias took it before adding, "It'll be good practice."

"For what?" Delias placed the bowl in front of Tenia, who started supervising her son feeding himself.

"For blowing Davan."

Tenia laughed. "You are so bad."

"Garrett likes me bad." Dana eased herself into the chair and picked up her spoon.

"Aye. 'Tis how you got pregnant with twins in the first place."

"Oh no. 'Tis because I was so good at being bad — or so bad at being good. Take your pick." Taking a tentative bite of stew, Dana chewed and looked across the table at Delias. "I don't think you need lessons on being bad."

"Because I'm too good to corrupt?" Delias asked dryly, resigned now to her friend's teasing.

"Because you're so good at being bad to Davan."

"I just follow your example."

"And I set such good ones." Dana took another bite of stew, chewed and swallowed. "Damn, 'tis good if I do say so myself."

"Don't break your arm patting yourself on the back," Delias said.

"I'd rather get Davan here to rub it." Dana looked slyly at Delias. "Among other areas to rub."

Delias raised a haughty brow. "My sciatica pain was in my back."

"Pshaw! You wish. I know where sciatica pain goes to, my little friend, and you had Davan rubbing it." Dana winked roguishly. "Tell me, are his hands as good as you thought?"

"Why? Do you want to try them out?"

Tenia gave a gurgle of amusement. "Garrett would kill any man who touched Dana! Davan would be running for his life."

"My honey pot does love me." Dana smiled smugly.

"I thought you were his honey pot?"

"My honey pot is just for him. Is that better?" When Tenia groaned and Delias mimicked being sick, she placed her hand on her swollen belly. "And look what happened when he sampled the honey pot once too often."

"Oh, Dana!" Tenia placed her hands over Vulya's ears.

"Just warning Del what could happen if she lets Davan sample her honey pot."

"Trust me," Delias said more placidly than she felt, "He will not ever be sampling my honey pot."

It was a merry hour later before the Reekas took their leave. They hadn't gone as far as the gate before Darvk was there, swinging a happily shrieking Vulya up into his arms. Darvk settled him onto one lean hip before bending down to press a tender kiss to Tenia's lips.

Straightening, he spied Delias and waved to her. "Feeling better, lass?"

"Just how many people know?" she demanded.

"Just me, Garrett, and our wenches." His grinned widely. "Afraid your parents or Red will hear?"

"I'd never hear the end of it. Please don't tell them."

"Ooohh, secrets," Dana said. "Lots of secrets."

Laughing, Darvk placed one hand on Dana's shoulder and gently moved her forward. "Wench, your husband awaits you."

"Summoned by He Who Thinks He Rules. How delightful."

"He said to tell you he's got a little surprise for you when you get home."

"That's how I ended up pregnant."

"She's in a mood," Tenia told Darvk. "Let's get her home so Garrett can deal with her."

"He wishes," Dana said pertly. "I deal with him and he likes it!"

"The man always was a glutton for punishment," Darvk remarked.

"The man likes his punishment."

"Incorrigible," Tenia informed Delias, while slipping an arm around her sister warrior's waist. "Come on, cousin. Home and bed."

"'Tis how I ended up - "

"Keep that thought to yourself."

"Just educating you, little cousin."

"I have two children, I don't think I need educating."

"'Tis not what you said last night," Darvk stated cheerfully.

"Your form of education is enlightening."

"Oh good, because I have some more education in mind for tonight."

"Really? Hurry up, Dana."

"Hey, no rushing the pregnant wench!"

Shaking her head and laughing, Delias watched as her friends walked out of sight. She could still hear their teasing after they'd turned the corner.

Looking up at the evening sky, she breathed deeply. Good friends, good life. She was lucky. She was also lucky that Davan had come when he did, or she could have been lying across the bench in agony waiting for someone for several hours or more. Just the thought made her shudder.

The first time she'd hurt her back, the Saalm medics had been on planet and they'd made her the cream. The healing properties brought quick relief, easing the spasming and inflammation within twenty minutes of it being applied. Followed by a healing sleep, the nerves were back to normal within several hours. She'd been warned to be especially careful when handling anything that required lifting or carrying and normally she was careful, but now and again she got careless and suffered the consequences.

Walking down the steps, she ambled along the pathway towards the gate. The evening was delightful, the breeze warm, the scent of night blossoms in the air. Children's laughter came from nearby, a man talking, a wench laughing. A hound barked in the distance and a lycat sat on a nearby gatepost, watching Delias curiously. Overhead a Daamen trading spaceship soared, angling upwards until it winked out of sight in space.

How she loved walking in the evenings, listening to the sights and sounds of a normal Daamen evening.

Taking a deep breath, she followed the pathway out of the gate and beside the cobbled road. She stopped several times to chat with friends also out for a stroll, or in their gardens. As the evening turned into night, people moved indoors and Delias found herself wandering up a quiet road and coming to a stop in front of a graceful, one-storey home that sprawled back on a large block of land. She didn't need the light of day for her to know it sprawled, because she knew this house. It belonged to Davan.

The gardens weren't as neatly tended as her parents' gardens, but they were cared for. Flowers and bushes grew in abundance, but tended to grow where their seeds took them. There was no real pattern to the gardens but she knew there was a pathway that meandered amongst the lush growth, and both day and night flyers frequented it along with Davan's two lycats and one old hound.

Now that she was here, should she just go up to the house and thank him? Her cheeks burned a little at the thought of seeing him face to face, knowing what he'd seen of her. For stars' sake, 'twas only your bottom! Nothing else! Her heart started to race at the memory of his palm stroking across her skin and she licked her lips. Mayhap she ought to leave it until tomorrow. But then he'd see her face. This way she could do it in the dimness of his veranda. Aye, 'twould be better. Dimness was good. No clear expression, no eye contact. I can do this. I can. Do it now, get it over with.

Before she could falter anymore, Delias pushed open the gate and strode up the pathway, skipped up the steps and approached the door. The wooden door was open and through the screen door she could see that the corridor beyond was dim fading into darkness further back, lit only faintly by the light coming from what she presumed was the lounge room or mayhap the kitchen. Music sounded quietly from somewhere, and she saw one of the lycats come out of the lit doorway and disappear into the depths of the house.

Now or never, Del. Do it. Squaring her shoulders, she knocked briskly. There was no answer, so she raised her hand to knock again when a deep voice came from behind her.

"Now why doesn't it surprise me to find you wandering around alone at night?"

Startled, Delias swung around to find Davan standing at the foot of the steps, his old hound yawning by his booted legs. The old hound gave a slow wag of his tail and slowly climbed the steps, stopping briefly beside Delias for an ear rub, which she fondly gave, before he crossed to a thick mattress lying in a sheltered corner and plopped down upon it with a contented sigh.

Delias transferred her gaze back to Davan to find that he'd come up the stairs and was looking down at her. He stood close, *really* close, and she gave a nervous clearing of her throat. "Um… Davan…" Thank God he couldn't see the blush in her cheeks. This man had seen her bare arsed, for stars' sake!

"Delias." In the dim light from the doorway she could see the glitter of his eyes as he looked directly down at her.

She was well used to titling her head back to look up at Daamen men, but she certainly had never noticed how their bodies emitted heat. Or mayhap 'twas just this man, and mayhap he was the only man she noticed who smelled… nice.

Oh stars, Del! Just thank him and run!

Taking a deep breath - *and boy, did he smell good* - Delias began, "I just wanted - "

"Come inside, lass." He reached past her and opened the door.

"Oh, nay, I just - "

"After you." He gestured.

Delias bit her lip. "'Tisn't necessary, I - "

His hand was at her waist - dear God, was it burning a hole through her gown? He felt so deliciously hot! - and he moved forward, his much larger body coming up against her so that she had only two choices - resist loudly or allow herself to be propelled inside. Or stay pressed up against his body, which was a tantalizing third choice.

Aghast at her wayward thoughts, Delias walked through the door, moving further into the house in an attempt to put some distance between herself and the intoxicating man who was right behind her.

Hoo boy, could she feel him behind her! All male heat and clean, masculine scent.

Giving herself a mental head slap to try and regain control of her unruly thoughts, she swung around, saying as she did so,

"Davan, I wanted to - " only to halt as she came smack up against his hard chest.

His big hands settled firmly on her upper arms, holding her against him when she would have stumbled back. "Careful, Del. You don't want to hurt yourself again."

Automatically she braced her hands on his chest, only to realize with horrified fascination that instead of the usual peacekeepers tunic he usually wore, he instead had on a simple, sleeveless vest that hung open, like most Daamen men, revealing the hard swells of muscle that were now pressed against her softer curves. Her breasts nestled against his upper abdomen, his strong thighs cradled her hips, and his skin was overly warm against her suddenly shaking palms. Dear God, did this man have a fire under his skin?

Tilting her head right back, she looked up into his face, seeing the hard planes silhouetted against the dimness in the hall. His features were partially shadowed, his blonde hair loose down his back and over his shoulders in a thick fall. But his eyes, stars above! His eyes glittered with a blue fire. That much she could make out in the dimness.

For a split second she thought he was furious with her once again and her heart quailed, but his hands started to gently run up and down her upper arms in a slow, hypnotic stroke, and his voice was deep and low as he asked, "Now, lass, what did you want?"

You. You, because you're doing strange things to me. You're making me feel strange things. If you weren't holding me against you, I'd be on my knees. And that certainly didn't help the images in her head that she was desperately trying to banish.

"I just… I wanted…" She stopped, swallowed, and began again. "I wanted to thank you."

"For what?"

"You know. My back."

"Ah. Aye." Those hands were now stroking down to her elbow, long, calloused fingers trailing lightly across the sensitive inner skin before smoothing back up her arms, then repeating the path. Davan's head lowered a little. "Your back… and…"

A little shiver went through Delias as his fingers trailed lightly along her inner elbow again. It was so delicious, so - "Nice…"

"'Twas?"

She tried to concentrate on her reason for coming to Davan's house, but it wasn't easy when his touch was sending little sparks skittering in their lazy wake. "I…aye. 'Twas nice of you to…. to…" She fought not to close her eyes and give herself up to the delicious sensations dancing across her skin. She took in a deep breath and that certainly didn't help, because she got a sense overload of masculine scent. Of Davan.

"To what?" His voice lowered even more, was huskier, like dark velvet.

"To…to rub the cream on my back and - " She cut the words off as heat pooled low in her belly at the memory of those big hands on her bottom, stroking so smoothly, so sure.

"And where else, Delias?" His head came lower as he bent over her, forcing her to arch back as he still held her close against his own body. His hands left her arms to slide one around her waist, the other around her back, supporting her as he bent her backwards.

Her senses were spinning. His thick, blonde hair tickled her skin as it pooled on her bare shoulders with his ever nearing bend. Her breathing was uneven, and she slid her tongue nervously across her lips as she held onto his arms, feeling the bulge and flex of hard muscle beneath her fingers. She gave a very poor, half hearted attempt to push him away, but then she gave up and just hung onto him.

His face now hovered just above hers, and she was well and truly bent back over his hands with no place to go but the floor if he released his hold on her. Wide-eyed, she looked up directly into brilliant blue eyes that glittered with the same fire she swore burned beneath his skin. How else could anyone explain such a hot man?

Thick lashes veiled his eyes briefly as he looked down at her lips. "Tell me, sweet Delias. Tell me where else I rubbed that cream."

"I can't…" She shivered at the unexpected sensation of a hard thigh sliding between her own softer thighs. It was a shock, but a delicious one, especially knowing the only thing keeping their flesh separate was the material of her gown and his pants.

"Shall I, sweet Delias?" His sinful mouth hovered a hairsbreadth above her trembling lips. "Shall I tell you where I rubbed that cream?" He angled his head slightly and his lips grazed her cheek lightly.

She thought her heart was going to hammer out of her chest and she shifted her head, following him, trying to get the satin feel of his lips against her own. Wanting him.

His breath was warm on her skin as he continued in that dark velvet voice, "I rubbed that cream on an alluring bottom. A luscious curve which fit perfectly in my palm." His lips sipped lightly, teasingly, at the corner of her mouth, and she moaned softly, gripping his arms as she pressed closer to him. "I traced the delectable arch, and I wanted more. I don't want to just trace that satiny skin, sweet Delias, I want to taste it."

His words were innocent when taken separately, but oh, so wicked when put together. Delias rubbed her thigh against his, one hand skimming up his arm to slide over his massive shoulder. "Please…"

"'Please' what?" His lips whispered above her own, so close they tickled her own lips, but still not close enough.

Her gaze locked dreamily with his. "Please… kiss me."

Chapter 3

*

Total surrender. It was what Davan had been seducing Delias into, with no shame and all gain. Her total surrender, and he knew he had it right here in his arms. He was taking that surrender and storming her gates. Literally.

The first touch of his lips to hers was light, caressing, almost teasing. A gentle press of silken skin to silken skin. God above, it was all he'd ever wanted, a taste of her, and now he had her.

Those soft lips moved against his and she arched closer, her small hands gripping his massive biceps as she sought to get nearer. Davan was more than happy to indulge that want, and he gathered her closer, so close that they were one from knee to breast. His thigh nudged that hot, secret place between her thighs and he was rewarded with her thigh sliding higher along his, opening her, giving him more access to shift even closer until his thigh was pressed hard against that secret spot he was going to plunder like a space pirate falling on stolen booty.

Delias's lips parted against his, and Davan swept inside, his tongue sweeping through her mouth, her taste exploding on his tongue, driving him almost wild with the need that ached in his groin. His blood was hot and heavy, like molten lava as it surged through his veins.

He ate at her mouth, devouring her, wanting more, knowing he was going to have more. Knowing he was going to have Delias. Finally have her. His desire for her ran so deep it unleashed the hidden emotions that had come to the surface in the last few days, and the surface cracked, and every emotion he'd suppressed raged forth, taking him over. It roared through him, consuming him, and he swept her up into his arms without breaking the contact of their lips.

Delias kissed him back as deeply, her little tongue flicking through his mouth, and her hand slid under his vest to

96

smooth over one hard swell of pectoral muscle. Her fingers left sparks on his skin in their wake, and it fuelled his carnal fire into a blaze that was almost out of control.

It took such effort not to pin her against the wall there and then and take her, to bury himself deep inside her wench's heat, that Davan actually took several steps towards the nearest wall before he regained a fraction of control to turn towards his bedroom instead.

When he lifted his head, Delias slid her lips to his throat, her mouth finding the pulse that beat so heavily there, and she laved it with her tongue. His knees nearly gave out then and there at such a small act that from her was so erotic. His staff bulged, almost painful in the confines of his pants.

It didn't matter that the corridor was dark, he knew his home like the back of his hand. Unerringly he strode to his bedroom, entering it to cross to his big bed. Releasing Delias's legs, he allowed her to slide down his body while keeping one arm around her waist. He didn't give her time to even think about where she was, he just managed to grate out 'lights dim' before claiming her lips again, pushing her further into mindless heat.

The lamp beside the bed lit to a soft glow, casting the bed in intimate light while keeping the rest of the room in dimness. Everything was focused on the big bed.

With one arm still around Delias's waist and his lips devouring hers, Davan reached out and grabbed the edge of the covers, wrenching them back with a careless yank to lie discarded at the end of the bed.

Delias's heat almost matched his own. He hadn't realized what passion beat beneath her cool surface, though he'd glimpsed it in her eyes—except when she'd looked at him. There had been only contempt, not the scorch of lust that he saw in the brilliant green depths now when those heavy lashes lifted to reveal her eyes to his gaze.

"Davan," she whispered huskily. "Oh God, Davan..."

His name on her lips was filled with sexual heat, and he

craved her nakedness against his. Hooking his fingers into the straps of her gown, he skimmed them down her arms, the bodice falling with it to reveal those luscious breasts behind the lacy support garment. He unsnapped the clasp at the front and the garment dropped to the floor, spilling those globes into his waiting palms.

Those breasts were made for him, he just knew it. The rightness of the silken skin, the little pink nipples that pebbled into his palms as he gently squeezed the delicate flesh, the way they fit into his big hands so perfectly. The whiteness of her skin stood out against the suntanned burnish of his hands. Just above her left breast was the delicate, silver mark that every Daamen wench was born with, a small incomplete circle on its side with a dainty scroll at each end curling back on itself. His fingers were like brands against her flesh, and he felt possessiveness sweep through him at the thought. The mark branded her as Daamen, and tonight he was going to brand her as his, brand her in and out with his seed, his scent, his touch. After tonight she would know that she belonged to him, that he claimed her and wasn't going to let her go.

Kissing his way down her throat and shoulders as he went, his hands smoothing down her satiny skin, Davan dropped to his knees and those tempting breasts were right there, the nipples begging for his touch, his kiss, his hot mouth.

But first... first... he looked up and captured her gaze, seeing the wanton need in the brilliant green depths of her eyes. Those well-kissed lips were red and plump, and her breath came unevenly as she saw the ardour for her he knew was plain on his face. He didn't bother trying to hide anything from her, his emotions clear on his face for her to read, to see, to understand. To know.

One small hand came out and entangled with his hair, and he saw the need and uncertainty combined in her gaze, and without further ado he leaned forward and engulfed her nipple in his mouth, sucking strongly.

Delias cried out, her knees buckling, and he caught her to

him with one arm around the backs of her thighs just under
her bottom. Holding her steady, he continued to suck, lashing
the tender bud with his tongue, wallowing in the luxury of
having all that soft, female flesh against his face. Every breath
he inhaled sucked her sweet scent deeper into his lungs until
it spilled out to fill very part of him, and he knew that no
matter where she went, he'd find her. Because he had her
scent now. And he intended for that scent to fill his bed, his
bedroom, and his home forever. He wanted to come home
and smell her as he walked up the path, to know she waited
for him, only for him.

Releasing the little bud, he nuzzled the satiny skin between
her breasts before taking possession of the other little nipple,
sucking on it strongly, plucking at her feminine strings so she
felt every suck clear through to her womb.

He felt her fingers in his hair gripping tightly, holding him
to her as she arched back before she released him to grip his
shoulders, leaning on him as she moaned. Lifting his head, he
saw that she was biting her lip, her cheeks rosy with desire,
and his hunger for her intensified.

Lowering his head again, he pressed his lips to her stomach,
licking into her belly button, making her gasp and push back
slightly at the suddenness of his movement.

Davan laughed huskily against her stomach, hooking his
fingers into the gown that pooled around her hips, and he slid
the silk down her hips along with her lacy panties, letting the
material pool at her feet. Automatically she lifted her foot to
step out of the gown, and he slid her sandals off. Now she was
finally naked and revealed to him fully. Sitting back on his
heels, Davan slid his hands down the backs of her thighs and
settled them behind her knees, his fingers running lightly up
and down the sensitive skin there as he looked his fill of her
nakedness.

Her slimness he knew, but the hidden treasures beneath
he'd only glimpsed through a wet gown. Now he saw it in all
its delicate glory. Her breasts were full, firm, the nipples

reddened from the attentions of his mouth, her waist small, almost spanned by his big hands, her hips a gentle roundness that tapered into slim legs and small feet. The small triangular patch of blonde hair at the apex of her thighs beckoned to him, and his staff jerked in response, stiffening more, pressing demandingly against the front of his pants, surging upward, seeking the moist heat that was hidden beneath the blonde patch.

Even though his body demanded release, Davan had one promise to himself to keep first. He wanted to taste her. Leaning forward, he inhaled her exotic scent, his hands coming up to grip her thighs and bring her forward.

"Davan, I..." Her voice wavered.

"One taste, sweet Delias." His eyes drifted closed as he approached that beckoning patch. "Just one taste."

"Davan, I don't think - " Her words choked off as soon as his tongue swept between her moist labia to stroke unerringly across the little clitoris hidden beyond.

She shuddered beneath his touch, grabbing onto his shoulders, her gasping breath filling the air. It was the sweetest sound Davan had ever heard, just as her taste was the most exotic he'd ever tasted. He lapped deeper into the heated moistness, his tongue pressing up against her perineum and rubbing.

Delias exploded, the orgasm ripping through her, and Davan surged upward, sweeping her up into his arms and placing her on the bed, jerking off his vest and kicking off his boots, watching her with hot eyes as she arched back, her nipples rosy, her eyes closed as the orgasm flooded her, her hands fisted into the sheet as she rode the wild crest.

It almost made him come to just watch her.

Stripping off his pants, he freed his staff which thrust up hard against his abdomen. Placing one knee on the bed at her hip, he swung himself over her, sliding his thighs between hers to widen the cradle as he sank down onto her. Keeping his upper weight off her by balancing on his forearms, he dipped his head down and caught her lips, plundering the depths of her mouth as he swallowed the whimpers that accompanied the orgasm as it slid back out into Eros.

He didn't give her time to come back, but lifted his head so he could watch her face as he drew back just enough to allow his staff to slide through the sheltering curls to part the tender lips hiding her secrets, and then he was nudging the entrance to her body.

Controlling his raging libido, he entered her slowly, stretching her untried body, and her eyes opened, the brilliant green depths hazy with remnants of the orgasm, the flickers of desire. Her eyes widened as she felt him slide deeper. Her arms came up, small hands sliding around his shoulders, smoothing across his skin as he lowered his chest to brush her breasts, her nipples pebbling hard against his swells of muscle.

"Delias." He breathed her name as he slid further home into that hot heat.

"Davan." She whispered his name in a voice like black velvet that licked across his skin.

"I need you." He lowered his head, his blonde hair spilling down around their faces, shutting them into a private world.

"Then take me."

"All of you," he whispered against her lips.

"You have me." Lifting her head, she touched her lips to his. "You always have." Sliding her hand behind his head, she drew him down the last scant millimetre to mould their mouths together.

Her mouth was as hot as her sheath, which clasped him, spasmed, and threw him over the edge of control.

He thrust the last few inches, breaking through the fragile barrier and burying himself deep inside her. The arching of her body, the sensuous slide of her legs against his, the way she reached for him, whimpering and wanting more, made the fire rage into a furnace, and he was swept away.

Bracing his hands on the mattress each side of her, Davan

withdrew and thrust home again, surging through the tightness of her sheath, her slickness easing the way, glorying in the way she responded to him.

It was as if she couldn't get enough. He sure as hell couldn't get enough. He wanted more, so much more, everything she had, everything she was, he wanted it all. He wanted her everything.

Her smaller frame was beneath him as he loomed over her, his staff claiming her body, the seed already leaking from the tip to brand her sheath. He took her mouth, plundering the depths as thoroughly as he plundered her body. His hips pumped as he filled her again and again, feeling the tide of prurience well up inside him.

Their combined scent filled the air, their skin slid across each other, hands felt, touched, mouths kissed and whispered, moaned and cried out, and their bodies melded together, his invading, hers receiving.

He thrust harder, feeling the pinnacle rising in front of him as he stoked their internal flames higher, his staff sliding through the wet, hot glove of her, her muscles gripping him and undulating, seeking to milk him. He pushed harder, his hands trapping hers and holding her wrists each side of her head. His hands pinning hers to the bed as surely as his hips pinned her down for their mutual pleasure.

He rode her hard, fast, and she arched into him, joining him on that wild ride as they both soared up that peak.

They teetered on the brink, and Davan stopped. For a split second in eternity he gazed down into her eyes, sharing his every emotion in one look, seeing her every emotion reflected in kind. Time stood still as they looked at each other, their breaths rasping in the stillness, and then he pulled back and thrust home one last time.

They both shattered, tipping over the edge. He arched backwards, his hips pinning hers down into the bed as his body held her prisoner to take his seed. His staff swelled, his scrotum pulling tight and releasing in a stream of seed that flushed through her channel, searing her, and her body took everything, spasming and milking him, her muscles clenching tight around him, seeking everything he had and taking it all. His hips postponed twice, straining forward as the last few spurts left him, and finally he'd given her everything.

Time had no meaning as they drifted through the gossamer clouds, floating slowly down to reality.

Davan lowered his head, his breathing uneven, choppy, to rest his forehead against hers, his nose touching the tip of hers. She opened her eyes dreamily and smiled up at him. Tenderly he kissed her before rolling onto his side and taking her with him, his arms around her gathering her into his body to hold her close. Tucking her head under his chin, he dropped a kiss onto her curls.

Delias snuggled close, her arm going around his waist, and within minutes she was asleep.

She felt so right in his arms, in his bed, in his home. With a sigh of utter contentment, Davan closed his eyes and slipped into sleep.

~ * ~

Manez couldn't believe how the Daamens didn't lock their doors. The fools were open to be robbed, but then again, you'd have to have a death wish to invade a Daamen's home uninvited.

He wasn't suicidal, but there was already a death wish riding him hard if he didn't find the object. The bloody thing was a spectre behind him, waiting to pounce in an agonizing way. He assured himself that he'd risk a Daamen's wrath rather than the wrath of those who awaited him.

Then again, neither was he an idiot. Bravado aside, he wouldn't have entered if anyone had been home. One blow from a Daamen's fist would have knocked him to kingdom come. Then again, knowing what waited for him if he failed in his mission... Talk about being caught between the devil and a black hole.

Thank all that was bloody unholy that no one was at home.

Czex spotted the crate first. It was sitting on one of the gleaming counters. Part of Manez wanted to just take the crate and run, but noting that it was open - damned curious female - he had to check, then if it wasn't in there they could search the house while no one was home.

The crate held jars of spices and herbs but nothing more. He searched twice, lining the jars up and even checking the contents, but there was nothing. The object was missing.

"Shit!" He looked around, desperation creeping through him. "Czex, search upstairs and I'll search downstairs. We have to find it!"

Czex disappeared upstairs and the hunt ensued. An hour later they met at the bottom of the staircase.

"Nothing," Czex said grimly.

"Shit! Hell!" Manez ran one hand agitatedly through his hair. "We need to go into the settlement, see if we can hear anything about the Peacekeepers having it."

"If they have it, we're dead."

As if Manez needed reminding.

They left the big house stealthily.

~ * ~

From the shadows of a nearby tree, the spectator watched through coldly glittering eyes.

And in the shadows of the next house, the watcher observed and waited.

~ * ~

Delias woke slowly, a smile on her face. Davan had woken her several times during the night with long, slow, drugging kisses, clever hands and hot mouth, and his body that had her fires burning out of control. Each time he brought her to orgasm, and each time after he cuddled her close and she slept, warm and fulfilled and safe, and more content than she could ever remember feeling in her whole life. It was just so right being in his sheltering arms.

Stretching luxuriously, she snuggled against the big body she was spooning. One arm around his lean waist, her hand rested on his muscle-ribbed abdomen. Her whole front was pressed against the back of Davan's muscular body, her thighs snugged up behind his big thighs, his muscular buttocks snugged into her groin, his skin so warm against her own and -

Oh stars! Davan! Her eyes widened in shock. Stiffening, she awoke completely from dreamy contemplation to harsh reality. *I slept with Davan! Nay!* She stared at the big back right in front of her eyes. Right against her naked body. *Oh God! We're both naked!*

Every memory came crashing back with vivid clarity. Hot skin, hot mouth, hot hands, hot bodies, hot words and hot sex. Just the memory was enough to elicit little fiery tongues of desire, but panic was also setting in.

She had to get away before he awoke to find her still in his bed.

With agonizing slowness, she carefully lifted her arm and started to withdraw it, easing away from the warmth of his big body at the same time, which was a damned shame, because he was so warm and big and safe and - *nay! Get away now while you still have some brain cells left!*

Delias hadn't retreated very far before a big hand suddenly clamped around her wrist and Davan rolled fast over onto his back.

Delias jerked back onto her knees, but the hand around her wrist was like a steel manacle keeping her by his side.

"I was waiting for you to do that," Davan said calmly.

Wide-eyed, Delias stammered, "You-you were?"

"Aye." Head resting on the pillow, he eyed her like a great lycat eyeing prey. "I knew you'd cut and run as soon as you realized what had happened between us." His blue-eyed gaze drifted down over her body, and when they lifted, they held a decided heat. "Come here."

"What? Nay!" Belatedly remembering her naked state, she grabbed the sheet and dragged it over her nakedness, an almost futile gesture because he was lying on it and she only had enough material to partially cover her breasts and drape across her thighs. For stars' sake, he's seen more of me than anyone ever has! Oh God, I lay with him! He was inside me! "Let go." Cheeks flaming and unable to meet his knowing gaze, she tugged at her wrist.

"And have you bolt? Nay."

"You have to let go!"

"Nay."

Anger mingled with embarrassment and she finally looked at him. And immediately forgot what she was going to say, because he was lying there in partial naked glory.

For several second all she could do was look at him lying in the bed. Really look at him. The covers were pushed down low over his lean hips, barely covering the long, thick staff that lay between his legs. His stomach was ribbed with muscle, and her gaze traced the swells upward to his massive pectorals, the smooth skin covering them she now knew was warm — almost hot — to touch. Like silk over steel. The bicep in his arm bulged and flexed as he lifted and bent his arm to rest his hand behind his head. His blonde hair was scattered on the pillow, and she remembered the silky feel of it against her skin as he'd trailed kisses across her body. She swallowed against the little pricks of heat that immediately tried to flare to life inside her at the memory.

"Delias." Her name was a soft, beguiling word on his lips, drawing her gaze to his face.

His dangerously handsome face, with the square jaw, the straight nose, the lips that were so masculine and had given her such pleasure, and had whispered such carnal words of love and passion during the magical hours of the night. Finally she met his gaze, those blue eyes that seemed to see straight into her very soul, those blue eyes that had seen her body as no other person ever had, those blue eyes that had gazed down at her as he filled her, his staff deep inside her bringing her to ecstasy while he watched, right before he took her mouth as he took her body.

Those blue eyes that looked at her so knowingly.

Delias felt heat, but also embarrassment, and for a split second she didn't know whether to yell at him, hit him, or just cry. She sure as hell couldn't hide from him, not with him shackling her wrist in one big hand.

Davan sat up suddenly, his big body moving with strength and grace. He didn't drag her closer, instead, his gaze softened. "We need to talk."

"Talk?" She started to shake her head.

"Aye, we do. 'Tisn't finished between us, Delias. 'Tis much to talk about."

"'Twas just one night, a mistake - "

"Never a mistake. I'm going to have a shower, then I'm going to go down and cook breakfast."

"Breakfast?" She stared at him.

"Aye, while you shower I'll cook breakfast, and you, lass, are going to join me."

"Are you insane?" She was dumbfounded. "I can't have breakfast with you!"

"Why not? We made love. What's breakfast in comparison?" With his hold on her wrist preventing her from pulling away, he leaned forward until they were almost nose to nose. "You will join me."

Before she could say anything, he released her wrist, turned away and swung out of bed. The covers fell from him and her mouth went dry at the strong, muscular lines of his body.

Unashamed of his nakedness, Davan walked around the bed and she hastily averted her eyes, kneeling on the big bed with the covers now clutched to her in both trembling hands. Her heart thumped crazily, and she waited to hear him close the bathroom door behind him so she could grab her clothes and run.

He didn't touch her, but she felt the heat of his body at her back as he stood close behind her. Breath coming unevenly, she looked sideways without moving her head but she couldn't see him. His unexpected warm breath on her cheek when he bent down behind her made her jump.

"Easy, little lass." A finger entwined in a lock of her hair. His voice was deep, sliding through her senses like black velvet. "But heed my words. Be here when I get out of the shower. Do not run. If you run, I'll track you down, Delias. I'll follow you, and I don't care who knows why."

"You wouldn't..."

"You know me, Delias." Those simple words conjured up a variety of images.

Aye, she knew him. Intimately. Physically. And more. She knew he'd keep his word. If she ran he'd follow, and he'd be relentless.

His lips grazed her ear, his deep voice calm, sure, and with a thread of steel. "Be here. Don't make me follow you."

She held her breath, biting her lip. Her heart was thumping so crazily she thought it was surely going to burst from her chest. A shiver went down her spine but she couldn't say if it was a thrill of fear at his words, or a thrill of something much more carnal as his silken hair spilled over her shoulder to tickle the swells of her breasts revealed above the tightly clenched sheet.

"'Tis just breakfast, Del." His lips touched the side of her neck lightly and her breath hitched at the sensation. How could a man's lips be so soft? "Just talk." He straightened abruptly and she felt the sudden loss of his body heat keenly. She listened for the bathroom door, but what she heard instead was that deep voice again. "Be here."

There was no click of a bathroom door closing. Within seconds she heard water running and she stole a glance over her shoulder at the door. It was open. He was in there and she was out here, and she could be out of the front door within minutes.

Be here when I get out of the shower. Do not run. If you run, I'll track you down, Delias. I'll follow you, and I don't care who knows why. The words resonated in her head and after several seconds of desperately deliberating, she knew she didn't want him tracking her down. She didn't want anyone to know she'd slept with him. Her arch enemy.

Oh God, she'd slept with the very man who disapproved of her! Only he sure as hell hadn't seemed to disapprove of her last night. His moans reverberated in the back of her mind, his groans of satisfaction, of carnal desire, his touch, the burning of his eyes, his kisses, the heat and passion for her.

It was not of a man who despised her. It was of a man who found her desirable, who made love to her as though he'd never get enough of her. Could a man make love to a wench like that if he despised her? Surely not. Surely... and besides, what about her?

Delias bit her lip, turning slowly on the bed so that she perched on the edge of it, dragging the covers closer against her. She'd fallen into his arms and had been totally debauched in her behaviour! She'd kissed him, touched him, done things with him she'd only ever heard about from her friends. And she'd enjoyed it. Revelled in it. *Wallowed decadently in it! Oh shooting stars of Cyron! What have I done? Why did I do it?*

"Keep thinking so hard and agonizing over things done, lass, and you'll give yourself a headache."

Delias looked up to find Davan leaving the bathroom, a towel draped low around his hips, his body looking so luscious she wanted to trace it with her fingertips and—Horrified at her wayward thoughts, she blushed and glanced away. *What the hell is wrong with me?*

"Del."

"What?" She shoved a thick curl back over her shoulder, trying to sound tough and uncaring, but her trembling words betrayed her.

"Go and have a shower." His tone was gentle. "Then meet me in the kitchen and we'll talk."

Talk? She was going to die of embarrassment, but she'd be absolutely mortified if he ended up chasing her down the road.

Without looking at him, she walked across to the bathroom,

the cover dragging along behind her because she refused to relinquish it. Davan might be comfortable walking around naked in front of her, but she sure wasn't comfortable with him that way!

She'd just made it to the doorway when an arm appeared before her, barring her way. Looking up and around, she was taken by surprise when Davan dropped a gentle kiss on her forehead and drew back. His eyes were kind. "Don't stress, lass." Removing his arm, he gave her a gentle push into the bathroom.

Closing the door firmly behind her, Delias dropped the sheet and looked around. The steam from his shower was filtering up through the skylight in the ceiling, but the scent of his soap was in the air. On the rack was slung two towels — one damp, the other clean and dry. One was his, the other obviously for her.

Seeing the two towels side by side in the one bathroom did funny things to her.

Berating herself for all kinds of a dreamy fool, she turned towards the shower, only to catch sight of her face in the mirror. Moving forward, she studied herself. Oh aye, she looked like a wench who had been thoroughly made love to, and who had revelled in it. Her face might be pale, but her lips were still swollen by his kisses, her eyes bright, and her hair fell around her shoulders in wild, curly abandon.

Wild because long fingers had stroked through her curls, hung on, used them to guide her head where he wanted her...

Delias's cheeks flushed at the memory and hastily she entered the shower, turning the hot, fragrant water on full, trying to wipe away the memories, but even the simple task of washing herself had her hands lingering where Davan's had, and every swipe of the slick, soap laden water across her skin

was a reminder of a rougher tongue that had stroked parts of herself she'd only ever fantasized about.

How the hell could she be getting all hot and bothered by just memories?

Shaking her head, Delias rinsed the soap away. She had to get downstairs, eat stupid breakfast, and then make a fast getaway. *No doubt the food will choke me, with Davan sitting across from me smirking and all knowing,* she assured herself. *Just get out there and get it over with, Del.*

Drying hurriedly, she peeked back into the bedroom to find her clothes neatly laid on the big bed. Even her delicate underwear was neatly laid beside her gown. Throwing the towel aside, she dressed hurriedly before heading back into the bathroom to hang the towel neatly on the rack. Glancing in the mirror again, she took note of her wild curls and searched for a brush. Sure enough, there was a brush and comb on the bench and she quickly dragged the brush through her hair before using one of Davan's ties to pull the rioting curls back at the nape in a ponytail.

"Now or never, Del," she told herself. "Time to face him."

Leaving the bedroom, she walked slowly down the corridor. The smell of food cooking floated to her and she felt her stomach rumble. It would seem nothing got in the way of nature. While she was sure she'd choke, her stomach was in ecstasy at the smells.

Coming to the door, she glanced in to see Davan placing a bowl of food down in the corner of the room for the old hound. The two lycats were waiting not so patiently on the floor near the stove.

Laughing, Davan took two bowls off the sink and placed them on the floor at the opposite wall to the old hound. "I'm sorry breakfast is late, little ones. I slept in."

Straightening, he saw Delias hovering in the doorway and his gaze slid over her warmly. "'Twas worth it."

She blushed to the tips of her toes and stepped back. "Um…about breakfast. I can't stay. I must go - "

"Nay." He didn't approach her, but his lazy stance was, she knew, deceiving. If she bolted, he'd be after her like a shot. Davan smiled. "Come in and sit down. I promise you I'm a good cook and won't poison you."

"We both slept in. You need to go to work - "

"Moreb is more than capable of covering for me for awhile." He gestured to the table as he moved back to the stove. "Sit."

Not knowing quite what else to do, Delias took the chair on the far side of the big table. He'd already set two places on opposite sides of the table with cutlery and glasses of berry juice. Between the two places stood a chilled jug containing more juice, and a small container of salt.

Chewing her bottom lip nervously, she eyed Davan's wide back as he moved with confidence at the stove. All he wore was a pair of trousers, the usual rough material she was used to seeing on the traders. His feet were bare, his chest was bare, and she was getting more flustered at the memory of waking up to find herself pressed to his bare back…and bare bottom.

Frantically trying to drag her attention away from the memory, she looked at the lycats who had finished their food and were now washing their whiskers. "I…um… I didn't know you had pets." Which was a damned lie, because she had always known this man was an animal lover and kept pets.

She dropped her forehead into her hand. Staying was a bad, bad idea.

Davan turned from the stove, a plate in each hand and a grin on his face which changed him from dangerously handsome to devastatingly boyish. Delias blinked. She'd never seen him grin with such merriment before — at least, to her.

Crossing to the table with an easy stride she envied, he placed the plate of steaming omelette on top of fried bread before her and took the seat opposite. "Nervous, Del?"

"What do you think?" she snapped, before recovering herself. "Nay."

Eyes crinkling at the corners in amusement, Davan picked up his fork. "Because you look it."

Gladly taking refuge in anger, Delias glared at him. "Well, excuse me for not looking the way you want me to look."

"You look exactly the way I want you to look. Thoroughly

ravished by me."

"I do not look ravished," she said stiffly, trying to control the blush that threatened to consume her.

With a gleam in his blue eyes, his gaze slid over her face and lower. "'Tis how I see you."

That gaze had her heart do a little leap, but she ruthlessly squashed any fluttering. "You said we had to talk. About what, I have no idea, because I have nothing to say about last night." Apart from oh my God! 'Twas amazing! To add action to words, she scooped up a forkful of omelette and put it in her mouth.

Thoughtfully, Davan watched her chew. It took all Delias's inner strength to meet his gaze, but she did so defiantly. He took another bite of food and chewed, all the time watching her with that thoughtful look on his face. It was unnerving.

"I thought you wanted to talk?" she pointed out almost accusingly.

"'Tis no hurry," he replied mildly. "I'm hungry, you're hungry, and so we'll eat first then talk."

"'Twasn't part of the deal."

"I don't remember any deal."

"Order, then. Your order."

The corners of his eyes crinkled in amusement again. "Oh, that order."

The wretched man was just like Red. Her blasted brother was so good at teasing, and it was a total surprise to find out Davan was a bit the same. However, seeing as she had never spoken to him except when absolutely necessary — and even then she did so bitingly — there'd been no other time they'd ever been together, and definitely not alone.

Except at the river the other night. Recalling that only made her angrier and deciding that she only wanted everything over with, she ignored him, keeping her eyes on the plate as she stubbornly ate without saying anything. He wanted to talk? Fine. Let him be the first to say anything.

After several minutes had passed with nothing being said,

she put the fork down, pushed the empty plate away, and picked up the glass of berry juice. The liquid was cool and sweet, and she swallowed gratefully. After three mouthfuls, she put the glass down and looked across the table at Davan.

Oh, what a surprise, he was finishing his breakfast calmly, not ruffled one bit by her ill humour. Polishing off the last of the fried bread, he lay his knife and fork down, pushed the plate aside and picked up the glass of berry juice. Raising it to his lips, he lifted his gaze to meet hers and arched one brow as he took a leisurely drink.

Pursing her lips, Delias folded her arms across her chest and leaned back in the chair. Anger was good; anger stopped her blushing like a giddy wench and gave her the strength to look directly at the man opposite her. The man who just hours before had been thrusting inside her. Deep inside her. Sucking in a sudden, sharp breath, she pushed the thought away.

It was a shame she couldn't push the little tingle deep inside her away.

Chapter 4

*

"Why do you dislike me so much?" Davan asked.

It was the last thing Delias had expected. "Pardon?"

"Why do you dislike me so much?"

"For the same reason you despise me." She narrowed her eyes at him. "Which makes me wonder, how come you took me to your bed when you despise me so much?"

"And I could ask you the same," he replied calmly.

"I have no idea," she said truthfully, because she honestly didn't know herself.

"And I don't despise you," he added.

"Oh, Davan!" She wanted to laugh outright, uncaring, but suddenly it hurt. "Please. Don't start pretending now."

His face was serious, his gaze steady. "I have never despised you, Delias."

"You can never look at me without disapproval. I'm not blind." Looking away, she swallowed the sudden lump in her throat. Stupid, stupid, stupid! One night in his bed and you're so bloody weak!

"'Tis what you really think?" he asked quietly.

She had to blink several times before she turned her head back to look coolly at him. "'Tis what I see with my own eyes, Davan. You can never look at me without disapproval."

He regarded her steadily. "I wasn't aware my feelings, however mistaken, were so apparent to you."

She shrugged. "It means nothing." Fingering an errant curl that brushed her cheek, she added, "Besides, mayhap last night was to teach me what to expect."

"Expect?"

Tucking the curl behind her ear, she met his gaze defiantly. "After the other night. When, as you so nicely put it, I put myself 'on display for others'."

With a sigh, Davan leaned back in his chair. "I knew 'twould come back to bite me in the arse."

———

"If Red had been there, he'd have kicked your arse."

"I'd have expected nothing less." Lifting his arm, he shoved one hand through his hair, his face rueful. "Lass, I am so sorry about that night."

"Why? I just proved your belief in me, didn't I?" she asked tartly.

"Nay. I lost my temper." Lowering his arm, he rested his elbow on the armrest of the chair. "Del, being alone in the river is dangerous and I was angry that you did it knowingly. I was angry that you swam on your own when merchants were in the settlement - "

"Which I didn't know," she pointed out.

"True. But nonetheless, 'tis valid reason for me to be angry. But for what followed, I apologize."

"Making me get out of the river naked without leaving?"

"You're not going to make this easy on me, are you?"

She arched one brow coolly.

He sighed. "I apologize for threatening to turn you over my knee."

Delias waited.

"I had no right."

She arched her other brow.

"I was wrong to threaten you with bodily harm." His eyes were steady. "Which I would never do."

"You were an arse."

A faint smile touched his lips. "You weren't exactly blameless."

"If 'tis your idea of an apology, 'tis poor."

The faint trace of humour fled. "Delias, I am so sorry."

"Humph."

He studied her. "But you're not blameless. "'Twas a damned stupid thing you did, Del."

All right, he was correct. It was a stupid thing to do. If her parents, brother, or any of their friends had seen her, she'd never have heard the end of it. Glancing up, she caught his gaze. "Fine. I agree."

It was his turn to raise one brow.

"And if you're waiting for a bloody apology, you'll be waiting a long time."

Davan gave an unexpected bark of laughter, his blue eyes twinkling. "You've been at the end of many a tongue lashing many times in your life, wench."

"How would you know?" She drummed her fingers irritably on the tabletop.

"We all know, Del. From the moment you could toddle you were in trouble. You're a stubborn wench, and it showed from the moment you wilfully disobeyed your father and ate the last of Red's birthday cake."

Surprised, she looked at him. "Birthday cake?"

"Aye. Red told me all about it at school the next day."

"That tattle-tale."

"He only tattled to his friends." Davan grinned. "I know your stubborn streak got you into a lot of trouble."

"Red the Tattle-Tale again?"

"Some. Other times 'twas from one of your parents talking to other parents. Del, you were a handful when you were young, and you're still a handful when you choose."

"Well, aren't you lucky I'm not your handful?"

"I can handle you."

"Huh!" The thought made her tingle, a little angrily, a little - *well, to be truthful, a little thrilled.* She looked him up and down disdainfully. "You wish."

Relaxed back in the chair, he eyed her with amusement and - oh, truthful time again, a little heat. *Oh boy.* "I can, do, and will."

Ignoring the little flutter of her heart, she tapped the table a fraction faster. "By bullying? You're good at that. Excel at it, in fact."

"If you call handling your tantrums 'bullying', then aye."

"I do not throw tantrums!"

He laughed again. *The bloody man was a tease.* With a huff, she folded her arms. "So are we going to sit here and discuss my behaviour, which obviously either causes you amusement or makes you despise me, or did you have something else to discuss?"

Amusement faded. "Delias, I do not despise you. Whatever gave you that idea?"

"Come on, Davan. Every time you look at me 'tis with disapproval."

He shook his head.

"'Tis been like that since you…"

One blonde brow arched inquiringly.

She blushed. "Nothing."

"'Tis something. Since I what?"

"Forget it." She started to push the chair back, only to find it immoveable. Glancing under the table, she saw Davan's foot hooked around one of the rungs of the chair. "Do you mind?"

"Aye, I do."

"Release the chair, you big oaf."

"Nay. Finish what you were saying."

With her chair close to the table and the armrests on either side of her, she was well and truly trapped. Unless she kicked him in the shin.

"Don't," he said, as though reading her mind. At her frown, he added, "I know exactly what you're thinking of doing, Delias, and 'twon't work anyway. I'm not letting you go until I find out what I did that makes you think I despise you."

"Why does it matter so much?" Why had she even said anything? 'Twas stupid, stupid of her to say anything at all about that day. As though she even cared.

His searching gaze locked with hers. "It matters to us."

Eagerly she latched onto that statement. "'Tis no 'us', Davan."

"Del." His tone was faintly chiding. "What happened that day?"

The man was relentless. Throwing herself back in the chair, she snapped, "You came across me swimming in the river."

He looked blankly at her. "You mean the other night? Lass, I already apologized for what I said."

"Nay, not then."

"Then when?"

"Do you really not remember?" Exasperated, she glared at him.

"Nay."

"You hadn't been a peacekeeper long when you came across me swimming alone in the river. I came out when you told me to and…" The memory still had the power to make her falter. To hurt her. Why the hell did it hurt her? The memory of his face when he saw her coming out of the water. Why should it even matter?

"Del?" Davan leaned forward, resting his forearms on the table.

Trying for nonchalance, she shrugged. "You were so disgusted with me. I remember the expression on your face. You could barely look at me. I started to greet you, and you simply told me off for swimming on my own and ordered me to go home."

There was silence in the kitchen and when she finally looked up at Davan, he was watching her with that steady look he had that made the recipient feel as though they were the only person who mattered. As though she mattered.

As if. Swallowing a stupid lump in her throat, she glanced away. Oh stars, surely she didn't have a bloody tear in her eye? *Damn it. Get a grip, Del!* "And every time I saw you after that, you were distant, stand-offish. It didn't take a genius to know that I disgusted you. That you despised me. Every time, Davan, every bloody time I was anywhere near you after that, you could hardly stand to be near me!" She was horrified to hear her voice rising at the end of that little speech, and even more horrifying was - *oh nay! Her breath had just hitched! She'd just… oh for God's sake! Nay!* Absolutely mortified, she took refuge in anger. "'Tis how I know you despise me, Davan!" And then she just had to sniff and spoil the whole façade.

Swiping at the lone tear that spilled from her eye to roll

down her cheek, she folded her arms defiantly and glared at him. "So there you have it. Satisfied?" His gaze was so compassionate. So warm. She wanted to slap him. "Don't bloody feel sorry for me, Davan. I don't need it. You can take your niceness and shove it up your - "

"Delias," he said with that niceness that made her teeth clench, "be quiet."

Gathering her dignity about her, she held her head high. "I want to go home. Will you please remove your big foot from my chair?"

He did so, but she'd only just shoved her chair back before he was around the table and kneeling beside her.

"If you're going to try and jolly me up, Davan, I swear to God I'll bust you."

"Just keep your tongue between your teeth for several minutes," he ordered gently, taking her fists into his hands and coaxing them open so that their fingers entwined.

"Look, I don't - "

"Or I'll kiss you senseless until you obey."

"Try it and I'll slap you silly."

"'Tis my fiery wench." With a sudden jerk on her hands, he pulled her down and kissed her quickly.

Almost immediately she was lost in the silken feel of his lips, his warm breath, his scent. It took all her determination to keep her thoughts in order. A very jumbled order, but at least she wasn't throwing herself at him and ripping off his pants. *Yet.*

He drew back but kept hold of her fingers. "You've had your say, lass, now 'tis my turn."

"Oh, good. I can hardly wait."

He ignored her sarcasm. "I do remember that day now. You were all of fourteen, and I was twenty. I took one look at you coming out of that water, all cool and wet and brimming with life and merriment, and I wanted you. I wanted to take you there on the banks of the river, Del."

Of everything he could have said, this stunned Delias.

"I wanted you more than anything right then," Davan continued. "Can you imagine how I felt? A man of twenty lusting after a young lass still in her youth? The disgust you saw, Del, was my disgust at myself, at my feelings. I ordered you home because I was afraid if you stood there in front of me any longer, with that beaming smile and your youthful beauty, I'd forget that I was sworn to protect all Daamens and I'd seduce you then and there." Taking a deep breath, Davan stroked his thumbs across the backs of her hands. "I was a man grown, and you still a young lass. Every time I saw you, I felt that same stab of lust, that same need. Of course I kept my distance, and I didn't allow us to become friendly. Unfortunately, 'twould seem that I did the job too well, for you grew up thinking I despised you. Delias, I am so sorry. I had no idea."

Dumbfounded, she didn't quite know what to say. "But - but you still look at me with disapproval."

He smiled ruefully. "Aye. I disapprove of the cold shoulder you give me, the scornful remarks, but 'twould seem I deserved it." He thought a second, and amended, "A little. I deserved it a little."

His words churned through her mind, but she wasn't so certain. "Are you sure you're not saying this because of last night?"

"Last night I set out to seduce you," he replied bluntly.

He'd certainly succeeded. Delias looked down to where his thumbs were still stroking the backs of her hands. Those big hands holding hers in a firm, yet gentle grip, had not so very long ago been stroking across her body. A blush stole through her cheeks and without looking at him, she said, "If 'tis so…"

"You're wondering why I waited until now to make a move?"

'Twould seem the man really could read her mind. She nodded without looking up.

"When I saw you the other night at the river, I was angry that you would place yourself in such danger."

Not the answer she wanted. Annoyed, Delias tugged at her hands but he didn't relinquish them.

"I didn't know why I reacted the way I'd done," he continued, ignoring her tugging. "With any other lass, I'd not have been so-so—"

"Nasty?" She gave up tugging on her hands and looked at him.

Immediately she was ensnared by the warmth in his eyes.

"I was going to say forceful." Davan's gaze remained steady. "I lost my temper when I'm normally calm, but I didn't know then 'twas because, as usual, you affected me."

"Huh."

"Tongue between your teeth, lass," he reminded her, a faint sparkle of amusement in his eyes.

Delias snorted but remained quiet.

"I was coming to apologize to you when I found you in pain." His hands slid up to her wrists. "I won't lie, I was glad 'twas me attending you and no other. And when I started rubbing that cream into you, seeing your pain, I wanted to ease it. You trusted me, and that need I had for you, that wanting and desire, resurfaced, and all I wanted to do was hold you, comfort you, keep you safe forever."

The intensity in his blue eyes was unnerving in a totally delicious way. Delias licked her lips and he followed the movement with eyes that grew hotter, but he resumed talking, lifting his gaze once more to ensnare hers.

"Delias, when I watched you sleeping on your bed, I knew then that I wanted you. Every feeling I had was back and I set out to seduce you. I admit that. And I did seduce you." His hands slid up to her elbows, his voice lowering, flowing through her like honey, rich and full of the promise of more. "I don't despise you, lass. I desire you. I want you. I love you."

Shocked, her mouth fell open.

"Aye," he said. "I'm not afraid to say it. I'm not afraid to shout it to the world. I love you, Del. I always have."

She didn't know what to say, what to think. Her body was about the only thing that knew how to react, for she swayed towards him.

Only to have him stop her with one big hand on her stomach. His eyes were serious, his tone even more so. "Is my hurting you the reason you disliked me, Del?"

Delias looked at him, at his dangerously handsome face, the eyes that were undeniably full of warmth and, aye, love. Could she love him back? Could she even like him at all? She'd disliked him for so long… *You slept with him and still you can ask yourself that?*

Subconscious voices weren't always helpful. Nor were they subtle.

She remembered all the times she'd known Davan was there before she'd even seen him. The knowledge that came from deep inside herself, the little prickle of awareness, the recognition of his body heat whenever he was near her, his very presence in the same vicinity as herself. The odd times she hadn't been aware of him, as soon as she noticed him, there'd been a filter of warmth go through her, followed sharply by… oh, be truthful. Rejection. She'd felt rejected. And so she'd immediately given him the cold shoulder, to show him she didn't care for him. Because it had hurt so much to know he despised her.

Well, how about that? Her girlish hurt feelings had followed her into adulthood, because she felt that hurtful pain of rejection even now, just thinking about it.

"Del, don't." Davan rose up on his knees to cradle her cheeks and tip her head up so that he could meet her eyes. "Don't dwell on the past, on misunderstandings and mistakes. I wish to God I could change things, that I could undo the hurt that I've caused you by trying to be so noble." Kissing her on the tip of her nose, he added softly, "I hurt you so much, lass, and I would sooner die than do that to you."

The man really could read her mind. Resting her forehead against his, she sighed. "I should have kicked your arse back then."

His laugh was rueful. "The follies of youth, lass."

They looked deeply into each other's eyes for several long minutes before Davan finally stated, "Del, I'm going to court you, and then after a respectable time we're going to wed."

Surprised, she jerked back to stare at him. "I beg your pardon?"

"Do you truly think I'm going to let you go again?"

"Davan, I hardly know you!"

"You know me enough to know I keep my word." His blue eyes were intent. "You'll be mine, Del. You are mine. I've wasted enough time due to my actions years ago. I'm not wasting anymore time in pretending."

She was floundering, both confused and partly ecstatic, but mostly confused. "Davan, I don't know what to say. I can't say that I love you, because I don't know. For so long I thought you hated me, and then after one night in your bed I'm supposed to believe you love me and everything is fine. I need time." How gauche did that sound? Almost desperately she looked into his eyes. "Please, try to understand. I don't mean to hurt you, or lead you on, or-or…" She shook her head. "Oh, hell."

Amusement resounded in his chuckle and when she lifted her head, she saw that his gaze was warm and the expression on his face tender. Loving. It was the loving that really rattled her. After the disapproving expression on his face that she'd previously thought was directed solely at her, to see it loving was still a shock.

Reaching up, he stroked her down one cheek, and she found herself turning her head slightly so that her cheek felt the heat of his calloused palm.

"Lass, I'll give you time, but not long. We've wasted too much time already. I'll come courting; I'll do all the right things. Take you out, get to really know you, and vice versa.

But know this, I won't be waiting forever to claim you. We will be wed soon."

His assuredness was mildly irritating. Tossing her head back, she looked down at him haughtily. "Don't be so sure of yourself, Peacekeeper. I'm my own wench, I don't take orders well."

His eyes sparkled. "I know what I want, wench, and I know what you want. I know what you need. A strong hand, a loving heart, and a lusty lover and friend, all right here." He gestured to himself. "And I'll be coming for you."

His words made her shiver inwardly in anticipation, but she still needed time to think. Not to mention that his confidence was still annoying.

This time when she stood up, he didn't stop her, but nor did he move back, which meant that as she stood her breasts brushed his nose, and when he tilted his head back to smile wickedly up at her, she saw the carnal gleam in his eyes. Her heart skipped a beat and she hurriedly side-stepped him.

"I'm going for a walk. I need to think. And before you say anything, aye, I am going alone."

With one powerful thrust of his thighs, Davan stood and towered over her. "'Tis daytime, sweet Delias. I'll not stop you. As long as you don't go far from the settlement."

"Oh, thank you very much." Still flustered and hiding it behind sarcasm, she flounced through the kitchen and to the front door. "Don't get comfortable thinking I'll do whatever you tell me, Davan, just because we spent a night together."

A long, muscular arm came over her shoulder and his big hand pushed the door open before her. "With you, Del, I expect anything." Humour filled the words. "But I'm not worried. I can handle you."

"Huh." Delias hurried down the steps, wanting to put some distance between herself and that big, warm body that was right behind her and playing havoc with her commonsense. "You wish."

"I know," he said.

~ * ~

Davan watched as Delias strode briskly down his path and

out of the gate.

On the pathway outside the gate, she glanced once at him, her cheeks flushing becomingly. "You're too sure of yourself, Peacekeeper."

He smiled at her.

Delias hurried away while he remained where he was, watching long after she'd disappeared from sight.

The old hound ambled out to sit at his feet, and he bent down and rubbed him behind the ears. "I am sure of myself, old friend."

The hound closed his eyes and leaned into Davan's hand.

"I'm sure because I know." A smile crossed Davan's face at the memory of Delias's surrender. The wench didn't know it, but she'd revealed a lot more than she thought she had during their passion-filled night. Closing his eyes, he remembered the words that had branded themselves into his heart.

"I need you." He lowered his head.

"Then take me."

"All of you," he whispered against her lips.

"You have me." Lifting her head, she touched her lips to his. "You always have."

~*~

Hidden behind one of the old trees that towered across the street, the watcher, eyes sharp, pondered. Things were taking unexpected turns and it didn't bode well. Complications weren't needed and this was a huge complication. All hell could break loose. This required careful planning.

The watcher moved away from the tree.

~ * ~

The spectator observed the house of the Daamen wench. Interesting things were happening, but the most important of all was no doubt going to flare soon. The spectator didn't want to miss a moment of it. How much to observe, how much to participate in, who to kill if needed… well, that last one didn't need much pondering. The spectator had that figured out already.

Manez sat at the far table in the tavern with his back to the room, hiding his furious expression from the Daamen men and women who came and left the tavern.

Czex tapped the ale mug nervously on the table. "There's no other way to do it, Manez. We have to get it and that woman is the only one who could know where it is. She has it."

"This whole bloody job is turning into a waking nightmare." Manez rubbed his forehead. "There're others who would kill to get their hands on it."

"And we'll be one of those killed if we don't get to it first." Czex glanced around the room before returning his attention to Manez. "So we need to get to that woman."

"It's not exactly a trading quest." Manez moodily contemplated the mug that Czex was tapping on the table. "There's no way we can just ask if she's seen it, and if so, to hand it over."

"Sure we can."

Manez glared at him.

Czex shrugged. "If she has it, she could still agree to us buying it from her. She might not know what it is."

"She's a female, you idiot, and a trader. Of course she's already looked!"

"But she hasn't handed it in to anyone, so maybe she hasn't," Czex argued. "It can't hurt to go and ask, can it?"

"And if she knows what it is but hasn't had time to hand it in or notify anyone?"

"Then we take it back by force."

"We hurt one hair on her head and we'll have every Daamen man and woman, and every Reeka warrior, after our blood. Our lives will be worth shit."

"So we'll have to ensure she doesn't alert anyone. We'll kill her and hide the body after we get what we want from her. And we get off this planet fast."

There was no other way. Grimly, Manez nodded. Time was wasting, and Death was tapping harder at his shoulder with every tick of the timer. "Wait for dark," he said, "when no one will see us."

~ * ~

When Davan strode into the Enforcer Building, he was met by Moreb who wore a very bland expression which never boded well.

"You're late to work," Moreb stated.

"Slept in."

"Really? You never sleep in."

"Well, I did today."

"Busy night?"

Strapping on the laser belt, Davan replied calmly, "You could say that."

"And yet you're looking incredibly energetic."

Oh aye, his friend knew something. Davan glanced at him. Still no expression on Moreb's face, though.

Moreb fingered the small, silver hoop in his left ear. "You know, I saw Delias this morn."

"Oh?"

"She looked… confused."

"Oh?" Davan imagined she was very confused, but it wouldn't be for long. He grinned to himself.

"Aye. Mayhap she was confused because she was coming out of your house."

"Mayhap." Davan sat down behind the scarred desk and skimmed through the messages on the viscomm.

"'Twas most odd, the wench coming from your house."

"Oh?" Oh aye, Moreb was bursting with curiosity.

Moreb perched on the edge of the desk, his gaze intent on Davan. "Now what would that fiery little wench want at your house?"

"Why would she want anything?"

"Why would she be visiting you?"

"Out of the goodness of her heart?"

Fingering his pursed lips, Moreb contemplated the ceiling. "And even more odd, 'twas no yells or screaming from your

———

128

house, no swearing, no sounds of feminine fury. Now what could that mean?"

"You need your hearing tested?" Davan deleted yet another message.

"Nay. I have a theory."

"Do tell."

"Well, seeing as how the wench went into your house last night and didn't leave until this morn, I have to say…"

Davan looked at him politely. "Aye?"

Unable to contain himself any longer, all pretence of blandness faded and Moreb said eagerly, "You hound! How the hell did you capture that wench? She hates your guts!"

"How elegantly put. But you, my friend, are wrong." Davan squinted at him. "How do you know she came to my house last night?"

"Saw the wench wandering around on her own yet again, so rather than risk her wrath by making her go home - risking her wrath is your job, by the way, not mine - I decided to follow her."

"Ah."

"I saw her go up to your house and you right behind her. Next thing, the door opened and you both went in."

Davan waited, both brows arched.

"So I went about my rounds," Moreb finished. "I didn't wait around. I figured if you needed rescuing, you'd contact me via the communicator." His eyes gleamed. "Did you need rescuing?"

Davan looked dryly at him.

"Ooohhh. Details! How the hell did you convince that wench to stay the night?" Moreb leaned closer, his hand resting on a pile of papers. "How the hell did you do it?"

Davan yanked on the pile of papers, thereby jerking Moreb's hand away and putting his friend off-balance. It gave him a great deal of satisfaction when Moreb barely saved himself from falling flat on his face.

Unfazed, Moreb righted himself and demanded, "Tell me!"

"Needing hints, friend?"

"Needing details!"

Placing the papers back on the desk, Davan settled back in the chair and linked his hands across his flat abdomen. After regarding his friend seriously for several seconds, he said, "I can't tell my secrets."

"You seduced her." Moreb's eyes lit up. "Oh stars! You seduced Delias! Red will kill you! Her father will kill you!"

"And yet you sound so pleased."

Moreb looked at Davan, and then his eyes narrowed. Davan could just about see the wheels turning in his brain. He waited.

Moreb's eyes widened. "You're wedding the wench!"

And there 'twas. Davan smiled slowly, feeling satisfaction well up in him at just the words. "Oh, aye, the wench is mine."

"How did you do that?" Moreb's mouth hung open in amazement. "How the hell did you convince her to marry you?"

"I told her."

"You told her? You told Delias?" There was absolute admiration on Moreb's face, along with incredulity. "And you live?"

"What can I say?" Davan's smile widened. "She loves me."

"She told you that?"

"She will."

"What the hell is that supposed to mean?"

"You know how confused she looked?"

"Aye."

Davan winked.

"Bloody hell." Moreb was impressed.

"Trust me, 'twas Heaven."

"Miracles do happen."

Davan's smile softened. "Aye, they do."

Moreb grinned suddenly. Reaching forward, he clapped Davan on the shoulder. "My congratulations, friend. Of course, I won't say a word to the lass until she realizes that you are correct. Mayhap I'll wait until the wedding day, just in case. I don't want her sharp tongue slicing ribbons off me."

Davan grinned back at him. "Knowing Del, 'twould be nothing left of you to glue back together. 'Twould be wise to wait."

"Not a word will pass my lips to anyone." Moreb rubbed his hands together gleefully. "Oh, I just can't wait to see Red's expression when he sees his baby sister being courted by you. He is going to bust a gut laughing!"

"Thanks for your support," Davan said dryly.

"And to think I thought the days here were getting too quiet." Laughing, Moreb stood and crossed to the doorway. "I'm off to start my rounds."

Knowing his friend wouldn't reveal their conversation, Davan waved him off. Moreb was the soul of discretion when needed and even though he'd be the butt of all Moreb's jokes from now on, Davan knew he could trust him.

His thoughts turned to Delias and he laughed softly. The poor little lass had been so confused that she'd left his house without a thought to anyone seeing her. He had no problems with anyone knowing she'd spent the night, he was damned proud of it, but Delias… damn, she'd looked so cute with that blush in her cheeks when she'd left.

Grinning to himself, Davan turned once more to the viscomm and the messages waiting for him. Tonight he'd seek the wench out, take her some flowers, steal a kiss or two, and a hell of a lot more, and work on sorting her confused feelings out for her. No doubt she'd give him the edge of her tongue, and he even looked forward to that. Now that he knew how he felt about her, and how she felt about him, even though she wasn't so sure, sparring with her was turning into a delight.

He couldn't wait to kiss her senseless.

Davan sighed. But business first…

Dealing with the messages was finally completed, and then he started sorting through the new wanted notices. Updating the listings of known space-pirates and outlaws, he noticed that one lot of space-pirates in particular had their reward doubled again. Sonja the space pirate and her crew of wenches. He shook his head. They'd been hitting deep into the Lawful Sector yet again and had incurred the wrath of the Aons. The Aon's space shuttle system had been hit several times, sometimes within mere hours of each other. Those wenches had nerve, he had to give them that. However, if they dared to hit a Daamen trade ship their hunting days would be over. So far they'd left the Daamens alone, he could only hope it stayed that way because he had a strong suspicion they'd prove formidable foes. Still, it'd be very unlikely for no space-pirate was fool enough to tangle with a Daamen trade ship.

Having finished updating the wanted system, he checked for messages from other parts of Daamen. Everything appeared quiet.

"Hello, Davan," a voice said quietly.

He looked up to see a Daamen wench dressed in a plain work tunic and sandals, far different to the pants, jacket and boots she normally wore as an Intergalactic Peace Ship Security Officer. Tall, slim, her brown hair pulled back into a glossy bun, the blonde streak in her hair catching the light, she looked steadily at him out of cobalt eyes. "Sabra! Nice to see you, lass. What are you doing here? Cam isn't back yet." Smiling, he pushed up out of his chair. "Are you on time off from the IPC ship?"

Sabra walked into the room and kicked the door shut with her heel. "Nay."

That one word combined with her serious face made him stop. Sabra was always friendly, a little guarded, which was to be expected given her past, but there twas nothing friendly about her persona today. One look at her expressionless eyes and he knew it was business that brought her to his Enforcer Building.

Moving slowly around the desk, Davan leaned back against

it and regarded her curiously. "What's wrong?"

"You're not going to like it," Sabra replied. "But you're going to listen."

Chapter 5

*

He eyed her closely. "Oh?"

"Aye. It concerns your wench."

"Delias?"

"You have more?"

He frowned. "What's wrong?"

"She's fine." Sabra leaned back against the door. "For now. But you have to listen closely and not go off half-cocked."

"I never go off half-cocked." Davan impatiently folded his arms. "You know me, Sabra."

"Aye, I do. I know you're as steady as a rock, but when it comes to the wenches you love, you Daamen men don't think straight." A small smile hovered around Sabra's lips. "And that I do know."

"Cam might be putty in your hands, lass, but I have a bit more control than that. Now tell me what's wrong."

Sabra tucked her hands into her pockets. "I'm tracking two outlaws who are currently in this settlement."

Davan was incredulous. "Outlaws? In my settlement?"

"You won't know these outlaws, they haven't popped up on the Peacekeepers' Wanted Listings."

"And why the hell is that?" Anger tinged his voice.

"Because Security has been tracking them and we couldn't have peacekeepers scaring them off." She looked pointedly at him. "'Twould be you, for starters."

"Security and their secrets." Disgusted, he shook his head. "You better have a damned good reason for allowing them into my settlement, wench." His eyes hardened. "And they better not be a threat to my people."

Sabra's gaze didn't waver. "Trust me, they're in more danger right now than our people."

"So why aren't you arresting them? What do these outlaws want here?" A sudden thought occurred to Davan and he straightened abruptly. "And what has this to do with Delias?"

———

"Ah, now 'tis the sticky part." Sabra didn't move. "'Twould seem the outlaws are watching her. But Davan—damn it, do not move!" She snapped upright and glared at him.

Davan strode forward. "Out of my way, Sabra. Now!"

"Right now Delias is safe." Placing one hand flat on his chest, Sabra shoved hard, to no avail. "Sit down, Davan, and let me explain."

"While my lass is being stalked by two bastards?" Without ceremony, Davan picked Sabra up under the arms and swung her, cursing, to the side. "Sorry, Sabra, you're moving."

"I thought you'd say that." Hands on hips, Sabra backed to the desk and perched on the edge of it.

Grabbing the handle, Davan yanked down. The handle didn't move and the door remained shut. Solidly shut. "What the..." He yanked again, then put his shoulder to it. The door was solid, built to withstand a Daamen's giant frame. It held fast. Turning angrily to Sabra, Davan growled, "Whatever you did to this bloody door, Sabra, you'll open it now!"

"Nay." She raised one hand coolly. "I knew you'd go off half-cocked. Now just listen to me."

Stalking across the room and around the desk, Davan jabbed the communicator button. "Moreb? Get over to Delias's place now and bring her back here." There was silence and he jabbed the button again. "Moreb? Damn it, answer me!" When the only answer was silence, he braced both hands on the desk and leaned forward, frustration and fury battling for supremacy. "Whatever Security shit you have going on here, Sabra, stop it now!"

Slipping down off the desk, she plopped down into the chair before his desk and surveyed him calmly. "I suggest you sit down and listen closely, Davan. Time is clipping along and while Delias is safe now, the longer we mess around, well, who knows?"

"Cam is going to hear about this." Davan was practically breathing fire, his fear for Delias's safety filling him.

"Tsk tsk, not very confidential of you, Davan." For several

seconds Sabra's cobalt eyes held a gleam of humour before she flicked one hand at his chair. "Sit and listen."

"Goddamn it, Sabra - "

"If you want to save Delias and a host of other men, wenches and children, you'll sit down, shut up, and listen to me." Her gaze narrowed. "Now, Peacekeeper."

He wanted to wring the wench's neck. With no other choice except blowing a hole in the wall, Davan folded his arms and glared down at her.

Sabra's gaze remained steady. "The outlaws are hunting something we know is pertinent to an investigation we're doing, but we're not sure exactly what 'tis. For some reason, they think Delias has it."

"Ridiculous. How would Delias get hold of something outlaws want?" And where was Delias now? Going for a walk. Alone. He bolted upright.

"Relax," Sabra said, obviously guessing his concern. "Delias is being watched at all times. We have the situation under control. So far."

"So far?" Davan glowered at her.

She ignored his outburst. "The outlaws have searched her house - "

"They *what*? When?"

"Last night while she was with you." Sabra linked her hands comfortably on her flat stomach. "They didn't find what they were searching for. I believe they're going to go back and pay her a visit."

He actually felt his stomach dip in fear. "When?"

"Possibly tonight. Darkness is what they work best with." Picking up the apple Moreb had left on the desk, she rubbed it on her tunic and took a bite out of it.

"And what do you intend to do about it?" Davan snapped. "Because I sure as hell know what I intend to do."

"You're going to do as I say. We're going to be watching and listening in to the outlaws and Delias. Once they have what they came for, we're going to take them."

"Just like that?" Agitated, Davan thrust his hand through his hair. "She could be hurt, Sabra, have you thought of that? What if she doesn't have what they want? What if they shoot or knife her?"

"'Tis a risk, but we're taking precautions."

"'Tis still a risk!"

"But one she's willing to take."

Stunned, Davan's mouth fell open. "What?"

Sabra took another bite of apple. "I had a little chat with Delias just an hour ago. She knows nothing of what they're searching for, and we had a hunt through her house and couldn't find anything unusual, either. So our only choice is to wait for the outlaws to reveal what 'tis they hunt."

Davan couldn't get one fact out of his head. "Del knows about this? She agreed to it?"

"Aye."

"My wench agreed to be the bait?"

"Aye." Sabra chewed thoughtfully. "But I'd expect nothing less. She has courage."

"That wench is putting herself in danger!" Unable to stay still, Davan strode around the room, his mind reeling. "Del could be seriously hurt, Sabra. I won't allow it!" Stopping before her chair, he leaned down, placed his hands on the armrests, and scowled down into her placid face. "I will not allow it."

"'Tis her choice."

"'Tis not!"

"Oh, I can't wait to see her face when you tell her that."

"Goddamn it, Sabra, what could possibly be worth the risk?"

Sabra stilled, her eyes going blank. "Illegal slavery, Davan. Children, men and wenches sold into illegal slavery. I will do whatever I have to, to stop it."

Cursing, Davan pushed upright and stepped back. Illegal slavery, people abducted from poor areas and sold into hellish lives. It was something most of the Lawful Sector abhorred, and something the Security had been infiltrating, that much he knew. But for Delias to offer herself as bait, it ate at his insides.

"What if 'twas Delias who was abducted, Davan?" Sabra tossed the apple core into the bin under the desk. "What if 'twas her abducted, raped, sold into sexual degradation or hard labour? Used and abused, hurt with no one to help her? To defend her? What if - "

"Stop!" Sucking in a deep breath, Davan tipped his head back and shut his eyes. "Don't." Just the thought of helpless people forced into that situation angered him. The thought of his precious Delias at the mercy of slavers, he couldn't bear even the thought.

"Delias is lucky, Davan," Sabra continued relentlessly. "The wenches of our world are protected. Others aren't so fortunate. What Delias is doing is - "

"Is risking her life." Rounding on Sabra, he repeated bitterly, "Delias is risking her life."

"'Twas her choice."

"Del has never been in this kind of situation, Sabra. She doesn't know what she's facing."

"She is no fool." Sabra's eyes softened a little. "I do understand. I did try to talk her out of it."

"Not enough, apparently." Jaw clenched, Davan looked towards the barred window. How could she even contemplate allowing his beloved Delias to put herself in such danger?

There was silence in the room for so long that he wondered if Sabra had left. He turned to find her still regarding him steadily. And then he remembered, she knew of abduction, of the horrors. It was no wonder she would do anything, but...

"Don't." Before he could say a word, she held up one hand, her eyes hardening. "Delias made this choice and 'tis one I won't make for her. I told her the dangers, the risks, but she made the choice."

"Let me talk to her."

She surprised him with a shrug. "Now, aye."

Davan started for the door, only to stop when a voice

snapped, "I'll do as I choose, Davan, you big oaf!"

Swinging around, he stared at Delias. She stood at the end of the room leading to the empty cells beyond. Behind her stood Moreb, who shrugged helplessly.

"She was at the back door and demanded that I let her in. So I did. I couldn't open it before, not even with the code. What's with that?" At Davan's glare, he hurriedly continued, "She made me wait with her in the cell hallway. We…uh…we heard everything." He grimaced. "Sorry, Davan. If I'd known - "

"You'd what?" Delias glared up at him. "Go running to Davan? Lock me up? You're as big an oaf as he is!"

Moreb rolled his eyes.

"And you can get that look off your face!" she continued to rant.

As far as Davan was concerned, she was the most beautiful wench in the universe, ranting and all, but that didn't make a difference in this situation. Striding across to her, he grabbed her upper arms and growled, "I forbid you to do this, Delias!"

Incredulous, she stared up at him. "You forbid me?"

"Uh-oh," muttered Moreb, backing away.

Sabra reached for another apple, polished it on her tunic and took a bite, watching with interest and amusement.

"Aye, I forbid you!" Hearing the boom in his voice, Davan belatedly lowered his tone. "Del, 'tis dangerous, and I won't allow you to risk yourself for - "

"For what? Other wenches? Children?" Hands on her hips, Delias glowered up at him, her plump lips pressed tightly together. "In case you've forgotten, Peacekeeper, I am my own wench. I make my own decisions."

"If your father or brother were here, you'd not be doing so," he retorted.

"They cannot make decisions for me. I'm of age!"

"Then I'm forbidding it."

"You big oaf, you think just because we had sex last night that you can dictate to me?"

Fascinated, Moreb listened and watched unashamedly.

Sabra chewed the apple and smiled.

Frustrated, Davan gave her a little shake. "What is between us has nothing to do with it!"

"Snarch shit!"

"Del, I won't lose you!"

"You won't lose me, I'll be right in your sights!"

"You could die, Del! Then what?" Just the words had fear spilling out of him. Cupping her cheeks in his hands, Davan leaned down and while looking directly into her eyes, he whispered, "Del, if you die, my life wouldn't be worth living."

The fury left her eyes, simply faded, and she reached up to place her small hands over his larger ones. "Davan, I won't die."

"How can you know that?" He didn't even notice the crack in his voice.

"Because you'll be watching out for me."

"Del, please, listen to me. Don't do this."

"When are you going to trust me?"

The words startled him. "I do trust you, lass."

"Nay." Her eyes were sad. "You still think of me as the young wench who swam by herself, the young wench who gets the tongue lashings, the young wench who is stubborn and gets into trouble."

"No change there," Moreb remarked, only to hold one hand up hastily when Delias glared at him. "Did I say that out loud? Apologies."

Sabra's grin widened.

Ignoring them all, Davan focussed on Delias, needing her to understand. "Lass, I do trust you. I just couldn't bear to see you hurt. 'Tis my job to catch criminals and protect others, not yours."

"'Tis everyone's job to help the law."

He sighed. "Del…"

"Davan, I'm doing this." Her gaze searched his, pleading for agreement. "I'm doing it under your watch. Sabra and Marly from the Security are here, and along with you and Moreb, that'll be a guard of four. I'll be safe, Davan. Really."

He could feel his reserve crumbling. He hated it, but deep inside he knew how determined she felt. Delias was a wench grown, he could only stop her doing so much, and deep inside him he knew that if he tossed her into a cell now for her own safety she'd never forgive him. Delias would always wonder how much he trusted her. But still, he had to make one last try.

"I would rather you didn't do this, lass. For me, don't do it."

Her eyes narrowed and she pulled back. "Don't try pulling the guilt-ridden, emotional crap on me, you big oaf." She smacked him sharply on his bulging bicep.

"Shit." He'd lost the argument.

Moreb guffawed, then tried to contain himself and look serious. Sabra took another bite of apple and raised one brow at Davan.

Keeping one hand at the small of Delias's back, he turned to face Sabra. "Much as I loathe the idea, 'twould seem the wench is set on it. What's the plan? And I'm warning you now," he added, still frustrated, "If I don't agree with it, you'll have to come up with another one, for I'll not risk Delias any more than has to be done."

"I think that decision should rest with me," Delias said tartly.

Davan glowered down at her. "You might have won the argument, wench, but in this I'll have the final say." Before she could give him the verbal blasting he could see brewing in her expression, he growled, "I'm the Head Peacekeeper, and you're under my protection, as both settler of this settlement, and my lover and future wife. So in this you will obey me." There was no way in hell he was giving in to her over this, it was his final decision.

Moreb sucked in his breath admiringly.

Delias was seething, Davan could see it in her burning eyes, and for a second he thought she was going to try and defy him on this as well—no chance in the universe, wench, for I'll not give on this—but instead she reached up, grabbed his tunic in one fist and tugged. Obligingly he bent down until they were almost nose to nose.

"You and I are going to have a little chat later about this obeying business," she hissed.

"As long as you do what I say, we can chat all you like." Oh, aye, he had immense satisfaction in the indignation that had her lifting her chin but before she could slice a verbal strip off him, he straightened and faced Sabra once more. "The plan?"

Feeling Delias start to sidle away, he slid his arm around her waist, pulling her hard up against him. The infuriating wench was still his wench and he wasn't about to let her go. Sabra started talking and he felt Delias finally start to relax against him as they listened.

The plan didn't make him happy and it took a lot of discussion to make it acceptable. Delias tried to change his mind but he held firm. Finally, with an exasperated huff, she folded her arms and capitulated.

Tough. When it came to Delias, he was going to ensure her safety any way he could, and if the stubborn wench insisted on being involved in this nightmare, then he was going to ensure her safety as much as possible.

~ * ~

The spectator watched from a distance. Perched high in a tree, blending with the environment, the shadows cast the figure in darkness amongst the thick, dark green foliage.

How interesting. Thoughtfully, the spectator watched the house. How long had it been since surveillance techniques had been called for? Nothing like sharpening old skills.

Two figures came into sight and the spectator watched coldly. Ah yes, it was Manez and Czex. It would seem they were after whatever they thought Delias had in her possession.

To make things even more interesting, the Head Peacekeeper had come calling carrying a bunch of flowers for

Delias. Sweet. And there she was, greeting him with a light peck to the cheek - *couldn't the wench get a little more eager? - ah, there it was.* He'd swept her up into his arms and backed her into the house, the door banging shut behind him. It'd be awhile before he came back out.

The spectator watched as Manez and Czex halted before drifting out of sight down another street. Glancing up at the late afternoon sun, the spectator calculated the time. No move would be made by Manez and Czex while the sun was still up, nor would the big peacekeeper be leaving for awhile. No lusty Daamen left his wench quickly.

Time for a break.

The spectator waited until all was quiet before swinging down from the tree, keeping close to the trunk. Other duties called. Later, when darkness fell, the fun would begin. Who was going to get to the so-badly wanted item first? The Security? The outlaws? Intriguing.

~ * ~

Delias watched as Davan prowled the rooms. His brow was furrowed in concentration as he checked the doors and windows.

"Someone is going to see you doing things not normally done," she pointed out.

"For once I wish we locked doors and windows. 'Tisn't safe."

"'Tis always safe." When he looked at her, she amended, "Almost always."

"And no one will see me," he added. "'Tis no lights on to backlight me."

"Ooohhh, I am so sorry I didn't realize that."

Turning to face her, he placed big hands on lean hips. "Sarcasm, wench, will get you nowhere."

"So why are you checking all the doors and windows when we're not locking them?"

His brow darkened. "I'm ensuring they all open with no problems."

"For when you come bursting in to my rescue?" She fluttered her eyelashes. "My hero."

For a man who was normally so good natured, Davan was seething. She could feel it, his frustration and dislike of the entire plan bubbling inside him.

Wrong.

His frustration and dislike of her being in the plan.

Tough. If he was interested in pursuing her, he had to live with her stubbornness.

She hadn't realized how stubborn he could be in turn, however. It was... titillating. And annoying. And his over-protectiveness was, oh, all right, 'twas titillating, too. It made her feel warm and protected. And damn edgy at times like this.

"Davan," she finally said in annoyance when he reappeared in the lounge and fiddled with the curtains. "Leave the damned doors and windows alone. Stars above, will you just stop?"

Turning to face her, he scowled. "I'm worried."

"In case I get hurt and you have to face my father and brother?"

"They are a worry," he conceded, "But my main worry is you."

Flopping down into one of the big armchairs, she replied, "No need to be. I won't tell on you."

Long legs crossed the room and she could feel that frustration emanating from him as he stopped in front of her chair. One brow arched, she looked up at him.

Squatting down before her, Davan opened his mouth.

"Don't." She placed one finger on his lips. "Don't start again. I'm not listening."

He nipped her finger and as she jerked it away and frowned, he said dryly, "'Tis no surprise."

"Look, Davan, if you're interested in pursuing me - "

"Pursuing you? I'm courting you, lass, and 'tis just the niceties. I'm wedding you, *very* soon."

"Huh." Quietly pleased, Delias tossed her head. "You haven't won any points yet."

"I beg to differ." The current events forgotten for the moment, his eyes crinkled at the corners in amusement. "Those moans last night and early this morn were quite clearly points being won."

"You wish." Just the memory made her heart beat a little faster, a blush climb her cheeks.

"I know." His voice lowered, his gaze running across her face, lingering on her lips before lifting once more to ensnare her gaze. "And after this is over, lass, I'm going to take you to bed and make love to you from dusk to dawn."

Oh God, he made her quiver in places she'd never quivered before! Feigning nonchalance, she studied her nails. "Only dusk to dawn?"

Big hands landed on her knees, slowly moving upwards, and there was no way she could lift her fascinated gaze from those hands working their way oh, so slowly, up her thighs.

"Nay, from dawn to dusk as well." His voice deepened, sliding across her senses like black velvet, just as his words slid through her like thick, hot molasses, full of promise and hot sweetness. "I'm going to kiss you and taste you all over, Delias. I'm going to touch and explore every crevice with my hands, my fingers, my tongue. 'Twill be no part of your body left untouched." His fingers slid under the hem of her gown and edged higher. "No part left untouched."

Her heart slowed, each beat becoming heavy. Moisture gathered between her thighs. Moistening her lips, she lifted her gaze to his.

God above, his eyes were hot. Promise was stamped all over his dangerously handsome features. The man wanted her then and there, she could see it, feel it. Heat emanated from his big body and he leaned closer, his big hands braced high on her thighs.

Holding her breath, she watched with widening eyes as he drew yet even nearer, his abdomen against her knees, the muscles in his arms flexing as he moved. Closer he came, closer still, and she could only wait with anticipation as his lips drew closer. His eyes held hers captive, never wavering once.

"You're mine, Delias," he said softly. "Never forget that. No person shall ever hurt you without facing my wrath, and 'twill be a wrath never seen before. If those bastards lay one hand on you tonight, I'll personally tear them limb from limb, Security here or not."

Alarm joined in with anticipation. "Davan, you can't do anything—"

His lips closed on hers, muffling her startled protest, and almost immediately she fell into the magic of his kiss. His lips were like silk, so soft for a man, yet so masculine at the same time. He gave no quarter, demanded everything, and shook her with the depth and intensity of his kiss.

He totally rattled her senses and sent her up in smoke. She felt like the fire of his passion for her swept from him to her, a sharing of heat that threatened to burn out of control.

Winding her arms around his neck, she pressed closer, her knees sliding on each side of his lean waist, her woman's heat coming to rest against his abdomen, the only thing separating them their clothes.

One of his hands slid up to span the small of her back, while the other slid up to rest between her shoulders, pulling her flush against him as he took total control. It was as though no matter what she did, he met it and took over, holding her for his caresses, his kisses. For himself. For her pleasure. Enforcing his claim on her, his mastery.

A Daamen man making sure his wench understood in no uncertain terms that she belonged to him.

When they drew apart, Delias looked deep into his eyes and finally she truly understood. There would be no running from Davan, no leaving him. She belonged to him. Truly belonged to him and no other, and he'd fight for her.

Fight to the death.

And that scared her, for tonight things would become dangerous and Davan wouldn't stand to see anything happen to her.

"Now," he stated softly, "You know."

"Davan." She started to panic. "Davan, you can't take things into your own hands tonight if something goes awry with the plan. You can' - —"

This time it was his finger against her lips, his gaze steady. "We follow the plan, but you are my first concern if something goes wrong. I will do whatever needs to be done."

For the first time she had second thoughts about the whole thing. At first she'd been angry that anyone would dare to enter her home uninvited and search for something. She'd been incensed, and more than willing to help the Security catch the bastards, even more so when she knew it involved helping those illegally abducted. But now…now she felt fear.

Davan mistook the alarm on her face. "'Tis not too late to back out, lass. Just say the word."

"Nay. Nay, I'm not afraid."

"You look it." His hand came up and he brushed a stray curl back behind her ear. "What alarms you so, then?"

"'Tis you." She looked at him. "I'm scared you'll do something reckless, that you'll get hurt."

"I won't."

"Davan, you promise me that no matter what happens tonight, you won't lose your temper." Grabbing his biceps, she squeezed. "Promise me you'll stick with the plan."

"Worried about me?" One blonde brow quirked and a small smile played around his lips. "'Tis sweet."

"'Tis no laughing matter, Davan!"

His amusement faded. "I'll be watching, Del. Whatever happens, I'll be with you." When she started to protest again, he stood with one powerful thrust of his legs. Looking down at her, he stated, "'Tis final."

It wasn't comforting at all. Chewing her lip, she watched as he prowled the room one last time. Getting out of the chair, she nervously wrung her hands. Now she not only had the outlaws to worry about, but Davan as well.

Almost as though he could read her thoughts, Davan crossed to her and slipped his hand around her nape, holding her for a gentle kiss on her forehead. "Don't worry, lass. Stick to the plan." And then he left the room.

Hurrying after him, Delias was just in time to see the front screen door close behind him. Moving to stand in the doorway, she watched as he strode down the path and out into the street. He waved to her, a smile on his lips but his eyes serious as they met her gaze briefly.

She waved back and watched him out of sight, his long legs striding smoothly, his big, muscled body moving with the grace of a giant man used to his build. The breeze played with the blonde hair that escaped the confines of the tie at his nape.

Feeling strangely alone with him gone, Delias slowly retreated back into the house. Her home seemed empty somehow, and she knew it was because the reassuring, comforting presence of Davan was gone. It was ridiculous how used to him she'd grown in such a short time.

"Big baby," she muttered to herself.

Time passed slowly, the dusk coming gradually, and she turned on the lights in the lounge and kitchen. Everything else stayed dark, as she normally kept it when home alone, only turning on those lights she needed.

The timer on the wall turned and it grew later. She had to admit to some nerves now. Why the hell didn't the outlaws come? Picking up an electronic book, she sat in the armchair and tried to read, but the words blurred into nothingness. She swore she heard every noise in the house, the normal noises of a house settling holding a more sinister aspect.

Knowing the house was being watched by Security and peacekeepers, she took a deep breath and tried to concentrate on the book.

Time passed. By midnight she was wondering if anyone was going to come. By two in the morn, she was more than ready to call it quits. Getting up from the chair, she tossed the electronic book onto the little table and stretched.

Something clicked in the stillness and she froze. Angling her head, she listened. No more sound but never being one to simply stand and wait, she started towards the noise.

"Hold your position," Sabra's voice sounded in her ear from the minute communicator attached to the inside of her earring.

It took all Delias's willpower to follow that order. Knowing someone was entering her house was stirring the latent anger inside her. Pretending to go about normal routine with someone entering her house didn't sit right with her. Then again, sitting in her lounge until two in the morn wasn't natural for her, either, so that made two new things in her life.

Pushing the wayward thoughts aside, Delias backed towards the window where the observers watching the house would have a clear view. The strategically placed minute cameras covered every room. Turning, she rearranged the flowers in the vase, her skin prickling with the knowledge that someone was closing in on her.

"How convenient of you to be waiting up for us."

The words had her whirling around, her hand coming to her throat in a gesture that wasn't all pretend. Waiting had stretched her nerves and even though expected, to actually see the intruders gave her goose-bumps.

"Who are you?' she automatically demanded sharply, forgetting her meeker role. "What are you doing in my house?"

Two men moved into the room, and one had a laser trained on her. She recognized them now as two of the new merchants who had arrived the day before. The one without the laser was bearded, his eyes hard, this thick lips moist as he dragged his lecherous gaze over her. The one with the laser was the one she instinctively knew was the leader between the two of them. His gaze flicked around the room before coming to rest on her once more.

"You have something we want," he stated.

"What are you doing in my house?" she repeated sharply.

"Try to act a little scared," Sabra whispered in her ear. "Scared is good."

Scared? Delias wanted to kick the bastards' arses. She should be a screaming bundle of fear, but all she felt was anger.

"The plan," Sabra reminded her.

Taking a deep breath, Delias clasped her hands together and adopted a more subdued tone. "What-what do you want? I don't have anything of yours."

The outlaws didn't waste time. The one holding the laser spoke harshly. "You have in your possession a crate of spices and herbs. There was something in that crate that belongs to us."

"Spices to sweeten your disposition?" she asked before she could bite her tongue. *Oops! Stupid wench!*

"Smart-mouthed bitch, isn't she?" The man with the thick lips moved in towards her. "I have uses for a mouth like that." He groped his crotch obscenely.

"Not in this lifetime," Delias snapped.

"Delias," Sabra's whispered admonishment cracked through her hearing like a whip.

"Hear that, Manez?" The thick-lipped man laughed coarsely. "I'm thinking we should have some fun with this bitch before we finish her off."

Oh, how she wished she could kick him in the balls. Instead, Delias reined in her irritation and shrunk back from him, her gaze going to the man with the laser, Manez. "I - I'm sorry. I just...what do you want?"

His eyes scanned her quickly, his look calculating. "I get the feeling you're not as meek and mild as you portray, female trader."

She had to patch up a bad situation now. Twining her fingers in the long, silken skirts of her gown, trying to appear more fearful than angry, Delias whispered. "Please, don't hurt me."

"Hurt you?" the thick-lipped man laughed. "Bitch, you're going to be screaming when I spread your legs and - "

"Czex, shut up!" Manez snarled.

Czex subsided but he still eyed her hungrily.

The man was vile and Delias suppressed a shudder of revulsion.

Manez strode right up to Delias and pressed the laser to her temple. "Now you're going to do exactly as I say, or my friend here is going to play with you while I watch, and then whatever's left of you will do my bidding. You can do this the easy way by following my orders, or you can do this the hard way by fighting first. Understand?"

The laser was definitely making her nervous, allowing her to push down her first impulse which was to tell him to go to hell. "I understand." She dropped her eyes.

There was silence in the room and she lifted her gaze to find Manez watching her with those ruthless eyes. When she meekly glanced aside, he reached out suddenly and grabbed her hair, jerking her up to him.

Gritting her teeth, she looked at him. If Davan was seeing this, he'd be gnashing his teeth. Blazing stars of hellfire, she was furious! No man had ever handled her like this! The only thing saving her from lashing out was her own sense of self-preservation that let her know this man, Manez, was a killer through and through.

"You don't fool me, Delias," Manez growled. "I've seen you at your work, I've heard you haggle with the merchants, and I've been around enough females to know when one is really scared, and when one isn't." His hand twisted more viciously into her hair, sending pain shooting through her scalp.

Reflexively, she grabbed his wrist. "Let go, you bastard!" The laser jabbing hard into her spine stilled her.

Manez studied her grimly. "You're not so scared, female trader. I see that look in your eyes, I know if you had a chance you'd fight us. But I'm not giving you that chance. One foot wrong and I'll shoot you. I'll kill you without a qualm.

Understand?"

"Aye." Wincing against the pain of his hold in her hair, she held still.

"Good." He released her but kept the laser pressed to her spine.

How she hated being so close to him, his long robes brushing her clothes. Inwardly she shrunk from him.

"The crate had this symbol on it." He bared his arm and she recognized the symbol inked onto it. "Where is the crate?"

"In the kitchen."

"Then let's go there."

He shoved her forward, the laser pressing into her spine in a painful prod. With no choice but to obey, Delias walked out of the room, passing the smirking Czex who reached out and trailed his fingers down her arm as she passed.

Part of her recoiled, another part wanted to slap him stupid, but commonsense prevailed and she merely gave him a withering glare. There was no use trying to pretend to be what she wasn't, not now that Manez knew her personality, but neither did it mean she had to be reckless. Keeping her mouth shut and her actions precise was as close to the plan as she could get. Playing the meek, frightened hostage hadn't worked, thanks to her own temper.

In the kitchen she motioned to the crate on the counter.

"Get it and empty the contents onto the table," Manez ordered.

Picking up the crate, she did as bidden, placing it on the table and taking the jars from it. Finally all the jars were lined up on the table and the crate stood empty.

They stood there, Delias between Manez and Czex, and all looked at the jars.

"So what's there?" Manez asked Delias.

"Jars of herbs and spices," she answered.

"I've checked those jars and there's nothing in them but what they're labelled with."

Delias shrugged. "I'd expect so."

"And the crate has nothing more in it, does it?"

"Nay."

"And this poses a problem."

Delias lifted her gaze from the jars to Manez. His eyes were cold, deadly, and she felt the first shiver of fear go through her.

"See, something I want was in that crate. You opened that crate, Delias. You know there was something else in it."

"'Twas nothing but these jars."

His expression never wavered. "You're lying, female, and I don't appreciate it."

Delias touched one of the jars. "I'm telling you, when I emptied the crate, there was nothing but these jars in there."

"I don't appreciate being lied to." His eyes flickered.

"What did it look like?" she asked. "Mayhap it fell out?"

The blow, when it came, was unexpected. The crack rent the room as his palm slammed into her cheek, knocking her to the floor. Searing pain burned through her cheek, she felt like it was on fire. Tears sprang unbidden to her eyes and pushing herself to her knees, she touched shaking fingers to her cheek. Shocked, she realized that for the first time in her life, she'd been struck with the pure intention of delivering pain.

Czex laughed.

Manez squatted down in front of her, his hands dangling between his knees, the laser loose in his hands. "Let's try it again, shall we?"

Chapter 6
*

"You bastard!" Her voice wobbled.

He shrugged. "You gave me no choice. Now tell me what you did with my disc that you took from the crate."

"Easy," Sabra whispered in her ear. "We're closing in. Don't provoke him."

Anger Manez? Delias had a sudden, fleeting fear that Davan would come hurtling through the door and kill him on the spot. No big loss, granted, but it wouldn't help those whose lives were balanced on her actions.

"The-the disc?" She sniffed and lifted her chin.

Manez waited, his stance for all the world one of having time on his side.

"I haven't seen it." When he raised his hand again, she flinched automatically, hating herself almost as soon as she'd done so.

"I see you're learning a little respect," he said smoothly. "Now let's try again. Where is the disc?"

He should be more worried about his life right now, there was no way he was going to walk away from the house in one piece now he'd hit her.

Swallowing, Delias started to push upright, only to have Czex grab her hair from behind.

"If Manez can't get answers from you, bitch, I can," he said hoarsely. "I'd love to persuade you."

"Czex." Manez jerked his head at him. "Release her."

With a final pat to her hair, Czex trailed his hand down her back to her bottom, giving it a little squeeze as he did so.

That bastard was going to pay for that liberty, she vowed. Later, he was really going to pay.

But right now Manez was the main threat and she sure hoped the Security and peacekeepers were closing in fast. They knew it was a disc they were looking for now.

"Lead him back to the lounge." Sabra's voice was hushed

and steady through the minute communicator, lending Delias courage.

"It - it's in the lounge." Delias started to push upright.

Grabbing her arm, Manez dragged her to her feet and looked down at her. His eyes were so blank, so devoid of expression that she shivered inwardly. The man seemed emotionless, except for anger.

"Don't try to fool me," he warned, his voice a quiet threat.

"I'm not."

He looked at her searchingly. "Reminders can be useful."

Delias had no idea what he meant, but she caught the flicker of his eyes and the sudden swing back of his arm, and she acted instinctively, throwing herself backwards.

His hand sailed harmlessly past her face, but before she could regain her footing, she was shoved face first to the floor, a knee slamming viciously into her back. She fleetingly caught a flash of silver out of the corner of her eye and fearing it was a dagger, she started to panic and tried to push upwards, drawing in breath to curse them soundly, only to be wrenched around onto her back and a hard hand slapped over her mouth.

Czex was grinning down at her as his hands pinned her shoulders to the floor. "Oh, bitch, you're going to be so good. I love a fighter."

Manez loomed over her. "You'd fetch a high price on the slave blocks in the Outlaw Sector."

Czex groped her breast.

Everything happened at once.

Delias clawed Czex's face and kicked out at Manez at the same time.

A roar filled the air and the glass from the skylight overhead shattered as a big body broke through and landed in a crouch directly behind Manez. Manez swung around to face the enraged giant straightening up. Eyes burning with fury, Davan glanced at Delias and the fury in his eyes turned ferocious when he looked again at Manez and roared, *"I'll kill you!"*

"Nay!" Delias screamed as Manez raised the laser, the whine of it lost in the voices and footsteps thundering through the house. "Davan!"

Manez didn't stand a chance. One powerful thrust of strong thighs and Davan was on him, his aim merciless. He snapped the bone in Mane's wrist, forcing him to drop the laser, and delivered a rapid tattoo of hard punches to him, bloodying his face and breaking his nose.

Sabra's voice snapped out orders in the communicator, and Delias knew the peacekeepers and Security were attacking.

A laser beam flared through the window, shattering the glass and burning a searing path across Czex's temple. It stunned him only momentarily and he tried to stagger to his feet as blood slid down the side of his face. He reached for Delias who frantically kicked out at him, her fear for Davan lending her strength, but she was no match for the laser he drew from the holster at his waist.

Slamming Manez into the wall, Davan swung around to attack Czex while Sabra snapped out an order for Czex to drop the laser, at the same time a tall figure dove cleanly through the window and crashed into Czex, bringing him down to the floor, the laser flying unfired from his hand to clatter against the far wall. Delias scrambled to her knees to see the Reeka warrior kneeling above a terrified Czex with a dagger held to his throat.

Davan knelt before Delias, touching her reddened cheek gently. "Oh, lass!"

"I'm fine," she insisted in a shaky voice. "Really."

Manez groaned and Davan surged to his feet, turning once more on the helpless outlaw. "You hurt my lass, you bastard! I'll kill you!"

Delias didn't know who to look at first, at Davan who was pounding on the outlaw, or the Reeka who, her cold eyes gleaming, was tracing the dagger blade around the front of Czex's throat, leaving a thin, red line in the wake of the blade. "Oh, Czex, how foolish are you? How desperate?"

Fascinated, Delias watched Czex's face whiten as he gasped out, "Reya!"

"So you remember me? I'm touched." Reya's pale green gaze slid to Delias briefly, assessingly, before returning to Czex. "You've signed your death warrant, Czex. Very careless of you."

Frantically, he grovelled. "Reya! Please - "

"Oh, not from me. You were just practice." Reya smiled coldly.

Sabra helped Delias to her feet. Giving her a quick study, she nodded. "You'll be a bit bruised and sore, but you'll live. However, my prisoner won't live much longer if you don't drag Davan off him."

Delias saw immediately what she meant. Manez was little more than a raw piece of meat under Davan's punishing fists. She'd never seen Davan so enraged. Uncaring that the man was unconscious, he continued to deliver one punishing blow after another.

"Davan!" Delias started towards him, pushing past Marly, another Security Officer who was attempting to stop Davan beating her prisoner to death.

Moreb was no help, he was zeroing in on Czex, whom Reya simply stepped away from and allowed the giant peacekeeper to drag to his feet and, with one savage blow, knock Czex unconscious.

"Davan!" Delias grabbed his arm, hanging on as the massive muscles of his bicep bulged up. "Davan, please!"

For a horrified second she thought he was going to ignore her but suddenly he stopped, dropping Manez like trash to lie on the floor. Whirling around, Davan looked down at her, and she saw the anguish in his eyes when he looked at her cheek.

"Del," he choked out. "Oh my God, Del!"

"Davan, 'tis all right." She reached up to touch his jaw. "I'm all right, honestly."

He swept her up into his arms, almost crushing her against

his chest as he hugged her fiercely. She was shocked to feel him shaking, and even more shocked when Sabra started to say something to him and he lifted his head to snarl at her, "Not now, Sabra!"

Unperturbed, Sabra stepped back, Marly beside her watching warily.

Reya watched coolly from where she sat on the end of the table, her booted feet swinging lazily above the floor while she twirled the dagger around the fingers of one hand.

Without a word, Davan turned on his heel and strode from the room, Delias clasped firmly in his arms.

"Davan, what - " she began.

"Don't," he hissed. "Just don't."

She could feel the coiled tension in him, the danger that filled the very air around him.

Without a word he carried her upstairs to her room where he sat her on the bed before going into the bathroom and coming back with a wet face washer. She sat still, not sure what to think, not sure what he was thinking, and to be truthful, not sure exactly what to say.

Kneeling by the bed, Davan gently placed the cold face washer against her cheek. It felt cool against the tenderness of her abused flesh, and she closed her eyes and sighed blissfully.

The silence stretched out and she opened her eyes. Davan's face was grim, his lips tight, and his eyes held a mixture of anger intermingled with worry for her.

"Well," she finally said. "That went well."

His eyes narrowed as he grated out, "Don't talk to me right now."

Startled, she leaned back from him.

Immediately his arm slid around her waist, pulling her to him as he said almost harshly, "And don't pull back from me. *Never* pull back from me." His chin rested on her shoulder and he tenderly tucked her chin onto his broad shoulder. His hand came to rest on the back of her head lightly, his fingers gently kneading her scalp. "Delias, just sit for a minute. Just sit."

Uncertain as to his mood, she obeyed. The gentle kneading was soothing to her sore scalp and as she relaxed against him, she felt his head shift and the brush of his lips against her ear. Snuggling into him, she sighed contentedly.

And then she got the jitters. She felt the tremble of her hands sift through to her body, and she pressed against him. "I'm not scared," she mumbled. "'Tis just delayed reaction."

"Then out of the two of us, you're the only one not scared," Davan said gruffly. "I was terrified for you." His arm tightened around her waist. "Oh, God, Del, you have no idea how I felt when that bastard slapped you, when that other low-life scum groped you. I wanted to beat them blind for the way they spoke to you, lass, and when they hurt you." A shudder went through him. "I know I was supposed to wait, that you weren't in mortal danger, but I couldn't, Del, I couldn't let them hurt you anymore." His arm tightened around her. "I wanted to kill them."

Sliding her arms around his neck, Delias turned her face and pressed her lips to his jaw. "I think you nearly accomplished that with Manez."

"You should have let me continue." He cradled her close.

"Not a good idea. Sabra wanted him alive."

"Having him alive is not worth your pain."

"Davan, 'twasn't that bad," she soothed.

"You didn't see the shock on your face when he hit you, Delias." Lifting his chin from her shoulder, he tenderly kissed her red cheek. "It tore a hole right through my heart."

Wanting to ease the pain in his eyes, Delias smiled. "You're really quite romantic. 'Tis not just flowers."

He shook his head. "'Tis no joking matter."

"I'm not joking. You are romantic."

Tracing his thumb gently across her cheek, Davan said softly, "You're not staying here tonight. You're coming home with me."

The thought of lying safe in his arms after tonight was

appealing and, to be truthful, right now she didn't like the idea of staying at home alone. Resting her forehead against his, she agreed. "As you command."

A rueful smile crossed his face. "If only you were as biddable in all things. Such as tonight's disaster."

"'Twas no disaster," she objected.

"Nay?" He arched one brow. "You got hurt, and for nothing, I might add. I should never have allowed it."

"Don't start that again." Sitting up, Delias caught a flash of silver from the corner of her eye and started. It was just her jewel box, but the other flash of silver... her eyes widened. "Davan!"

"You're hurt?" Immediately anxious, he started to run his hands over her. "Where? Del, where - "

"Nay." She pushed his hands away. "I remember something!"

"What?"

"Come on!" Giving him a light shove, she stood up when he moved back and made for the door.

Davan was close behind her as she ran down the stairs.

Sabra looked around as she came into the kitchen. Sitting in a chair at the table, she had her hands around a mug of steaming hot una. Reya sat on the opposite side of the table, her expression as cold and calm as usual, her warrior's clothes that she always wore showing off her feminine strength. The silver armband on her upper arm was a stark contrast to her tanned skin, and her long, wild, red/gold curls hung thickly down her back. There was no trace of glass in the kitchen, they'd obviously cleaned it up.

"Delias." Sabra glanced from her to Davan and back again. "Everything all right?"

"I think it might be great!" Dropping to her knees beside the counter, Delias angled her head down and scanned the floor. A glint of silver caught her eye and reaching under the counter, she clasped a small, cold object and pulled it out. Coming upright onto her knees, she waved the object in the air. "Could this be the disc he was looking for?"

Sabra stared at the disc before getting to her feet and crossing to Delias's side. Reaching out, she took the small, slim disc from Delias, whipped out a handcomp from her jacket pocket, slid the disc in and waited.

Delias watched anxiously as Sabra scanned the contents on the handcomp. A slow, satisfied smile crossed Sabra's lips, and when she looked up at Delias, she said quietly, "'Tis it! How did you know where 'twas?"

"I saw it when I was knocked to the floor by Manez." Delias looked around and up at Davan. "Remember when I hurt my back? I dropped the crate and it fell open. The disc must have been inside and rolled under the counter without my knowing it."

Sabra's eyes gleamed. "'Tis what we've been searching for, what the outlaws have been searching for. Delias, do you realize what you've done?"

"Found it?"

"You've given us a golden opportunity to save hundreds of lives!"

Delias grinned. "We did it!"

"We certainly did!"

Reya raised one fine brow. "Well done, Delias."

Delias switched her attention from Sabra, who was hastily pressing keys on the hand comp, to the Reeka warrior. "What were you doing here, anyway? Were you passing by?"

Reya took a sip of una. "Actually, I noticed Manez and Czex in the settlement and I knew they were up to something. I noticed the watcher, there," she gestured to Sabra, "following them, and I knew something big was up. Not being invited to the party, I took it upon myself to polish up my surveillance skills and keep watch on you."

"Me?"

"I saw them watching you and then going into your house. I kept watch on you all."

"Did you know?" Davan asked Sabra, his tone still reserved,

more than obviously still not happy with the way things had progressed.

"Of course." Sabra shrugged. "Reya and I spotted each other watching Manez and Czex. 'Tis how I knew those pair of silly bastards were in more danger than Delias was. After all," she winked at Reya, "everyone knows that once a Reeka has you in her sights, you're doomed."

Reya raised her mug in salute.

Pocketing the handcomp, Sabra looked up at Davan. "I know you'd love to do something nasty to me right now, Davan, and I don't blame you. I didn't want Delias to get hurt. But trust me, I would have given my life to protect her from serious harm. You know that, right?"

Davan gazed at her for several seconds before he relaxed. "Aye, I know. 'Twas just that when that bastard hit her I saw red. I know Del wasn't in mortal danger, but..." He shook his head. "I'm sorry if I spoke rough to you, lass. 'Twas just fear for Del."

"As long as we're all right." Sabra gazed steadily up at him. "I count you as my friend, Davan. I never want to damage that friendship."

Smiling, Davan reached out and ruffled her hair. "We're all right, lass."

A shadow lifted from Sabra's eyes, and she moved across to Delias, carefully removing the small communicator from her earring. "I thank you so much, Delias. Not many would do what you did today. I'm proud to know you."

Uncomfortable, Delias shrugged. "'Tis fine. As long as it helps someone."

"More than you know." Sabra drained the mug of una and placed it on the sink. "Coming, warrior? I've some prisoners to take to the IPS, and you have a daughter to attend."

"Aye, I must fetch her from Tenia's." Unfolding her tall, slim frame from the chair, Reya nodded coolly at Delias. "Glad you're all right, little sister." Her gaze flicked to Davan. "Not a word to Maverk when he comes back about tonight."

"You wish," he retorted.

Her smile was as cold as a winter pond, the glint in her eyes that of glaciers. Turning, she followed Sabra from the room.

Davan helped Delias up from her kneeling position from the floor but before he could say anything, Sabra glanced around the door. "Davan?"

"Aye?"

"Moreb said to tell you he'll do the legal notes. He said 'tis no need to return to the Enforcer Building tonight."

"Thanks."

Sabra disappeared again and Davan slid an arm around Delias's shoulders to draw her against his side. "Let's go home, lass."

Outside was quiet and Moreb appeared out of the darkness. He looked soberly down at Delias, his normal merry expression absent. "I'm glad you're all right, lass. I'm sorry you got hurt."

"I'm fine." Delias smiled up at him. "Manez and Czex are hurt far worse than me."

"'Tis lucky they're not dead," Davan growled.

Moreb switched his gaze to his friend and boss. "Sabra had to get them off planet quick. We had angry traders and their families waiting to string them up then and there. Word spread fast."

Delias glanced around at the quiet street.

Moreb correctly guessed her thoughts. "It took awhile to assure them you're fine and in Davan's excellent care. I convinced them all to go home, that we had everything under control." Suddenly he grinned broadly. "Reya helped convince them. I won't repeat what she said, but it worked."

Delias could imagine.

"But they'll be around tomorrow," Davan finished. "Everyone wanting to help."

Moreb shrugged. "'Tis the way of it. We'd all do the same."

"Aye." He reached out and slapped his friend on the arm. "I thank you."

"Just doing my job." Moreb winked at Delias. "Of course, one of your butter cakes with pink frosting would go down a treat."

She laughed. "'Tis a promise."

Moreb and Davan exchanged a few more words, then Davan steered Delias out of the path and onto the street. Holding her tucked into his side, they walked down the streets and to his home.

~ * ~

Lying back in the big bed, Davan listened to the shower. Delias had insisted on showering once they'd gotten back to his home, insisting that scrambling around on the floor made her feel dirty, but he had a strong suspicion 'twas the memory of Czex's hand groping her breast that made her feel dirtier.

His fists clenched. Just the memory of that bastard touching her, his lewd threats…he should have broken the bastard's neck when he'd had the chance. At least Czex and Manez would never see the light of day again. Cardrak, the prison planet, was their final destination.

Closing his eyes, he tried to relax but all he could see was Delias's shocked face when she was slapped. The tears in her eyes that she'd blinked away. It had taken all his strength, the echoes of her earlier pleadings in his ear, to stick to the plan that had made him stay still as he watched through the skylight from the space in the ceiling. Until Manez had tried to slap her again, then he felt his control slipping dangerously. When Czex had groped her, that had snapped it completely and regardless of the outcome that Security wanted, he couldn't stand by any longer. He'd dived in to save his beloved Del.

Well, hell, it had all turned out well. Delias had found the disc, and he'd nearly killed the man who'd hurt her, so he figured the outcome was good. It would have been better if he'd been able to kill both outlaw bastards, but Del was safe and that was all that mattered now.

"Um… Davan?"

Opening his eyes, he turned his head to see Delias standing in the doorway of the bathroom, a towel wrapped around her slim figure. He smiled. "Aye?"

"I forgot to bring a nightgown."

"You don't need one." He held out one hand to her. "Come here."

She hesitated and he waggled his fingers. Slowly she crossed the floor and he couldn't help but think how cute she was. Fiery one minute, shy the next. As she came to a stop beside the bed, he lifted the covers and winked. "Makes two of us naked. Get in."

Delias blushed but she laughed as well. Dropping the towel, she quickly slid under the covers and into the big bed, snuggling up to him without hesitation.

"Mmm, nice." Davan slid an arm around her shoulders and held her close.

Tipping her head back, she smiled up at him. "Too forward? You want me on my side of the bed?"

"You stay right where you are." He dropped a kiss on the tip of her nose. "'Tis just where you should be, and 'twill be your permanent spot very soon."

"So sure of yourself." She tsked. "What about the courting?"

"Speed courting. We're being wed as soon as your parents and brother are back."

Delias went still. "Oh?"

Lifting his head from the pillow, Davan looked down at her. "Something wrong? Because I'm telling you now, 'tis how 'tis going to be done."

"Just wondering how I'm going to explain to them why I'm wedding my arch enemy."

"Opposites attract?"

She laughed.

Thoroughly enchanted by her, Davan caught her mouth, kissing her at first laughingly, then slowly deepening it as desire flared between them. She reached for him, her hands soft against his skin, sending sparks skittering along his nerve endings where she touched.

Heat pooled low in his loins, spreading out, filling his manhood so it lifted, stiffening, searching for the hot moistness to ease it, to spill its seed deep inside the hot haven that was made perfectly for just him.

Davan rolled carefully over Delias, keeping his upper weight off her on his forearms. Her eyes were hot with carnal desire, brilliant green pools of hot promises. Her soft lips were red and swollen from his kisses.

Oh aye, she was his.

"You're looking satisfied," she murmured, leaning up to nibble the corner of his mouth and sending sparks skittering in all directions. "Should I know about what?"

His smile was pure sexual heat. "You're mine. Forever." Dipping his head, he scraped his teeth across the pulse that was beating an erratic tattoo in her throat.

"Mmmm." She arched up, pressing her breasts against his chest. "Anything else?"

"Aye." He pressed a hot, open-mouthed kiss on her sinfully full lips before lifting his head and looking down at her. "I forbid you to ever do anything like you did tonight. Kick, scream, do whatever you want, I forbid it."

She opened her eyes and met his serious gaze. After several seconds, she whispered huskily, "You're telling me this now?"

"Aye." Threading his fingers through her silky curls, he gently kneaded her scalp. "Because I love you. Because 'twould kill me to see you in that situation again. I can't allow it, Del."

Pulling his head down, she kissed him slow and sweet, sliding her foot up the back of his muscular calf in a slow glide that had him almost sweating with ardour.

Of all things, he hadn't quite expected her to react like this. He hadn't even expected to say the words until later, but they'd just fallen out when he'd looked down at her lying so soft and passionate and safe in his arms.

When she drew back from him, she looked him straight in

the eyes and said softly, "All right."

"All right?" Was he hearing correctly? Delias was agreeing to his forbidding?

"Aye." She smiled. "I didn't particularly like being knocked around. I find I don't have the stomach for it. I like my excitement from only two things."

Relief filled him, but he was still wary. "And 'twould be what?"

"Pitching my skills against the merchants to get great deals." Her smile turned hotter. "And pitching my wits against you and seeing the results."

Davan blinked and then he laughed. "You witch."

"'Tis all the excitement I need." She slid her hand down his chest then around his back, trailing her fingers in the small of his back, making him catch his breath. "Threats of punishment from you also do strange things to me." She winked saucily. "'Tis all I'm admitting for now."

Sliding his thigh between her smooth ones, Davan parted her legs and settled in the cradle of her hips. He watched her eyes darken, the brilliant green of her irises going erotically hazy as the length and breadth of his staff pressed against her stomach.

"So you're saying you accept my forbidding only because it suits you?"

"Oh aye." Her hands cupped his buttocks, nails digging in lightly. "Did you expect complete obedience?"

As he looked down at her and saw the warm laughter and desire combined in her eyes, love warmed him, sweeping out of his heart and filling his body. "With you, Del, I expect a life of love and laughter and headaches."

"No surprises there, then." Sliding her hands up to the back of his head, she pulled him down to press light, soft kisses across his mouth. When he sought to capture her lips and deepen the kiss, she evaded him. "Davan?"

Hearing the seriousness of her tone, he met her gaze questioningly. "Aye, lass?"

She studied him so intently, he wondered what she was thinking. A slow smile spread across her face. "I love you."

He smiled back. "I know you do."

Surprise flitted across her pretty face, and then she slapped him smartly on one of his bulging biceps. "Presumptuous oaf!" But amused laughter filled her tone as well.

Laughing, Davan captured both her hands and pinned them above her head easily in one big hand. Looking down at her, he said with mock seriousness, "I can see I need to take you in hand again. 'Tis long overdue."

"Oh, really?" She wiggled beneath him, her soft body doing all kinds of crazy, erotic things to his own. "I don't take well to being told what to do, peacekeeper."

"Never mind, my fiery, sweet little Del." He shifted his hips, his staff sliding unerringly between the slick lips sheltering the entrance to her body. Wet heat immediately engulfed the tip of his staff as he lodged at the entrance to her body.

Delias moaned, trying to arch up, but he held her pinned down with his hips as he raked a hungry tongue across one pink nipple, making her catch her breath. Smiling against the plump softness of her breast, he glanced up to ensnare her ardour-filled gaze. "I can handle you." His hand slid down between their bodies, his fingers finding the little bud hidden amongst the folds of her femininity. He stroked it and was rewarded by Delias's moan as she bit her bottom lip. "I will handle you." He laughed softly, nuzzling her nipple with his mouth as his finger played the little nub between her thighs. "I am handling you."

"Oh, God!" She burst out. "Davan!"

He felt the first ripple go through her and marvelled at how easily she came to peak. Removing his hand, lifting his head, he reared over her and drove deep, watching her face as his pumping hips drove him deeper inside her.

Her throat arched back as she gave herself over to every sensation that bombarded her, and Davan rode her hard, wanting to imprint himself inside her once again. He thrust into her, losing himself in the slick heat that gripped him like a hot glove, her inner muscles clenching onto him as though not wanting to ever let him go. Long, slim legs lifted and wrapped around his waist, pressing him closer, and he drove deeper, a tidal wave of concupiscence taking him over.

He craved her, needed her, wanted every bit of her, and even as his body took her, invading and plundering and laying claim to her once more, he leaned down, hungry for her taste, capturing her mouth with a voracity she met.

Delias kissed him back as hungrily, almost insatiable as she plundered his mouth in turn, her hands catching at his back, then his shoulders, short nails raking over his skin lightly enough not to mark, but enough to drive him onwards, to let him know how much she wanted him.

He drove home hard, burying himself deep inside her, his hands curved around her shoulders from behind, holding her in place to accept his last thrusts. Once, twice, three times he drove deep, and Delias cried out his name, her sheath clenching and convulsing around his staff. The hot rapacity of it flung him out into a shattering space of pure, unadulterated eroticism.

Davan had no idea how long he was out there, only that when he finally came to, he was lying on top of Delias, his head beside hers on the pillow, his face buried in the wild blonde curls that carried her sweet scent.

"Oh, God," Delias whispered shakily.

Immediately he summoned the strength to roll off her, gathering her into his arms as he did so to take her with him. "Sorry, lass," he gasped, his heart still stuttering.

"Not you," she said breathlessly. "Well, aye, 'twas you, but not your weight." Cuddling close, she sighed and relaxed again.

He felt her heart thumping against his side, and thoroughly sated and unashamedly satisfied, he rubbed his cheek on the top of her head where she rested on his shoulder. "'Twas good, aye?"

She laughed. "Looking for compliments?"

"Nay. I have it in your reaction."

"If I had the energy, I'd smack you for that."

"Feeling like another tussle?" He stretched in utter contentment. "Give me a few minutes."

"Nothing wrong with your ego." Delias patted his stomach before resting her palm on his chest. "Aye, you did good."

"You're a hot little piece yourself, lass." He ran his hand down her back and palmed one rounded buttock. "A real little star burst."

"Sweet talker."

Contented silence fell upon the room, and Davan listened as Delias's breath evened out and slowed. He thought she'd gone to sleep when she muttered, "Davan?"

"Aye?"

"About the forbidding thing and the handling thing."

His lips quirked. "Aye?"

"We're going to have a talk about that crap later."

"Looking forward to it, lass, looking forward to it."

Delias fell asleep and he rolled onto his side, wrapping both arms around her and cradling her close. Resting his chin atop her head, feeling her even breaths against his skin, he smiled.

Aye, life would be love, laughter and headaches, he had no doubt, but life without the fiery Del by his side would be incredibly dull.

Davan felt the two lycats jump on the end of the bed. He grinned to himself when he felt Delias move in her sleep, automatically making room when one of the lycats cuddled up behind her. A loud purring filled the room.

Utterly content, the love of his life safely in his arms, Davan closed his eyes.

~ * ~

The water was warm and Delias drew a deep sigh of contentment as she trod water and looked up at the moon overhead. Night flyers sung in the darkness of the trees and fish splashed nearby.

It was an almost perfect night.

A deep voice cut through the peace. "I hope you have a good explanation for swimming alone at night, wench."

Turning around in the water, she grinned at the giant standing on the bank with his arms akimbo and hands on lean hips. "Why, if 'tisn't the Head Peacekeeper of this settlement."

"Oh, aye, 'tis the Head Peacekeeper, the man who maintains law and order, and hunts those who break the law. Such as you."

"I am so scared." Lazily paddling around in a circle, she looked coyly at him over her shoulder. "Got a message about a lawbreaker, did you?"

Davan's face was in shadow, his voice stern. "I did. A message at two in the morn, to be precise."

"Tsk-tsk. Now who could have messaged you at this time of the morn? 'Tis criminal."

"'Tis criminal when I'm supposed to be getting my beauty sleep."

"Do tell." Treading water again, she arched one brow.

"Aye. 'Tis a wedding today."

"Is the lucky wench anyone I know?"

"Possibly. The poor man you definitely know."

Delias made kissy sounds. "So, 'tis a wedding today and a law breaker now. You are busy. What are you going to do, Peacekeeper?"

"Are you coming out, wench?"

"Make me."

"You do like to test my patience, don't you?"

Amused, she tossed her head and paddled out a little further into the lazily flowing river. "'Tis my answer, Peacekeeper.

"Your last chance, wench. You come out, or I'm coming in."

"Ooohhh, I'm so afraid!"

He toed off his boots and slowly peeled off his tunic. "Lawbreakers should be dealt with severely."

"Oh, someone please help me. Please save me from the big, bad-tempered peacekeeper," she drawled, and paddled out a little further.

Glancing again over her shoulder, she saw him skim his trousers down over strong legs and when he straightened, her heart picked up pace. The moonlight picked out every rise and valley of his massive muscles, silhouetting his strong frame to perfection.

Delias licked her lips. "The peacekeeper is making me wet." Angling her head, she amended, "Wetter, actually." The silence was laden with a heavy feeling of heat and lust, and she could almost taste the carnal desire in the air. She grinned. "What say you, Peacekeeper? Want to spank me for being so bad?"

Within seconds Davan was in the water and stroking towards her, his arms thrusting smoothly through the water.

Still treading water, Delias watched as he dove under the water. No doubt the lusty man was circling her. Moving around slowly, she eyed the water. He'd be coming up soon, and she wriggled in anticipation.

Fingers were suddenly around her ankles, and she sucked in a deep breath, expecting to be yanked under the water, but instead those fingers trailed slowly up her legs, leaving little trails of sparks in their pathway. The fingers behind her knees tickled, and she automatically started to pull back, only to have a big hand come up between her thighs and cup her womanhood.

"Oh, stars!" She forgot to tread and would have slid straight under the water except that Davan surged up in front of her, his hands circling her waist to hold her up.

Clasped close against him, her breasts pressed against his naked chest and the heat from his slick skin penetrated her, soaking through to her very core.

Delias drank her fill of him. His blonde hair was darkened from the water and droplets slid down the strong planes of his face. The small, silver hoop in his left ear winked in the moonlight. Rivulets ran down his shoulders, and she slid her hands along the smooth skin, tracing the swell of muscles until her arms slid around his neck and she nestled closer to him.

"Well," she breathed, meeting his glittering gaze.

"The lawbreaker," he returned, his voice dangerously soft.

"The peacekeeper." She winked. "Here to punish me for messaging him at two in the morn."

"Here to punish you for being in the river alone. Again. At night. Again." His knee nudged her thighs apart and Davan nestled the core of her against his hot skin. "Naked. Again. Such a bad wench, Delias."

Delias flashed him a full on smile.

Leaning forward, he breathed hotly against her lips, "Del, I am going to have to take you in hand again." He claimed her mouth in a hot swoop, muffling her jeering laugh and turning her insides to hot lava as he ravished her mouth.

So hot. His skin like satin over steel. His mouth so carnal, so knowing, one big hand sliding beneath the water to caress her buttock, smoothing and stroking over it, tracing the crease between her cheeks with a teasing finger. Fire dove straight to her core, and the feel of his hot, thick brand against her stomach had her rubbing against him.

When he lifted his head, Delias said breathlessly, "If 'tis your idea of punishment, Peacekeeper, please, I've been a very bad wench."

"God, Del, I am so glad!"

Giggling, Delias nestled closer, resting her forearms across his broad shoulders. Davan held her close, treading water for the both of them, laughter sparkling in his eyes, the lust making them even darker and more intent.

Tenderly, she dropped a light kiss next to his mouth. "I am so glad your lip is better."

"Your brother hits hard."

Trailing her lips higher, she pressed a soft kiss to the corner of his eye. "I am so glad your black eye has faded in time for the wedding."

"Your father hits as hard as your brother."

"I told them both off." Drawing her head back, she gazed into his eyes, her amusement fading. "I never wanted them to hit you, Davan."

Davan shrugged. "I'd expect no less. I allowed you to place yourself in danger. I would react the same if I had been in their place."

Delias frowned.

"Besides," he added with a rueful grin, "'Twas your mother tearing strips off me verbally that really hurt."

"I am so sorry."

"Trust me, I got off easy."

She arched one brow. "How so?"

"If my parents had been alive, I'd have been in line for more verbal strip tearing."

"'Twas partly my fault, too."

Amused, Davan eyed her. "I know you got huge verbal strips torn off you."

"Pooh!" She tossed her head. "I'm used to it, remember?"

"Oh boy, do I know that."

Ignoring his laughter, Delias trailed her fingers across one broad shoulder. "They really like you, you know."

"Oh, aye, I know. Your father said 'twas my turn to handle you. Now he could rest."

"He did not."

"Red said he could stop eyeballing all the men chasing after your skirts, and your mother just gave a sigh of relief."

"You lie."

"Your father said he wasn't going to give you away at the wedding, he was going to throw you to me as he rushed by."

Controlling her amusement, Delias said haughtily, "For that, you're going to be all alone on our wedding night, just you and your hand."

"Oh, nay, my fiery little wench, my hand will be busy with your body." His teeth flashed white. "Both hands. All over your body. All night."

She gave him a shove. "Mayhap we better both return to our

respective homes and wait for tonight then. You'll need all your strength to catch me when my father throws me to you."

The chuckle that rumbled up through his chest rocked against her breasts, almost robbing her of breath. "You called me out here, now you have to deal with the consequences."

"'Tis so?" Lifting her legs, she wrapped them around his waist, satisfaction oozing through her at his sharp intake of breath as she nestled her womanhood against his staff. "Well, I do hear that you should have one last rehearsal to make sure everything goes all right... on the night." She winked and added huskily, "If you know what I mean."

Pursing his lips, he frowned. "I'm not sure. You have to show me."

"Ooohhh." She wriggled and laughed when he groaned and clasped her hips to hold her still, his staff surging hot between them. "So I'm in charge?"

"Right now, Del, you're killing me."

"You mean you're surrendering to me?"

His eyes narrowed to brilliant blue slits. "I'm still in charge."

"You don't look like you're in charge." Rubbing the tip of her nose against his, she smiled sultrily. "I bet you couldn't forbid me anything right now, could you, Davan?"

"Wrong, saucy wench." Resting his forehead against hers, he looked deeply into her eyes, his grin wicked. "I forbid you to ever look at another man the way you look at me now. I forbid you to ever leave me. I forbid you to ever be out of our bed for even one night. I forbid you to ever leave my side."

"'Tis a lot of forbidding." She pursed her lips. "I'd need something in return."

"Hmmm, let's see. Me forever, my handling you, my dealing with you, my sorting out your tantrums. Did I leave anything out?"

"I don't know," she replied, amused. "'Tis your fantasy."

"Sweet Del, you *are* my fantasy."

Cam & Sabra

Soul – finding love is part of it, trust is another, and Cam is
intent on his soul mate cresting that last hurdle.

Chapter 1

*

"So."

Sabra didn't look up from the viscomm screen. "What?"

Freeman leaned back in the chair and swung his booted heels up on the desk. "So you let a friend get hurt to obtain information."

Scanning the contents on the screen, Sabra noted the names. "'Tis what you heard?"

"Yep."

"Then it must be so."

"That's cold, Sabra." He gave a fake shudder. "Even for Security."

"Freeman, you'd sell your own mother for information, so don't even try playing horrified."

"But you're not me."

Glancing up, Sabra ran her gaze assessingly over him. He smiled brightly at her. Freeman was handsome in a rough-hewn kind of way. Lean. Tall, which meant he was on eye-level with her. Brown hair, sparkling brown eyes, winning smile and a carefree manner that belied the razor-sharp intelligence which made him one of the top IPS Security Officers. He also had a razor-sharp, sardonic wit which he liked to use on his friends and foes alike.

"Nay, I'm not like you," she said.

"Jealous?"

"I'm trying to bear up under that particular disappointment."

"You wound me."

"Tempting." She dropped her gaze back to the viscomm.

"So, tell me." Freeman swivelled the chair from side to side. "How the hell did you manage not to get yourself hung by the Head Peacekeeper, Davan, for allowing his little piece of fluff to get hurt?"

"That little piece of fluff is as tall as you." Sabra tapped a name on the screen and a file came up.

"In comparison to the gigantic Davan, Delias is a little piece of fluff." Freeman regarded her with a mixture of curiosity and amusement. "So how did you manage not to be lynched by Davan?"

"Because Davan has more brains than you."

"You can't tell me he wasn't foaming at the mouth when Delias got slapped around."

The memory wasn't one Sabra liked. "Freeman, haven't you got anything better to do than bug me?"

"No." She didn't have to look up to know that his eyes were sparkling. "Am I bugging you?"

"You have too much time on your hands." Reducing the file to the corner of the viscomm screen, Sabra brought up a new file, added a heap of names and touched Freeman's name on her keyboard. "This will keep you busy."

Instantly suspicious, he stopped swivelling the chair around and eyed her. "What did you just do?"

"Go check your viscomm." Bringing up the original file, Sabra waved one hand at him. "Bye bye."

He stared at her for several seconds before getting slowly to his feet. "You just sent all those overdue reports to me, didn't you?"

"Uleah will expect them by morn."

"Morning?" Freeman let loose an oath. "Damn it, Sabra! It's ten o'clock at night now!"

"Then you'd better get busy."

A crafty expression crossed Freeman's face. "You weren't going to have them done by morning, anyway, so he won't be expecting them." He started to lower himself back into the chair. "Now, about Davan - "

"I sent a message to Uleah's viscomm to say that you had taken over the reports and would have them to him
personally by morn." Leaning back in the chair, Sabra linked her hands upon her flat abdomen and smiled widely at her friend's now frowning face. "Better get a move on if you hope

to have a few hours sleep tonight."

"You are mean." Pushing upright, Freeman shook his finger at her. "Vindictive. Meanly vindictive."

"How you do flatter me." She fluttered her eyelashes at him.

Turning on his heel, Freeman crossed the room to his desk, flicked on the viscomm and cast a stunned look at the listings of files now awaiting his attention.

"Aye, I'm cold." Grinning, Sabra turned back to her viscomm. "And now I feel so much better."

Dropping into his chair with a scowl, Freeman growled, "Did I mention vindictive?"

"Why, nay, I don't believe so." Cupping one hand to her ear, she angled her head to one side. "Please, mention it."

Shaking his head, Freeman brought up one of the files and started tapping on the keyboard. "You are soooo vindictive."

"Music to my ears."

Leaving Freeman muttering to himself, Sabra returned her attention to the names listed on the viscomm, but her thoughts weren't completely on her work. In a far corner of her mind niggled a worrisome thought, one she squashed ruthlessly, refusing to allow it to surface. Ignoring the little needling, she focussed on the listing.

Aye, she recognized several of the names. Two were new, but that was good, for it meant that several more illegal slavers had been unearthed. Now she just had to pinpoint their last known locations.

The hunt was on.

~ * ~

The hover tray was full.

Dropping the last sack of grain onto it, Red gave a sigh of relief. "Cam, I cannot lift anything else."

"Poor lad is weak from charming the tavern wenches last night." Aamun looked up from where he was totalling the cargo on a handtronic. "Cam, you need to give him some time to rest."

Striding down the ramp, Cam clapped his hand on Red's

brawny shoulder. "Better go and rest, Red. We're just heading into the settlement to deliver these goods to the merchant, then 'tis just a nice meal and drink at the tavern—"

"A few hours with some sweet wenches," Borga added with a huge grin.

"And while we're gone, you can catch up on some sleep," Cam finished.

Red's brows shot up almost to his shaggy hairline. "And leave you bastards to give the wenches a bad impression of Daamen traders? I need to be there to show them how a real Daamen treats a wench."

"Only if we want them running from us." Jase grinned from his lounging position against the side of the Daamen trade spaceship. "Only one man here can really show those lasses a good time, and - "

"'Tis me," Borga butted in.

Red jumped him, bringing him down in a flying tackle. Cursing and laughing, they rolled across the grass.

Aamun shook his head sadly at Cam. "These young, unwed Daamens."

"Aye," Cam agreed, side-stepping the grappling Red and Borga, "With no sweet lass of their own, they're doomed to chase every comely wench's skirts. Sad."

"Very sad."

Jase scoffed. "Poor old wed traders, tied to one wench's skirts. 'Tis jealousy I hear, I'm sure." He turned to Simon. "What do you hear?"

"Jealousy," Simon replied promptly. "But never mind, my friends, we'll wench wild enough for you two as well."

Aamun rolled his eyes.

Thinking of his own comely wench, Cam watched Red and Borga wrestling across the grass. Ah, his sweet little Sabra. How he missed her. He wondered where she was, what she was up to... what danger stalked her, what danger she strode boldly into on her latest hunt.

The thought was enough to dim his enjoyment of the

moment and he turned to the hover tray and started to fasten the ties around the load, leaving his friends and crewmates placing bets on the outcome of the impromptu wrestling match and cheering on the participants.

It was pointless worrying so much, he knew, for Sabra could very well be sitting safe inside a Security ship assessing information, or even getting ready to return home. A small smile crept across his lips as he adjusted a tie. It had been a few weeks since she'd last been home on Daamen with him, hopefully it would be time again soon. Tonight she was supposed to be contacting him, mayhap she'd have news of her return soon. He couldn't wait to speak to her again.

"We love them so," Aamun said quietly as he came up beside him. "'Tis hard enough to leave them for several months at a time when trading, as I do my beloved Mina, but what you have to shoulder, my friend, is quite a burden at times, aye?"

Cam snapped the tie in place before placing one hand on the big crate and turning to face his friend. "If Sabra is happy, I am happy."

"Truthfully?" Aamun's gaze was searching.

"Aye." Being the only other married man aboard ship, Cam knew Aamun had more of an understanding than their unwed friends. "Sabra isn't the stay-at-home type, Aamun. I wouldn't expect her to be so."

"She'd be safer."

"Aye, 'tis no doubt, but her past has forged her into what she is, and I love her regardless."

Aamun nodded and half smiled.

For a split second, Cam had a feeling of aloneness. Aye, Aamun had more of an understanding than Cam's unwed friends, but he didn't really understand Sabra, not as Cam did. He didn't really know everything Sabra had been through, only some of it, the same as the other Daamens. One night Sabra had entrusted him with everything, and it was something Cam treasured, for he was the only one she'd ever told.

The ties between himself and Sabra might not be completely understood by everyone, the knowledge that they lived such different lives, but it suited them both and that was all that mattered. Mostly it mattered to Cam that his beloved Sabra was happy.

Feeling more cheerful, he turned back to the wrestling pair on the ground and raised one brow. "Is either of them actually winning?"

"Beats me," Jase replied, "But 'tis entertaining!"

~ * ~

The darkness of the room was unrelieved. In the darkness came the sound of sobs, the odd whimper, a muted voice. The very air stunk of unwashed bodies and dirty feet shuffled on the wooden floor.

Looking up, she wondered if anyone was even looking for them anymore.

The dull pound of boots sounded from far off, muffled but threatening to the listeners who scrambled towards the back of the room. The silence in the room was fraught with tension.

~ * ~

Uleah studied the information on the big screen in the wall. "So this is confirmed?"

"By our source, aye," Sabra replied.

Sitting on the other side of the table, Freeman yawned and blinked but remained focused on the screen. One thing her friend and fellow security officer was good at was rising above his tiredness. Sabra didn't feel a shred of remorse. She had no doubt he was already plotting revenge.

Looking back at Uleah, Sabra waited.

The Security Chief turned back to the table. "I think we have enough information for several of you to go to the area and see what you can find."

It was just what Sabra had been hoping he'd say. "We can be gone in the hour."

"Better make it two hours." Uleah looked wryly at Freeman.

183

"I doubt he's going to be moving very fast."

"He's just a dedicated worker." Standing, Sabra picked up the handtronic. "He couldn't wait to get a start on those reports, could you, Freeman?"

Freeman just looked at her.

Uleah's eyes twinkled. "I do like dedicated workers."

Freeman snorted.

"Come on, sleepy babe." Sabra crooked a finger at Freeman. "We have work to do."

"I'm overworked." Pushing upright, Freeman stifled another yawn. "However, unlike some, I do my work. All of it. Myself."

"See?" Sabra walked to the door. "Dedicated. You do us proud, Freeman."

"You better watch your back, Daamen, that's all I'm saying."

Glancing over her shoulder at him, she smirked. "I'm so scared. I might have to tell Cam to come and save me from the big, bad Security Officer."

"Knowing Cam, he'd be here in a flash and ripping my arms off. But you're not the kind to squeal for help, so I'm not worried. Revenge, Daamen, is so sweet. I can taste it now."

Sabra laughed.

"Meanwhile," Freeman said, "I'll notify Marly and get her to commandeer a spaceship."

"Aye. I'll go download all the information we need onto the Central Navigation Board, so Security from here can track our flight patterns, then I'll pack a few things."

They parted company and Sabra headed to Security Central which was located deep down near the bottom of the massive Intergalactic Peace Ship. Security Central branched out from several corridors, each one leading to contained areas only accessible by Security. Entering the main Central area, Sabra nodded to several Security Operators controlling the Galaxy Watch System. Maps from different areas of the galaxy lined the walls and information scrolled almost continuously on eight viscomm screens. The Security Operators worked with efficient speed, directing the information to relevant Security Officers working in different parts of the galaxy. New lines appeared on the maps, faded, brightened, disappeared or multiplied according to information directed there by both the Security Operators and the Security Officers.

Five Security Officers monitored the maps and relayed messages back to the Security Officers affected, and sent other information to different planet Peacekeepers according to needs.

Giving them all a brief nod, Sabra sat down in a vacant chair in the corner of the room and keyed her code into the Security Navigational System, and once it gave her access, she typed in the known coordinates of where she was heading, as well as Freeman's, Marly's and her own personal codes, followed by the job number, which notified the monitoring Security Officers of who was involved in the job.

She hadn't finished when a message from Marly came on her handtronic with the code of the spaceship they were going to be taking, and she entered the code into the System, effectively locking the tracking system onto the ship.

The information scrolled through the System and one of the monitoring Security Officers nodded across to her while touching the map that showed every section of the Intergalactic Peace Ship. In the security docking bay, a small yellow light appeared, indicating the spaceship she and her workmates would be taking.

Having done what she could for now, Sabra headed back to her cabin to pack. The cabins set aside for Security were comfortable, informal and roomy, but it wasn't meant to be home. However, because Cam often shared this cabin with her, to Sabra it was home. Her second home was on Daamen, in the home she also shared with Cam.

In fact, wherever Cam was, was home.

Glancing up from the drawer where she was pulling clean underwear, she looked at the image photo on the drawer top. Dropping the underwear back into the drawer, she reached out and picked up the frame, bringing it down to study it.

Cam was laughing out at the image-taker, his brown eyes, so dark as to be almost black, bright with fun and life. Thick, glossy black hair hung down his back and over his broad shoulders in cascading curls. The faint scar above his left brow and another from his left ear to partway across his cheek added to his dangerously handsome face. The small silver hoop all the Daamens wore in their left earlobe added a piratical air.

The image had been taken as Cam had turned, laughing at something she'd said, and she caught him in a moment that she treasured because the image was so natural, was so him. Laughing, happy, her gentle giant, friend from childhood, saviour of her soul, and holder of her heart.

"You know," she said to the image, "before you came along, I was never poetical." Stroking her finger down the scar on his cheek, she smiled a little. "Before you came along, I never thought my life would be anything else but being a bounty hunter. Now I'm a wife and Security Officer. Life takes funny turns." Gazing at the face of her beloved Cam, her smile faded.

Would he approve of what she'd done? Somehow she doubted it. Knowingly allowing a friend to be hurt... Abruptly placing the frame back on the drawer top, she returned to packing. What was done was done. No turning back. She'd started a hunt that had to be seen through to the end regardless of personal feelings.

Damn it, when she'd been a bounty hunter her loyalty had been to her pack. Now her duty extended to a far greater extent. Sometimes being a bounty hunter had been easier.

Straightening, she slung the bag over her shoulder and crossed the cabin, turning into the little hall and striding to the door to her apartment. Without a backward glance she strode through the door as it slid open and walked away, knowing it slid securely shut behind her and locked.

Being a Security Officer meant greater responsibilities, and she'd done and seen things that the general population of the Lawful Sector would never know, and the records were forever logged into the Intergalactic Peace Ship Security.

"Heard what you did to Freeman." Marly fell into step beside her, her gaze amused.

"For that, I must take all the credit," Sabra returned, glad to turn her thoughts elsewhere. She glanced down at the redheaded Security Officer whose head came to her shoulder.

"Wish I could have seen his face." Marly gave a short, harsh bark of laughter. "I certainly heard all about it."

"He's a whiny babe."

"I take offense at that." Freeman came out of a side door and fell into step on Sabra's other side, his bag slung over his shoulder. "And Marly's as vindictive as you for taking delight in my bad treatment."

"Your misery is my delight," Marly informed him.

Freeman sneered at her.

Marly smiled nastily.

"I can see you're all in good spirits." Uleah said, watching from the lift as they approached.

"Fighting fit, Sir," Freeman informed him.

"When he's not falling down on the job and snoring," Marly added.

Sabra just raised her brows at Uleah when he looked at her.

"I'm here to see you to your ship," Uleah informed them.

"He wants to make sure you don't divert back to bed," Marly told Freeman.

"I'm surprised you got out of yours. You weren't occupying it alone," he shot back.

"Jealous? I'm sure I saw some woman run out of your cabin naked and screaming at midnight."

"At midnight I was still working on overdue reports." Freeman glanced at Sabra's impassive face. "Apparently I'm dedicated."

Sabra smiled serenely, enjoying the byplay.

"Yes, well..." Uleah stepped aside as the lift door slid open and two women and a man emerged.

They glanced at the Security Officers, their gazes both wary and only slightly friendly. Sabra recognized them as Planet Representatives and well used to the wariness with which Security was regarded, she eyed them impassively, taking a perverse delight in the quickening of the Representatives' steps away from them.

Turning her gaze back to Uleah, she found him regarding her with amusement. "What?"

Uleah shook his head.

"He's just being polite," Freeman said. "He's laughing at your intimidation methods."

Sabra raised one brow.

"Don't try to pretend you don't know."

"I notice you're not even trying to pretend to be polite."

"I'm honest. Politeness has nothing to do with it."

"We noticed," Marly remarked.

"You're polite, not honest." Freeman paused, thought a second, and added, "Scratch the polite part."

"Up yours, Freeman."

"Only in your dreams, babe." He leered. "Unless...?"

Marly faked an exaggerated shudder.

"It's going to be a long trip," Uleah said to Sabra.

"Been there, done that, ignored them both the whole way." Sabra walked into the vacant lift.

Uleah grinned.

Still trading sharp barbs, Marly and Freeman followed them into the lift.

Personally, Sabra liked listening to the sharp retorts her friends traded almost constantly. It reminded her of the harsh humour of her pack. Once-pack, she reminded herself, but still her family. Not blood, but family by ties forged by pain, loyalty and a brotherhood that could never be understood by outsiders. The pack had saved her life, patched her up and accepted her into their midst. The bounty hunter pack was still her family, regardless.

Which reminded her, the pack was heading through the Lawful Sector in a couple of months time and she had to ensure she was home on Daamen so they could visit. If she couldn't be home, she was damned sure going to meet them in space and spend some time with them, Security or not. She felt a tingle of pleasure at the thought of seeing them again.

Uleah was silent as the lift took them down to the Security docking bay and Sabra wondered if he missed the days when he used to go out on missions. Being higher in rank had to suck sometimes, especially missing out on the action. It might very well be her lot one day.

Shrugging the thought away, she stepped out of the lift as the doors slid open and followed Marly to the ship she'd commandeered for them.

"Oh, for stars' sake," Freeman complained. "Could you pick anything smaller?"

"Don't sweat it," Marly replied snidely, "You're big ego and swollen head will fit inside."

"If not, we can always snag him on a cable and tow him behind us." Ignoring Freeman's sardonic response and Marly's laughter, Sabra turned to Uleah. "Anything else we need to know?"

"I'm sure you all have it in hand." Uleah looked at them all. "Just be careful."

"Always," Freeman responded immediately.

"I'll look after him, don't worry." Marly patted Freeman's arm.

"I knew you were hot for me."

She punched his arm.

"Ooohhh, I like it rough, Marly. How did you know?"

Uleah shook his head. "I can only say I'm glad you're going with them and not me, Sabra."

"I'm good at tuning them out." Sabra nodded to him. "We'll be in contact once we find something out."

The Chief Security's expression sobered. "You take care." He looked at Marly and Freeman. "All of you."

———

Freeman saluted him. "I'll watch the fragile flowers, Sir, you can count on me."

Marly rolled her eyes. "Geez, that's scraping the bottom of the barrel."

Sabra just nodded to Uleah and strode up the ramp and into the ship, her companions following, still bickering as usual. Once inside, she dumped her bag in the robe of one of the four sleeping cabins and went back to the control cabin. Marly was already strapped into the pilot's chair, her fingers flowing smoothly across the control panel as she started the spaceship. Freeman entered seconds later and dropped into the co-pilot's chair, his movements mimicking Marly's as he did the checks.

Taking the seat at the back of the cabin in front of the viscomm, Sabra started to sort through the information loaded there, sorting them into the sections they needed for the hunt. Leaving the flying of the ship to her friends, she immersed herself in the information. She didn't even notice when the ship left the docking bay and speared into space.

~ * ~

The little settlement was hit in the early hours of the morning. The sharp flare of lasers split the night, screams echoed through the still air, and coarse orders were snarled out.

Fire seared the night, lighting the surroundings. A woman fled, holding her baby in her arms. She ran, hoping no one saw her, only to stumble to a halt as a shape loomed out of the darkness. The fire light behind her lit up a face, the

expression on him so cruel and brutal that she sank to her knees.

"Do you think to run?" he rasped.

"Please," she wept. "Please, I beg you! My baby - "

"Is in the way," he interrupted, raising the laser in one meaty fist. "Put it down."

She hugged the wailing baby closer. "Please, I beg of you! I'll give you anything! Anything!"

Impatiently he reached out and fisted one hand into the

delicate lace of the baby's clothes.

The mother reacted instantly, surging to her feet and clawing with her free hand at his face, her nails raking bleeding wounds down across his eye and over his cheek.

"You bitch!" he swore, and shot her point blank.

The baby's wails stopped instantly. Both mother and baby were silent, the ground beneath them turning red with their combined blood.

Swiping at the blood trickling down his face, Matheus stepped over the corpses without care and strode in the direction of the burning settlement. One dead woman and her useless baby didn't matter, not when there was more meat being rounded up, more small settlements to hit, more people to enslave and sell in the Outlaw Sector. Lately business had been very profitable.

Within the hour the only thing left of the little settlement were smouldering ruins and the corpses of the too young and too old. By dawn, carrion eaters settled to feast.

~ * ~

She looked up as the doors creaked open above, a sliver of light briefly lighting up the hole. Sobs sounded, voices raised in protest. A grunt of pain, and then bodies came hurrying through the hole, dropping down into the depths to land painfully on the floor as they were pushed through the opening above. They barely had time to scramble out of the way before more women and young girls of various ages tumbled through to land on the floor.

Crouched in the corner, she caught a glimpse of the men above just before the door slammed shut again, the lock snicking into place.

The newly arrived women were crying, some sobbing hysterically. She didn't rush to offer sympathy, to comfort the terrified captives. Instead, she stayed in the corner.

Survival at all costs. Whatever it entailed, she would survive. She just had to wait for her chance.

Several hours later the door above opened again and the

women and girls pressed against the wall as the light flared on. A staircase slid out from the wall and four men from above stepped down them into the cargo hold.

"Line up against the wall," one of the men snarled. "Face forward!"

This could be her chance! Knowing what was coming, she stood against the wall, her eyes forward, heart thumping painfully in her chest. Smoothing her hair quickly, she glanced to the side.

He came along the line slowly, his hard-eyed gaze assessing each woman, each girl. Now and again he stopped, his hand reaching out to grab a girl's chin and force her head up while he studied her. One of the newly arrived women stepped forward, objecting, and was clubbed ruthlessly to the floor by one of the men flanking him, his laser butt wielded with deadly accuracy.

The girl started to cry and Matheus released her and moved onward, assessing each woman. Most were silent now, frightened, avoiding his gaze.

He drew level to her and she raised her eyes, met his gaze boldly, but not too boldly. Just enough, she hoped, to intrigue him. To catch even just the tiniest bit of his attention.

The only way out of the hole was with this man.

Matheus drew level with her, his gaze travelling disinterestedly over her face. His eyes narrowed when she didn't look away and he reached out abruptly, his fingers digging cruelly into her cheeks as he wrenched her head to each side. One hand came up to viciously squeeze her small breasts and she managed not to wince.

Grabbing a handful of her hair, he jerked her from the line and threw her towards one of the men flanking him. "This one."

She'd thought it'd be easier, but she was mistaken. She knew it wouldn't be pleasant, but hadn't expected the brutality. Dragged from the hole, she'd been taken to a cabin, stripped by two men who laughed at her pale, thin body, who shoved her into a bath and rubbed her lewdly, who washed her with vicious, deviant thoroughness, who shoved her into a red satin gown and propelled her, now in shock and hurting, to where Matheus awaited her.

And then the hurting turned to pain, and finally to agony.

She'd made a very big mistake.

~ * ~

Walking through the smouldering ruins, Sabra studied the ground. Kicking aside some of the rubble, she moved further into the burned house.

"Someone really did a job on this place." Marly looked up from the handtronic she was using to film the scene. "One guess who."

Freeman remained kneeling by a body. "Going by the fact that those left are the old and too young, I'd say the illegal slavers have struck again."

Moving further away from the ruins, Sabra spotted the bodies lying further away. Crossing to them, she gazed down at the corpse of a young wench and a tiny babe.

They'd tried to run, the wench seeking to save her babe from the illegal slavers. The attempt had been in vain, for she'd died as well as the babe.

Mayhap that would have been her wish, to die with her babe rather than see her child torn from her arms and murdered. Sabra had seen it all before as a bounty hunter, a parent giving their life for their child. Hell, she'd hung outlaws who were parents and seen their children handed over to relatives.

Shoving her hands into the pockets of her jacket, she looked up into the sky. The sun was slipping beyond the horizon, the moon waiting to ride free. In the distance she saw the lights of the peacekeeper pursuit crafts closing in, in response to the message Freeman had sent the nearest settlement. The night's work was nowhere near done.

And she'd missed contacting Cam on the viscomm.

"Hope the peacekeepers have an idea of where those slavers are heading." Marly moved up beside Sabra and stared down

193

at the corpses. "Shit, they didn't stand a chance."

"The innocent rarely do," Sabra murmured.

"But we're going to even the odds."

Freeman moved up on Sabra's other side and watched the pursuit crafts circle overhead. All humour was gone from his face, his expression grim and hard.

The two pursuit crafts landed nearby and two peacekeepers disembarked. Their faces were just as grim when they drew near. The sun disappeared and in the gloom shadows made hollows in their faces.

"Security." One of the peacekeepers nodded to Freeman. "Thanks for contacting us."

"I'm Freeman." Freeman gestured to Sabra and Marly. "These are my fellow Security Officers, Sabra and Marly."

The peacekeeper nodded to them. "I'm Sanka, Head Peacekeeper of Uraj, which is the nearest settlement to here, as you know. This is my peacekeeper, Hendle."

After exchanging brief hellos, they all turned back to the settlement.

"The illegal slavers who did this," Sabra began, "do you know where they might be headed?"

Sanka shook his head. "Could be anywhere."

"Have anymore been hit today?"

"No. This is the first in this area that I'm aware of." Sanka looked grimly down at the body of the wench and the babe. "Some of these settlers had relations in other settlements. I'll have to start organizing for the bodies to be retrieved and relatives to identify them."

Marly walked further out and continued recording, the light from the pursuit crafts lighting up the area.

"I want the names of the missing and the dead sent to the link that we'll enter into the Enforcer Building's logs," Sabra said. "I also want the names of the relatives and where they live, sent."

Sanka nodded.

They spent more time searching the ruins but Sabra knew

the illegal slavers were too careful to leave anything behind that would identify them.

Not to worry, she'd find them. The Security would find them. Looking up at the moon now riding high in the sky, she smiled slightly. She had contacts that could help.

More ships had arrived as the Security spaceship left the settlement.

"Are we going to continue on our original course?" Marly queried as Sabra entered the cabin.

"Aye. 'Tis not too far from here." Sitting before the viscomm, Sabra contacted the IPS Security and relayed the latest news. By the time she'd amassed the latest news in turn from the IPS Security monitoring the galaxy maps, it was late.

Freeman had already turned in to bed and Sabra left Marly putting the space ship on autopilot.

Entering her cabin, she sat down at the viscomm and sighed. Cam would be long asleep by now, sleeping the sleep of someone who loved his life and wasn't troubled by faces of the dead and suffering. There was no reason for him to be troubled, he was so kind and good-natured, never hurting anyone unless provoked and even then it had to be something really bad, such as threatening those he loved. Nay, Cam slept the sleep of the deserving.

Glancing at the copy image photo sitting beside the viscomm, she smiled at the laughing, dark eyes in the dangerously handsome face. Her big, gentle rogue. Her one bright light when things were so dark around her.

Flicking on the viscomm, she logged into Cam's personal viscomm and smiled. "Hey, sleepyhead. I know you're off in the land of nod. I'm sorry I missed our call time. Something came up." Such as dead innocents and babes. I bet you would have had tears in your eyes if you'd seen that babe. "I promise to make it up to you somehow. I'll contact you tomorrow night, all right?" She hesitated, missing him keenly. "Ah well. Love you, Cam." Reaching out, she flicked the viscomm off, leaned back in her chair and sighed.

~ * ~

The planet shuttle rocked under the laser fire that blew through the engines. Wires sparked, computers blew. Smoke filled the cabin.

From the compartment behind him, the pilot heard the screams of the passengers. He stumbled to his feet, hitting the alarm button to alert nearby law authorities of the attack.

The door separating the pilot's cabin from the passengers' compartment blew inwards and the pilot was flung backwards. He blinked up from his prone position on the floor in time to see the guard's body drop to the floor, a charred hole in his back, his eyes wide open in shocked death.

A hulking man stepped over the body, his booted feet planting themselves heavily on the floor. Looking down at the pilot, he rasped, "You don't look so good, pilot."

The pilot wiped the blood trickling down the side of his face. "What do you want? Are you space pirates?"

The man laughed gratingly. "My name is Matheus."

The pilot looked blankly up at him.

"I'm your death."

Before the pilot could say anything, the laser in Matheus's hand lifted and flared, the beam going straight through him and into the control panel of the wall. His head thunked down on the floor as Matheus swung on his heel and walked out.

The smell of burned flesh was ripe in the pilot's nose, and he knew he was dying.

He heard Matheus snap orders to gather the people, to kill the old and the very young. The screams filled the air, the flare of lasers, and he knew more than he was dying that day.

It wasn't long before the only sounds were those of the flames licking through the crippled planet shuttle and his rattling breath. Sparks exploded from the console and he felt his life slipping away.

~ * ~

Cam awoke early and the first thing he did was get out of bed and look at the viscomm on the table on the far wall. His heart leaped when he saw that there was a message from Sabra. Sitting in the chair, he tapped her sign on the screen and immediately her face appeared. Almost hungrily, he studied her. She looked her usual quiet, intense self.

Her voice was low and husky, stroking through his senses like velvet. "Hey, sleepyhead. I know you're off in the land of nod. I'm sorry I missed our call time. Something came up." The cobalt blue of her eyes darkened slightly, a sure sign to those that knew her that the something that had come up wasn't pleasant. "I promise to make it up to you somehow. I'll contact you tomorrow night, all right?" She hesitated, then gave a half smile that he knew she had no idea held a trace of wistfulness. "Ah well. Love you, Cam." The screen went dark.

Cam saved the message, then repeated it, stilling the recording at the end before it could go blank again. Leaning back in the chair, he drank his fill of her image on the viscomm screen.

Her hair was in the customary bun she wore when working, the thick streak of blonde hair startling amongst the rich brown tresses. How he loved to stroke his fingers through that silky fall of hair when she wore it loose. Her cobalt eyes, so intense and fathomless, held shadows he didn't like to see. His lass should never have shadows in her eyes. Reaching out one finger, he traced down her high cheekbones, wishing he was doing so for real. Her lips were soft, pink and plump, and tasted as sweet as berries. That little chin was a true indication of her stubbornness. Cam smiled, love sweeping warmly through him. "I miss you, sweet lass."

His gaze wandered lower and he saw that she was dressed in the usual IPS Security uniform of brown jacket and white shirt, and even though he couldn't see further than her waist, he knew she wore brown pants and low-heeled black boots.

In uniform she looked officious and a touch forbidding to those who didn't know her, but when off-duty and on Daamen, she dressed in the work tunic or flowing gown of a Daamen wench. Sometimes she dressed in pants, boots and shirt, but mostly she wore the clothes she knew pleased Cam. Or thought pleased Cam. He was just glad to have her safely at home regardless of what she wore. Personally, he liked her naked and underneath him. He grinned, knowing the tart reply he always got when he told her that, which was often. That tartness was usually followed by a wrestling match and then hot loving. Oh, aye, he surely did enjoy telling her how he liked her beneath him, over and over.

Aye, he missed his lass, and he meant to be near the viscomm tonight in case she contacted him again. Flicking off the viscomm, he stood and stretched. If Sabra got into the middle of something nasty, she wouldn't be able to contact him. Sometimes that happened. It was something he'd grown to accept. Not like, but accept.

Meanwhile, work called. Showering, he dressed and went out into the corridor. Some of his friends were stirring. Shamon, as usual, was being woken by Heddam. The man did love to sleep late and early morns didn't agree with him. Cam grinned as he heard Shamon cursing Heddam out.

Simon met him in the dining cabin. "Got a call from a merchant down in Ordra, on Merconita. He's got a shipment of xeon cloth, marcora herbs and venya wine. He says he knows some of the Daamen traders were interested awhile back if he got some in his possession, and now he has he wants to know if we'd swing by and have a look at it, mayhap do some trading."

"Can't see why not." Cam poured a mug of hot una. "'Tis not far out of our way and that shipment will be worth a lot. Let the Trade Base know of our change of plans and altered flight pattern. Better let Garret know, too." He grinned widely. "Don't want him to think we're running wild with his ship."

Simon laughed. "He couldn't care what you do as his acting captain, Cam. He's too busy trying to keep Dana in line."

"Dana has him running in circles."

"Even more so now she's due to give birth any day." Aamun strolled into the cabin. "Speaking of wenches having their men running in circles, have you heard from Sabra?"

"Are you suggesting she has me running in circles?" Cam took a sip of hot una and eyed his friend over the rim of the mug.

"Suggesting? Hell nay!" Aamun snorted in amusement. "Just stating a fact."

"As if you're any different when you're home with your Mina," Simon put in on his way to the door.

"Mina knows I'm boss," Aamun retorted.

Simon guffawed.

"She does!" Aamun yelled at his departing back. Turning to an amused Cam, he said, "Mina knows."

"Of course she does." And Cam knew very well that Aamun would drop everything in an instant to be by his wife's side if she but said a single word of need.

"Man has to be master of his home," Aamun continued, peering into the food counter and debating his many choices.

"Oh, aye."

"We have to set an example for the young men."

Jase ambled in the door, Heddam and a sleepy Shamon following. "What?"

Aamun slid the glass screen back and drew out a platter of fruit. "We men have to set an example to you young blokes on how to be masters of your own home. To let your wenches know you're boss."

Cam grinned widely.

"Because you're such a fine example," Jase returned. Placing one hand on his muscular chest, he fluttered his eyelashes and pitched his voice high. "Oh, Aamun, you big, manly stud. How you make my heart flutter." Mincing forward, he swung his hips from side to side.

Shamon winced. "I think my eyes are starting to burn in their sockets."

Stopping before Aamun, Jase bent his knees so he was far below Aamun's eye level, and he continued shrilly, "You big, masterly man. Show me who's boss, you stud. Take me in your arms. Kiss me." Pursing up his lips, he made kissy sounds.

"Show us how you handle this, Aamun," Heddam invited cheerfully. "We need to learn."

"Mayhap we should film it for future reference?" Cam suggested.

"I need a bucket," Shamon said. "I'm going to hurl any second."

Aamun eyed Jase witheringly.

"Come on, big boy." Jase looked coyly up at him. "Am I being naughty? Are you going to spank me and show me who's master?" Turning around, he proffered his rear. "Spank me, big boy! Master me!"

"Big mistake," Cam observed.

Jase seemed to realize his mistake almost in the same instant that Aamun planted his boot on Jase's backside and shoved.

Jase careened over the floor and smacked into Heddam, bringing them both to the floor in a kicking, cursing, laughing heap.

"I feel so much better," Aamun remarked to Cam.

"Nothing like beating up the crew first thing in the morn to get the blood flowing," Cam agreed.

The rest of the traders arrived and breakfast was had amidst the usual chatter. Cam informed them of the change of plans and they started discussing the worth of the cargo awaiting their inspection.

~ * ~

The planet shuttle was a burned out hulk floating in space. Several bodies, blackened and twisted, lay on the floor. The peacekeepers looked grimly around.

"There were more than just these few passengers," one of the peacekeepers informed the Head Peacekeeper.

Sanka pinched the bridge of his nose. "Hell." Taking a deep breath, he looked at the other peacekeeper coming from the ruined pilots' cabin. "Did you get the recording box?"

Hendle nodded.

"The pilot's dead now?"

"Yes. He told us some things, though, before he died."

"He named the attackers?"

"Some man named Matheus. He said they came for the passengers."

Sanka sighed. "Let's tow this ship in and call Security."

By the time they got back to Uraj, Security was waiting for them in the Enforcement Building. Freeman left to investigate the burned out planet shuttle, Marly took the recording box from Hendle and disappeared with it into the depths of the Enforcement Building, and Sabra waited by the window, her face expressionless, her form still. Those cobalt blue eyes of hers watched Sanka with an intensity that he had no doubt made many an outlaw squirm. That gaze didn't exactly make him rest easy.

"The pilot managed to tell Hendle a few things before he died," Sanka informed her as he sank into his chair.

Her gaze switched to Hendle.

The peacekeeper stated quietly, "The man who shot him was called Matheus. He told the pilot his name. The pilot heard them gathering the people together, heard him give the order to kill the very young and old. They took the rest."

"Illegal slavers." Crossing to the galaxy map on the wall, Sabra studied it. "They were close by."

Sanka looked across at the map. "The settlement they hit last night wasn't far off."

He watched as she studied the map, her slim figure moving slowly from one side to the other as she paced the length of it. Her hand dipped into her jacket pocket and she withdrew an apple, rubbed it on the jacket lapel and bit into it. Chewing the bite of apple, she stopped here and there, studying the map, tracing different pathways with a finger while considering each line.

Freeman entered, his gaze going briefly to where Sabra was pacing the length of the map and back. He looked at Sanka. "The screening system was destroyed, so we can't get a look at Matheus. Did the pilot describe him at all?"

Hendle spoke up. "Apparently Matheus is big, huge even. Built like a stone wall. Has one eye, a patch over the other."

Sabra turned around. "'Tis a little distinctive."

"There are many people with a patch over their eye," Sanka pointed out.

"But with prosthesis eyes available, why go for a patch?" Sabra took another bite of apple. "A patch can be used to intimidate, make one appear more dangerous, rougher. A scare factor."

"Or maybe he just didn't find a false eye to suit him." Marly came through the door in the rear of the room. "Vanity."

Freeman raised one brow. "Then by all accounts the man needs a makeover. He doesn't sound very vain."

"You'd know."

"Bite my arse."

"You wish, deviant."

"Yeah, I wish. Want a bite? Come on, you know you want to."

Sanka expected Sabra to speak harshly to her fellow Security Officers, for he'd pegged her as being in charge, but she ignored them, her gaze thoughtful as she contemplated something silently.

Tossing the apple core in the bin, she crossed to the viscomm on his desk. Sanka got out of her way, getting up and moving back curiously. With several taps, Sabra was into the outlaw register, combing quickly through and entering data with a speed and efficiency that had him raising his brows in admiration.

Whatever information she came up with, he didn't see. The viscomm went blank and the Enforcement Building logo came on as she straightened up.

He looked questioningly at her.

"I just have to look into a few more things," she told him. "We'll be in touch."

"But did you find what you were looking for?"

"Mayhap." She started for the door. "Keep me informed of anything unusual happening in the area."

He could only watch as the Security Officers left the Building.

"Well." Hendle looked at Sanka. "Now what?"

Frustrated, Sanka taped into the viscomm but he couldn't track the pathway Sabra had followed on his viscomm. Cursing, he sank back into his seat. "Right now all we can do is keep our eyes and ears open, put out feelers and report to Security like they ask. And..." He sighed. "And start contacting the families of those killed and taken from the planet shuttle. Hendle, organize for the undertaker to take the bodies and hold them until their families arrive."

~ * ~

Once in the spaceship, Sabra hustled Marly and Freeman into the control cabin. Standing before the galaxy map, she looked at Marly. "What did you find out from the recording box?"

Marly flicked on the viscomm. "I transferred the recording to our systems. Mostly it's just the orders you hear given by the slavers, the screams and shots, the fires." Her eyes gleamed. "But there's something else in the background. Give me a few minutes and I should be able to separate it from the rest of the noise." Picking up the ear phones attached to the viscomm, she slid the tiny ear pieces into her ears and started to work on the recording.

Sabra switched her gaze to where Freeman leaned against the doorframe. "What did you find on the planet shuttle?"

"It may mean nothing, but I found this under a crispy." Freeman held out a tiny silver article between his finger and thumb.

"Crispy?" She carefully took the tiny object from him.

"Burned body."

"Your vocabulary astounds me." Placing the object in her palm, Sabra frowned down at it. Small, a partial disc, it was flattened and bent out of shape. "'Tis what?"

"No idea." Freeman rubbed his chin. "I thought maybe a dinno from some settlement."

"Could be." She turned it over. "But I don't think so. 'Tis like no dinno I've ever seen."

"Maybe it's part of some jewellery from one of the travellers. Came off and was damaged during the attack."

"Could be. It looks like it originally had a small stone in of some kind." Sabra touched the indent in the centre of the misshapen disc. "Scan it into the data banks, see if Security back on the IPS came come up with something."

Freeman took the disc from her and went to the viscomm on the other side of the cabin.

Sabra turned back to the galaxy map. Taking the thin tracer tool, she placed it on the map and started making lines, linking them up.

Freeman, finished with his task, came back to stand just behind her. He studied the map. "What am I looking at?"

"A galaxy map."

"Really? I'm astounded."

"Doesn't surprise me." Sabra touched the map. "These are the planets that have been hit by the illegal slavers. They only hit a settlement here and there, never close together. Now, I entered the data into the viscomm at the Enforcer Building and I've noticed that a few planet shuttles have been hit lately also."

"Not by space pirates, I'm guessing."

"'Tis been assumed so, but I'm wondering about the accuracy of those findings." Sabra pointed to the linked lines. "Here are the settlements hit, and here are the planet shuttles. Five planet shuttles in all, and all of them not far from the settlements attacked not long before."

Plucking the earphones from her ears, Marly turned in her chair to listen.

Freeman leaned back against her chair, crossing his ankles. "That means they're now following a pattern. Beforehand it was just settlements, and now its planet shuttles as well.

Presuming your assumption is correct."

"'Twould seem so." Sabra tapped the tip of the tracer tool against her chin. "Hit a settlement, then hit a planet shuttle close by. Space pirates get blamed for the planet shuttle. Illegal slavers for the settlement hits."

"Could be the space pirates and the illegal slavers are working together," Marly pointed out.

"Definitely a possibility, but this Matheus strikes me as the kind of man who likes to oversee his own dirty work."

"I take it this means that as soon as we get word of an attack on a settlement, we find out the closest planet shuttle near to it and hightail it into space and hope we get there before them?"

Sabra smiled. "Or we get onto the planet shuttle and meet the slavers ourselves."

Freeman's smile was all teeth. "I do like that plan."

"Now if only we knew what settlement would be hit next," Sabra mused. "Going by this map, it could be anywhere."

"Certainly narrows the field down," Freeman said sardonically.

"I might have part of that answer," Marly said.

Sabra and Freeman turned to her.

"Listen to this." Marly turned back to the viscomm. "I managed to separate the noise from what I heard in the background."

The viscomm hissed, static in the distance. Far off they heard the screams, harsh voices, and laser fire. But separated off, amidst a high-pitched squeal, they heard several words,

broken up, some of the letters missing, but they could still make out something.

"Can you get it any clearer?" Sabra queried.

"That's the best I can do." Marly shook her head. "But it gives us a couple of possibilities."

Freeman brought up the letters onto the screen and they all regarded them thoughtfully.

"It looks to be the name of a planet," Freeman said. "Maybe a settlement."

"And if we find that settlement," Sabra added, "We might get there before the attack. Marly, narrow the letters down and bring up the planets and settlements with those letters."

Freeman rolled his eyes when the listing came up. "Oh, this'll be easy."

Ignoring him, Sabra looked from the siting to the galaxy map. "Put the names against the sections hit already."

This time the listings came down to several settlements on one planet.

"And there you go." Sabra's eyes gleamed. "Not far away, either." She straightened. "Freeman, contact the peacekeepers from those settlements. Warn them to stay alert but they are under no circumstances to approach anyone. They're to monitor the skies for unknown aircraft and send any reported sightings to the IPS Security. And they're to alert us immediately before they do anything."

Leaning back in the chair, Marly folded her arms across her chest. "And what are we going to do meanwhile?"

Sabra studied the map and smiled. "We're going to wait right here." She placed the tip of the pointer on a section of a planet. "This settlement is in the middle of the three settlements whose names contain those letters you found. From this settlement we should be able to respond fast to any attack."

"Oh goody, right in the middle of a potential hot zone." Marly's eyes gleamed. "I like it."

"I knew you liked it rough," Freeman commented.

"Rougher than you can do, Freeman."

"Try me, baby."

"I'd break you, make you go home crying to your mummy."

"Ooohhh." He faked a delicious shiver. "You turn me on, baby!"

Sabra studied the map. The middle of a potential hot zone. Oh, aye, she liked the idea, too.

The hunt was well on its way and she loved every second of it. Only now she was impatient to face the illegal slavers.

The closer she was on their trail, the more she wanted to see their faces, watch their eyes... hang them high.

Rolling her shoulders, she smiled to herself. Inside the Security still beat the heart of a bounty hunter.

~ * ~

Lip swollen, one eye blackened, she huddled in the corner of the big bed. Naked, blood on her thighs, she contemplated what she'd done. Would she have changed it? She shuddered. No. Survival at all costs.

Chapter 2

*

The merchant was beaming, he was so happy. He stood to the side adding up the credits on his handtronic. Beside him was a hover tray loaded with goods the Daamen traders had sold to him. Beside the giant Daamen traders was a hover tray that they were loading with the valuable xeon cloth, marcora herbs and venya wine. The merchant had gotten a great deal, and the Daamens were equally as happy.

Taking one side of the heavy crate containing the cloth, Cam lifted, his muscles bulging in his arms. Simon, on the other side, gave a grunt.

"Young blokes today." Aamun shook his head as he passed them with a barrel of venya wine on his broad shoulder. "No stamina."

"I'm saving it for the lasses later," Simon said as he lowered his side of the crate onto the hover tray. "I'm certainly not using it all up on work!"

"Nice to know where your priorities lay." Cam let the crate go and together they pushed it into the middle of the hover tray.

"Man has to know where to draw the line," Simon agreed. "Have to show those wenches just where my stamina lies. Namely, in bed with them."

Aamun rolled his eyes.

"Gotta admire the persistency." Jase dumped a heavy cloth bundle of herbs on the hover tray. "Mainly because 'tis all he gets — persistence."

"That doesn't even make sense," Simon objected.

"You persist, the wenches are disappointed."

"Jealousy is an ugly thing."

"So's the truth."

Cam grinned.

"Hey! Cam!"

He looked around as Borga hurried through the open

doorway of the merchant's building. "Aye?"

"You'll never guess who I spotted in this very settlement." Borga's eyes were bright, his grin wide.

"Who?"

"Sabra."

Heat leaping, Cam turned fully around from the hover tray. "Sabra?"

"Aye. I saw her going into the Enforcement Building with two of her cronies, that weirdo Freeman, and that wench with the nasty tongue, Marly."

"She must be working here or nearby," Simon mused. "I wonder what is happening?"

"Something must be going down." Jase leaned against the crate on the hover tray. "She could be just passing through."

Cam pushed back from the hover tray. Sabra here meant something was up. She wouldn't have told him she was heading here, mainly because she hadn't known of his change of direction. He could meet up with her, spend a couple of hours with her or even a few minutes, depending on how urgent her job was and what she was planning. But even a few minutes with her in his arms was better than nothing.

"Why waste time here?" Jase looked at Cam. "Go get her."

Though he longed to do just that, Cam shook his head slowly. "Not while she's in the Enforcer Building. Besides, the lass would have seen our ship in the docking bay; she'll know we're here."

"She won't know 'tis you," Jase pointed out.

"I bet she will," Borga said. "As soon as she saw the Daamen trading spaceship, she'd have put in a call to the Daamen Trade Base to find out who is here. That wench will know 'tis Cam."

"Then she'll hunt you down as soon as her business is dealt with." Jase grinned broadly at Cam. "We'll make sure we spend the rest of the day in the tavern while you await your little delight in the ship."

"Thank you so much," Cam replied dryly.

Impatience rode him hard while he forced himself to continue to assist his friends loading the hover tray. Aye, he wanted to go and find her right now, but Sabra in security mode wasn't to be trifled with, for her work was dangerous and distractions could cost her life. Nay, she'd come to him when she could, and he knew she'd come to him before she left the planet to continue her mission.

For Cam the time dragged. When the hover tray was loaded, the traders walked beside it back to the docking bay as it skimmed above the ground. Cam saw the three ships that had been there in the docking bay when they'd landed, but now he saw that a small spaceship, dull and nondescript, was docked one vacant bay over from the trade ship. No one was around.

Which meant Sabra wasn't there yet.

Unloading the hover tray and packing the cargo securely in the cargo hold only took a portion of his attention.

"Are you coming into the settlement for a drink?" Aamun queried as the last of the cargo was secured.

"Nay. I'm waiting here for Sabra."

"She could be awhile." Aamun's expression was understanding. "It might help keep you occupied."

"Nay." Cam shook his head again. "I'd rather wait here. You all go, have a fun time. We won't be leaving until morn or..." He hesitated.

"Or an extra day or two," Borga finished with a knowing laugh. "In case your lass is still here."

Jase nudged Heddam. "I do believe our captain is blushing."

"And how cute he looks." Heddam smiled sweetly.

"Up yours," Cam said gruffly.

"Ooohhh I do believe he is flustered!" Borga cooed. "How sweet!"

"Keep that up, Borga, and you'll be on cleaning duty."

"Oh my!" He placed one hand on his massive chest and sucked in a breath. "Cam's gone all authoritative on me! I like it! Ooohhh, I'm thrilled!"

"The lad's been without female company for too long."

Aamun gave Borga a shove towards the ramp leading out of the cargo hold. "A week without a soft, warm bosom and he's eyeing the rest of us with a gleam in his eye."

"Why, Aamun, I didn't know you cared!"

"Next trip, I'm locking my door."

"Trust me, you don't have the shape I crave." Borga made an hour glass shape in the air with his big hands. "Big bosom, big hips, a lush bottom I can hang onto, a sweet face... oh, 'tis a wench I'm talking about! Which, you big bastard, you surely aren't, so your virtue is safe with me." Borga shuddered. "I may need all night with a comely wench or two to get that picture out of my mind."

Cam watched as his friends, laughing and talking, trod down the ramp and strode towards the settlement. He smiled. Aye the trading life was the life for him, so thank God he'd been born a Daamen. Now his day would be complete if a certain wench arrived very soon. He looked across at the much smaller spaceship.

Several hours dragged past slowly and Cam occupied himself by contacting the Daamen Trade Base with a listing of the purchases he had, in case a nearby planet wanted to trade with the newest items before he bartered them to any other merchant. He contacted his family on Daamen and chatted to his mother briefly before linking to Garret.

His friend's face came onto the viscomm, his shaggy brown hair in a haphazard ponytail. His usually merry grey eyes were a little glassy.

"Hard night?" Cam asked in amusement.

"I swear the wench is trying to drive me mad," Garret retorted. "Every move she made, every little sound, I'm awake. 'Tis been the same for three nights now."

"Mayhap you need to relax, friend."

"Relax? Dana went on a bloody walk yesterday, I had no idea where she went. I had to search the whole settlement to find her."

Vastly entertained, Cam nodded encouragingly.

"Do you know where I found her?"

"Nay."

"Having a nap at Reya's house. Can you believe it? I'm going out of my mind worrying where she is, and she's napping at Reya's house!"

"And why would she be napping at her cousin's house?" Though Cam could guess.

"She said she needed a rest from me. Can you imagine that? A rest from me." Garret was indignant.

"You hover over the lass like an old man."

"I'm about to become a father, Cam, and Dana is about to become a mother, but tell her that!"

"I'm sure she's fully aware of it."

"And still she insists on waltzing around the settlement when she should be home here with me, resting in bed."

"Dana is not the sort of wench to lie around resting, Garret." Cam laughed.

"She should be resting. She's pregnant with twins, doesn't seem concerned - "

"You're worrying enough for the both of you."

"That wench needs to learn to obey!"

"Dana? Learn to obey?" Cam guffawed. "I think you need the rest, Garret."

"Can you believe that my mother says the exact same thing? That even bloody Darvk and Maverk are laughing at me? Hell, I brought her younger brother Rominac here to back me up and he's saying the same thing as everyone else."

"You don't say?"

"And now you're laughing at me."

"What can I say? 'Tis the best entertainment we've had, watching you hover around Dana and drive her mad."

"She could give birth any day, any minute - "

"Any night?"

"Laugh it up, Cam. One day this could be you and then we'll see who has the last laugh."

"Mayhap if you spent more time away trading and less time

at home, Dana wouldn't be pregnant," Cam pointed out.

"Are you insane? I need that wench - I mean that wench needs me around to watch her."

"Of course she does. It has nothing to do with you following her around with your tongue hanging out, ready to do her every bidding."

"I swear, Cam, I'm worried sick about her. Her belly is like a balloon, she needs help getting up, and she has these weird carvings."

"I hear 'tis normal."

"I can't bear it. What if something goes wrong? What if she's on her own and goes into..." Garret's face paled. "Labour?"

"The wench is never on her own," Cam reassured him. "You know everyone is keeping an eye on her for you. 'Tis *you* everyone is worried about."

"I'm never getting her pregnant again," Garret declared. "I'm getting a triple order of sterility potion. I'm going to drink a whole bottle every time I bed that wench."

"The rate you bed her, Garret, you'll need a cargo hold full just for one trip home."

"I don't know what you mean."

"Hell, every time we're on planet you're dragging her off alone. You're addicted to her."

Garret smiled dreamily. "She's a beautiful wench. Hot, sharp tongued..."

"Disobedient."

The dreamy look vanished. "Which reminds me, she should be back from her walk with Delias."

"She'll be fine."

"Nay." Garret jumped up. "I'm going looking for her. I swear, she'll make me an old man before my time." The screen went dark.

Chuckling, Cam leaned back in the chair.

And then everything inside him tightened, every instinct on the alert.

He scented her, the faint flowery scent that slid into his

senses. He felt her, the warmth, the undeniable spark between them. And then her arms were sliding around his shoulders, her hands sliding down his naked chest between the open vest. Her breath was warm against his neck as she pressed a soft, hot kiss against his pulse that was beating hard at her presence.

"Miss me, lover?"

Heat, hot and heavy, slammed low in his groin.

Cam acted fast, his hand reaching up and hooking around one of her upper arms, pulling her around quickly, his other hand coming around to support her back as she was swung in a half circle, the backs of her legs hitting the armrest, and she tipped back onto his lap.

It took mere seconds.

Mere seconds to have her in his arms, her slim, soft body against his, and his arms holding her close, one hand behind her shoulders, the other cradling the back of her head, his fingers sinking into the silky hair as he held her for his kiss.

Cam took her mouth hungrily, devouring her, his tongue sweeping inside to reclaim her taste, to fill himself with her nectar. Everything that was her he craved.

Her arms were around his neck, holding him just as close as she strained towards him, pressing her breasts against his chest, her lips sipping at his just as hungrily.

Sabra. His beloved Sabra was with him once again and Cam was washed away on a tide of pure, carnal heat. The need to bury himself inside her, to brand her as his once more with his seed, with his very presence, with his scent on her skin. To let all and sundry know she was his.

To mark her again, as he always did.

He stood quickly, clasping her close in his arms. He barely registered how he got them to his cabin. He didn't remember even getting on the platform lift. He'd have taken her on the floor of the control cabin if some distant part of him hadn't been aware enough to not want any of the traders to unwittingly catch them there. Not for anything would he risk embarrassing his lass.

Not once did he relinquish his kiss during the fast trip from the control cabin on the second floor up to his cabin on the third floor.

He kicked the door to his cabin shut behind him, lowering Sabra to stand on the floor before him, and still he kissed her hungrily, even as his hands stripped her of her clothes with urgency. He slid the band from her bun, glorying in the silky texture of rich tresses that tumbled in a thick fall over her shoulders.

She greeted his hunger with her own, and within minutes they were both naked on the big bunk, her on her back beneath him as he rolled over onto her, his hips cradled against hers, his thighs forcing her legs wider, as she bent her knees.

Their gazes met, meshed, and for several seconds they simply looked into each other's eyes. Their ragged breathing filled the cabin, their scents entwined.

His hands braced either side of her on the thick mattress, Cam drank his fill of her, her cheeks flushed, her eyes bright with passion, her lips swollen from his almost ruthless kisses. Every breath she drew pressed her small, pink nipples against his chest. Her hands against his sides slid around to rest in the small of his back.

They didn't need any words.

He shifted, drew back slightly, the tip of him sliding between her slick folds to nudge unerringly at the entrance to her body. She was wet for him, the hot dampness eased the way. One thrust and he was inside, pushing mercilessly up to the hilt, buried so deep inside her he didn't know where he ended and she began.

His name echoed in the room as Sabra arched her throat, and he immediately licked at the pulse that pounded within the elegant length. Fastening his lips on it, he almost sucked hard, wanting to mark her as he always did, but again that little voice far in the reaches of his mind cautioned him, warning him that she had to go out with his mark - *God aye, his mark!* - go and face outlaws, space pirates, traitors, stars knew who, with a love bite on her neck for all to see.

He almost wept, his dominant side roaring a protest as he angled away, dragging his teeth down to her shoulder, licking the hollow there as she undulated against him.

His hips thrust, his staff shoving hard through the hot, wet folds of her sheath.

She met him thrust for thrust, straining up against him, moaning his name. Capturing his mouth when he slanted a kiss across her cheek. Her small tongue licked deep, her flavour bursting through him.

God, he could never have enough of her, never get enough. He could spend every second of his life like this with her, and it still wouldn't be enough.

He wanted to mark her, needed to mark her, to leave his passion's bite on her as he always did. But there was only one way, one intimate kiss he could give her that he ached to give her. An intimate kiss he'd not been able to share with her because of her past.

But now... now the need was there full force, the need to mark her, to at least lay the mark where he knew he'd see it, where she would see it.

When he withdrew from her, Sabra whimpered a protest, and he kissed her reassuringly. Purposefully, he kissed his way down her shoulder, over her breasts, sucking on the pert nipples as he went, savouring the soft, yet hard, texture of the little buds in his hot mouth.

Lower still he went, his tongue dipping into her belly button.

And then he brought his mouth lower still, lower where he craved, his chin brushing the curls on her mound. Oh aye, there'd been small ventures, but her stiffening, the uncertainty in her eyes, had always stopped him. He'd never do anything to upset his beloved Sabra.

Cam looked up the length of her body to see her watching him. Desire still blazed in her fathomless eyes, but a hint of shadow was there as well. It was enough to send him sliding up her body, his hands tunnelling into her hair as he came over her.

Tenderness welled up inside him, mingling with the heat that thrummed through him, and he dropped a gentle kiss on the tip of her nose.

"Cam," she whispered.

"'Tis all right, sweet lass," he soothed. "One day."

"Aye." And she claimed his mouth again.

Like a switch, the tenderness fled to be replaced with the hunger that always burned out of control when he was with her. His staff swelled and he shifted his hips, sliding deep inside her once again, feeling her inner muscles clamp around him.

The molten lava of desire that pooled in his groin surged into his staff, stiffening it even more until it ached almost unbearably. Every stroke back through her clasping sheath was a sweet torture, every push back inside her a dominant victory.

His heart hammered, thundering in his ears as his hips pumped faster, harder, and when her slim legs lifted and wrapped around his waist, opening her fully up to him, he could only clench his teeth and shove hard into her welcoming body.

His seed was slipping from the tip of his staff, a slick heat that slid along the walls of her sheath, mingling with her own wet heat.

He felt the ripple go through her, her hands on his back pressing down along his spine as she tried to push upwards, even though his hips pinned her to the bunk. She shuddered beneath him, her muscles clenching hard as she started to climb the peak he was pushing her so expertly, so hotly, up to.

Cam thrust harder, faster, his blood roaring through his veins, his libido rushing out of control fast, his carnal desire for her swelling deep inside him, his scrotum pulling tight, and he pumped short, hard, barely withdrawing from her before slamming back in again. Only his hand clamping onto the headboard of the bunk prevented him from shoving them higher up the bunk.

His hunger burned out of control, bright lights flaring behind his eyes, burning his vision as his blood seared through him, as the soft body of his beloved wife beneath him pressed closer, rubbed, strained against him. He heard her cry out, her voice husky, his name riding the air, pulling at him, and he was lost.

His hips pistoned, once, twice, three times and more, and his seed burst from him, hot, pouring deep, swallowed by her womanhood, her muscles milking him dry.

Flung out over the peak, a part of him stayed with Sabra, a part of him that never forgot her even in the throes of a shattering climax. He swore he could almost see her in that splintering light. She stayed with him, her body against his, his hips pressing hers into the mattress as they rode out their passion.

Each still so aware of the other.

The prurient waves crashed over them, rolling them, dragging them under before finally slipping back, allowing them to drift back down, exhausted but laughing softly as they opened their eyes and looked at each other.

Still atop her, Cam rested on his forearms and dipped his head down to drop a soft kiss on her lips. "I love you, Sabra."

"I love you, Cam."

He rolled off her onto his back, his hand reaching out to clasp hers, their fingers entwining, as he closed his eyes and waited for his ragged breathing to come under control.

The silence in the cabin was comfortable, intimate. As attuned to her as he was, Cam was instantly aware when Sabra's mood changed slightly.

Opening his eyes, he rolled onto his side and studied her face. She was looking up at the ceiling, biting her lip.

"Sabra?" he said softly. "What troubles you?"

She turned her head on the pillow, her gaze meeting his.

"About... you know."

"Nay. What?"

Her cheeks coloured. "When you want to go... down there."

Ah, now he understood. "Aye?"

"I can't yet. I'm sorry."

He could see the sorrow in her eyes. "Sabra, 'tis all right."

"No, 'tisn't." Her fingers squeezed his lightly. "Love making between us should be shared. My issues make it hard for you."

His heart went out to her. Coming up onto one elbow, he reached out with his other hand and ran his thumb over her lips. "'Tis never hard with you, sweet lass. I'm a patient man. One day you'll be ready and I'll be here. Don't worry about it." Leaning over, he kissed her tenderly on the lips. "You are a hot wench, my hot wench. Never think you leave me wanting. You give everything of yourself, and I take it all. I give you all I have. One day we'll share a little more, but 'twill be when you're ready. Meanwhile," he grinned down at her, his eyes twinkling. "Meanwhile, you hot little wench, you burn my boots off with just one look."

Cam was relieved to see the shadow lift from her eyes, and when she laughed, he grabbed her around the waist and swung her over him. Her shriek was wholly feminine, and he knew 'twas one that no one else ever heard but himself. With Cam, Sabra felt free to be who she was, to be fun-loving and passionate. It was an exterior she rarely showed others, apart from the laughing. But even then, her laughter was never as free as when she was with him. Even though she laughed with the bounty hunter pack she called family, it wasn't the same as when she was with Cam. With him, she was simply Sabra, his little wench, his childhood friend, his lover and wife. Only he knew her innermost, secretive thoughts and feelings.

How he revelled in that knowledge.

~ * ~

"Ready the ship." Matheus studied the galaxy map. "We've another pick-up to make."

His cronies laughed harshly, their amusement hard.

"And there's something else to take care of." Matheus turned to Harten, his second-in-command. "You will take care of it."

"My pleasure."

Turning back to the galaxy map, Matheus continued studying the worlds. There were places to see, people to take, bodies to sell.

~ * ~

Sabra walked into the dining cabin, tucking a stray strand of hair behind her ear that had escaped her bun. Her gaze fell on Cam where he leaned against the long food counter, a mug of steaming una in one hand.

Dark eyes twinkling, he eyed her over the rim. His long, curly hair was neatly fastened back in its usual ponytail. The man was like a dangerous dessert, delicious and tempting and with a devilish side to him.

"I rather preferred you dishevelled and naked in my bunk," he drawled.

"We can't all have what we want all the time." Crossing to him, she went up on tiptoes and when he obligingly leaned down, she kissed him lightly on the lips.

"Mmmm." He smacked his lips. "Yummy."

She laughed.

Sliding an arm around her waist, Cam handed her a glass of icy berry juice - and aye, he knew her favourite and kept it on the ship at all times - and led her over to the big armchairs that were fastened to the floor on the other side of the dining cabin. Sabra slouched down in one of the armchairs and he sat in the one opposite.

"So," he said, "here on business? Or just passing through?"

"Isn't passing through and business the same thing?"

"Oh, lass." He shook his head in mock sadness. "'Tis no answer."

Sabra grinned and took a sip of the berry juice, savouring the sweetness.

"I heard about that little ruckus back home."

Sabra's smile faded. "Oh?"

"Aye." Cam rested the mug on the armrest and laconically rested one booted ankle on the opposite knee. "Davan has been tied up in knots almost ever since, so they tell me."

"Really?" She studied Cam's face, trying to gauge what he was thinking. As usual, his expression was calm, his gaze steady.

"Overly protective now and driving Delias crazy. Though," he winked, "he was always hovering over her and driving her crazy, so 'tis no big change there."

"Nay." Sabra took another sip of juice.

Cam's gaze sharpened. "Something wrong, lass?"

"You've heard nothing else?"

"I heard you and Marly were there."

"And?"

One dark brow rose. "And?"

The condensation from the glass was cold against her fingers. "Did you hear why Delias got into that situation?"

"Because you asked her to help." There was no condemnation on his face, but his expression was thoughtful as he watched her.

"Aye, I did." Placing the glass down on the low coffee table, Sabra leaned back in the armchair, placed her elbows on the armrests and rested her chin on her linked hands.

Cam studied her quietly.

She met his gaze steadily, wondering what he was thinking. A little afraid to know.

"All right, lass," he finally said. "What troubles you?"

"What makes you think I'm troubled?"

"Sabra." There was a hint of censure in his deep voice.

Just the way he said her name so simply made her heart leap a little. Sabra rubbed her bottom lip with her thumb while she wondered exactly how to broach the subject.

As usual, he knew her thoughts. "Sabra, you had good reason for what you did."

"Are you so sure?"

"Absolutely."

"One day you might not think so. One day I could make a decision that you won't like."

"Lass." He leaned forward in the chair, his dark eyes so knowing. "Liking a decision has nothing to do with it. No matter what you say or do, I'll be there for you. Always."

She had to swallow the stupid lump that came into her throat.

Reaching out, he placed one big hand on her knee and squeezed gently. "Nothing you could do would ever make me think less of you."

"You can't tell me that you approve of me placing Delias in a position to get hurt."

"You were there," he replied simply.

"You have absolute faith in me."

"Of course."

"One day I could disappoint you."

Not one more word passed his lips. Instead, he caught her hand, tugged her up and pulled her to him and down onto his lap. Wrapping his arms around her, he cuddled her against him and tucked her head under his chin.

It was such a simple, warm gesture of love and acceptance, and it made her relax totally. With a sigh, she snuggled closer.

The peace didn't last long. Her communicator on her jacket gave a small beep and with a sigh, she sat upright, pulled the ear piece from her pocket and slid it into her ear out of sight. "Aye?"

"A settlement has been hit," Marly's voice came through clearly.

"Coming." Sabra looked at Cam.

"Work calling?" he guessed.

"Aye." Leaning forward, she kissed him gently on the lips. "I love you, Cam."

"I love you, Sabra."

It was the same words they always said to each other when

they parted. Neither had to say out loud that those words could be the last they ever heard the other speak, but it was a knowledge between them.

Cam walked her to the bottom of the trade ship ramp. He kissed her one last time, soft but quick, and she left the safe, warm haven of his arms and strode over to the small ship where Marly and Freeman waited.

Just before she entered the ship, she glanced over her shoulder to see her big, gentle giant leaning against one of the iron ramp arms, his gaze on her. He smiled slightly and raised his hand. She smiled back and then entered the spaceship.

Once on board, Marly greeted her with news. She didn't even notice the change in herself. Minutes ago she'd been Cam's wife, now she was a Security Officer, and the hunt had just become more intensified.

~ * ~

The peacekeepers were grimfaced as they went about their business. The ruins smouldered, the bodies were fresh. Carrion eaters circled the skies awaiting the chance to feast on dead flesh.

Miles away a planet shuttle lifted from a settlement, the travellers settling in for the long flight to the next planet.

Out in space, a spaceship, bristling with lasers, waited for the next prey. In one of the cabins, a woman knew she'd done something to survive for a little longer, and she cried.

~ * ~

How he loved the fear on the faces of the travellers. Harten strode down the aisle, his laser in one fist. These travellers were quiet, fearful, but none tried to fight. Some of the women sobbed and he saw some really pretty ones amongst them. One in particular he wanted, the one with the rich brown hair with that intriguing blonde patch in it.

Four of his men spread out along the big planet shuttle, two behind him ready to round up the travellers and two moving into the next carriage.

Stopping beside her seat, he gestured with his laser. "Stand up."

She did so slowly, surprising him with how tall she was, at least half a head taller than himself. What a novelty, not many women stood this tall. Her head was bowed.

Grabbing her chin in hard fingers, he jerked her face up. Oh yes, this one was pretty, all right. Cobalt eyes, so piercing and... hard?

Startled, he blinked. He couldn't believe it when metal pressed against his abdomen and he looked down to see the tip of a laser resting against his abdomen.

"Surprise," she said softly.

"What the - "

"You're under arrest, arsehole."

Recovering from his surprise, Harten gave a harsh bark of laughter. "Me?"

One fine, dark brow arched. "You think you shouldn't be?"

"I think you're a dumb bitch." His upper lip curled as he glanced around at the other travellers huddled in their seats. "I don't see anyone else willing to help you. You're incredibly stupid to think you can take me on your own."

"What makes you think I'm on my own?"

"Problem?" One of men called from the end of the carriage.

It was more than obvious that his men didn't have a clue that this woman had him at laser point, but Harten wasn't worried. "Nothing I can't handle," he called back.

The woman looked him directly in the eye, not a sign of fear on her pretty face. He'd soon fix that. "I'll have you grovelling at my feet within the hour," he promised her.

The tip of the laser pressed harder against his abdomen. "'Tis right?"

"Yeah." He grabbed her wrist. "Kill me if you can."

"I'd rather you just come with me, all nice and quiet."

"Harten?" One of his men called.

"Not now," he grated.

"There's something wrong with these travellers!"

Harten glared over his shoulder. "Damn it! Deal with it! I'm busy!"

"There're no travellers here!"

"What the hell are you on about? I can see the bloody travellers myself!"

"I'm telling you, Harten, they're not real!"

Ignoring the laser tip against his abdomen, Harten reached out to grab the nearest traveller only to have his hand go through thin air. The traveller wavered in his seat, popped and was gone.

In front of his disbelieving eyes, every traveller vanished.

"Surprised now?" the woman drawled.

"What the hell...?" He swung his head around and glared up at her.

"A little visual imaging." She pressed the tip harder against him. "Hands up, slaver. You're under arrest."

"By you and what army?"

"I don't need an army." She smiled. "I'm IPS Security."

The word sent a chill down his spine. He stared at her, and then he cursed. His hand at her wrist jerked, wrenching her hand away, but she moved fast. Faster than he'd ever seen anyone move.

One second her laser was in her right hand, the hand he wrenched away, and the next a steel blade was pricking his ribs from her left hand.

"Harten!" One of men yelled.

And then everything went to Hell in seconds.

There was a loud curse, a shout, and the sizzle of laser fire. Crackling through the communicator in his ears was the sound of an attack on his spaceship, laser fire, and screaming, his men cursing, the sound of orders shouted.

And then he didn't care about the problems on his ship, because his attention was diverted by the dagger blade sliding between his ribs and the woman's knee slamming into his balls. Harten fell in a silently screaming heap, pain clawing brutally through him from his abused privates, while blood slid down his abdomen to soak into his shirt.

———

In the far reaches of his mind, he could only feel incredulity. Surely his men were coming? Surely someone was coming? Surely...?

A booted foot slammed down on the ground in front of his face, but he couldn't look up. Eyes screwed shut against the pain, he rolled and moaned, bile searing the back of his throat.

"He's not on board the spaceship," a female voice sounded nearby.

"The peacekeepers searched everything?"

"Freeman helped them. Every part of that spaceship has been searched. The only ones there are the prisoners and the illegal slavers. There's no sign of Matheus."

Fingers grabbed a handful of his hair and Harten's head was jerked up. "Where is your bastard captain?"

He moaned.

"Last chance, Harten. Where's Matheus?"

All he wanted to do was curl up in a ball and die, his balls sending waves of pain surging through him.

The next thing, pain exploded through his head as it was cracked against the floor of the planet shuttle.

"Shit!" He swore, half crying with pain, half in fury.

"Whoa," the female voice said in amusement. "Tough love, Sabra."

"A wench has to do what a wench has to do." His head was rapped against the floor again. "Where is Matheus?"

If he said one word, Matheus would hunt him down and kill him—slowly.

"Your ship has been boarded and taken over by peacekeepers. Those of your men left alive are under arrest. No one is going to rescue you, Harten. You're on your own."

Opening his eyes a fraction, Harten looked up into cobalt eyes that gazed back at him without mercy. If he didn't say anything, this cold-hearted bitch was going to -

"If you're going to start slicing and dicing," the female voice said again, "Let me know. I don't want blood on my boots again. I hate cleaning blood off my boots."

"So stand back," the cold-hearted bitch named Sabra said as she squatted over him and pricked the point of her dagger under his chin. "Because I'm going to start slicing until I get an answer."

At first Harten didn't believe her, didn't think any woman had the guts to carry through on a threat like that, but when the dagger whipped from side to side with impressive speed, he could only stare incredulously up at her as she wiped the blade on his shirt.

And then he felt it, the warm, slippery slide of his own blood down his throat. Panicking, he grabbed his throat, his hand coming away drenched in blood, and he opened his mouth to start screaming, only to stop when the tip of the dagger slid between his lips to press against his tongue.

"You're not dying yet," the Security Officer called Sabra said quietly. "The only words I want to hear from you are the ones telling me where Matheus is. You don't tell me and I'm going to skin you strip by strip. I've already made my first cut, it won't take much to continue."

Sweat poured down Harten's face as he stared up at the expressionless face above him. At first he'd been captured by her prettiness, but now... now he saw the ruthless light in her eyes. He recognised the outfit she wore as IPS Security, so he knew she spoke the truth. He also knew Security was a sometimes shady group, slipping in and out of trouble spots, doing things most of the Lawful Sector had no idea of and probably never would. Security was the stuff of nightmares for those law breakers they fixed their sights on.

And Security had fixed their sights on illegal slavers. On Matheus and his crew.

They were all doomed.

The dagger slid down over his lip and chin, a trickle of blood following as she cut shallowly.

"No!" He screamed. "I'll tell!"

The dagger stilled and she looked down at him with those fathomless eyes.

The warm blood trickling over his chin was making him sick. Spilling anyone else's blood was fine, torturing someone else was fine, but being on the receiving end was something he couldn't handle. Like most bullies.

"One of the prisoners told us of a fortune," he said.

The Security Officer's eyes were intent.

"She told Matheus that her betrothed was rich, that he had in his possession jewellery handed down through his family. It was worth a lot of dinnos."

"And you expect me to believe that Matheus went after that jewellery? When he has a fortune in slaves in his cages?"

"Some of that jewellery is worth more than several shiploads of slaves." Harten wiped his hand across his chin, his guts churning as he stared at the crimson mass on his palm. "He was going to not only get the jewellery but also take the family and hold them for ransom."

"He's a real piece of work," the female voice out of his sight said again. "Makes me all warm and fuzzy inside."

"What's the name of this woman who gave Matheus this information?"

"Nedula."

"Is she still alive?"

"Yes. She traded the information for her life."

Sabra stared down at Harten before straightening. Sheathing the dagger at her waist, she looked at someone out of his vision. "He's all yours."

~ * ~

The prisoners were a sorry looking lot. Bedraggled, bloody, bruised, but none severely wounded.

"No surprise there," Freeman said when one of the peacekeepers commented on it. "Matheus wouldn't want to damage the merchandise."

"That's cold."

"That's business."

Sabra looked around at the women. Huddled in a group, they didn't look very happy. Dazed, a little shocked, stunned. None were happy. No wonder, when most of them had lost loved ones in the attacks. The men who came in hugged some of the women, obviously family or wedded partners, but some sat and wept.

This was something none of them would ever forget.

Marly entered the room and spoke quietly to Sabra. "We've found the woman, Nedula."

Without a word, Sabra followed her to another of the ship's cabins. On the bunk, pressed back against the wall, sat a young wench. Even though her face was battered and bruised, she could see that she was normally a beautiful wench. She noted the torn gown, the bruises on the flesh behind the tattered material where it gaped open.

Nedula had her knees to her chin, her blonde hair straggling down her back.

"You gave Matheus information," Sabra stated bluntly.

The peacekeeper standing near the door looked startled at her flat tone.

Nedula's eyes were dull. "Matheus raped me."

"What did you tell him?"

"He raped me several times. He beat me up."

"What did you tell him, Nedula?"

The wench wiped the tears from her bruised cheeks. "I did what I had to do. I thought if I gave myself to him, that he'd be more lenient, but I was mistaken."

Sabra studied her. Aye, she had been raped and beaten and she was sorry for that, but now it was something else she needed. "You told him that your betrothed has a fortune in jewellery. Where does he live?"

Nedula looked up at her. "Uraj."

Not far off. "When did he leave?"

"An hour ago."

"What's the name of your betrothed?"

Her face crumpled as tears spilled down her cheeks. "Uri."

Sabra swung on her heel. "Marly, contact Sanka. Tell him—"

"Wait!"

She halted, glancing back over her shoulder at Nedula.

"I love him," Nedula wept. "I love Uri."

"You betrayed him," Sabra said bluntly.

"I did it to survive! I didn't mean to... I didn't want..."

"You betrayed him, and yet Matheus was still going to sell you. Did you truly think he would let you go?"

"I thought..." Nedula looked lost. "I thought he might."

"People like Matheus don't care, Nedula. All you've done is hand him more victims. In fact, you gave him the one person you should have protected."

Nedula's face crumpled and big sobs started to shake her body. "I love him!"

Shaking her head, Sabra strode from the room.

Marly glanced up at her curiously. "What?"

"She betrayed him."

"To live. To survive."

"To survive, you don't betray those you love."

"Some might." Marly shrugged. "Some do."

"Would you?"

Marly looked at Freeman who was approaching them holding his handtronic in one hand. "If it was Freeman, I'd sacrifice him in a heartbeat."

"I heard that, you nasty slag."

"Speak dirty to me, lover."

Freeman raised a haughty brow.

Ignoring them both, Sabra strode down one of the tunnels that connected the illegal slavers' ship to the small Security ship. The second tunnel connected the peacekeepers' ship to the illegal slavers' ship. Marly and Freeman followed on her heels, still throwing insults at each other.

Dropping down into the seat in front of the galaxy map, Sabra gazed at it unseeingly. Nedula had sacrificed her betrothed in exchange for her life. Bartered love against her body. Wanting one thing bad enough to give anything for it. Betraying a loved one for her life. Doing anything to get what she wanted, regardless of the cost to others.

Sabra drummed her fingertips on the armrests of the chair. How far would she go to get Matheus? Her loved ones she was loyal to, but others...?

Chapter 3
*

The settlement was quiet. The big house on the outskirts was even quieter. Blood spattered the walls, furniture was overturned, and in the middle of the room a man lay almost unconscious on the floor.

Matheus sat in the chair sliding the gold chains through his fingers. How beautiful, how rich the colour, how expensive. He glanced at the man on the floor. Now if only he could get this bastard to talk, tell him where his sisters were, he could grab them and leave the settlement with none being the wiser.

Jaken peered out of the window. "It all seems quiet."

"I don't want to hang around for long. We've been here awhile as it is, thanks to this fool being out visiting. Wasted my precious time." Matheus dropped the chains into the bag and pulled out a ring, admiring the jewel that winked in the light. "Just have to wait until this useless cretin awakens and then I'll get the whereabouts of his sisters from him. They'll be worth a fortune as well." He rubbed the jewel. "They're near, I just know it."

"Sooner or later they'll come for him," Meka agreed.

Minutes ticked past before the man on the floor started to stir. Immediately Meka dragged him upright and shoved him into a chair, holding him there by a hand gripping the back of his neck, fingers biting into the flesh.

"Now, Uri." Matheus leaned forward, his forearm resting on his thigh. "Tell me where your sisters are."

"No." Uri's voice was a rasp, and he coughed and spat blood.

The blow to the side of his kidneys nearly collapsed the bloodied man.

"We don't have to be so harsh about all this." Matheus laughed suddenly. "Oh, hell, why not? A little blood-letting is good for the soul."

Meka drew a small, thin pipe from his belt and balanced it in his hand. From the ends of the pipe hung small, iron balls swinging from small chains. Moving around to face Uri, he drew the pipe back then swung it hard and fast. The small balls cracked against Uri's jaw, and he would have fallen from the chair if it wasn't for Jaken shoving him back. The pipe cracked again, the small ball swinging to smash with deadly accuracy against the other side of his jaw, effectively cracking the bone. Agony flared in Uri's eyes. Blood poured anew from his mouth, and he cried out.

"Stop!" A girl's voice screamed. "Stop!"

"No!" Even though every movement would have been agony, Uri tried to push upright.

A young girl, no more than twelve, ran into the room. Crying, she ran to Uri, throwing her arms around his neck.

Uri held her close, his broken fingers hanging uselessly but his palms against her back. Tears filled his eyes as he hugged her.

Crying, she buried her face against his bloodied neck.

"How sweet." Matheus stood up. "One sister. Where's the other?"

"Away." Every word was agony with his broken jaw.

"If you won't tell me, then I'll take this sweet little piece and make her give up her sister."

Uri tried to fight when Matheus grabbed her arm and jerked her away from him, but the ball from Meka's pipe slammed into the back of his head, disorientating him, and he fell to his knees on the floor.

Matheus dragged the girl kicking and screaming over to the sofa, pushing her down and grabbing the neckline of her delicate frock. Leaning down, he snarled, "Tell me where your sister is, or I'll rape you here and now."

She was terrified, he could see it in her eyes, and it gave him the surge of lust that fear always rewarded him with, but her refusal, her damned loyalty to her sister, that angered him. He hated loyalty.

He'd show her just how much.

In one savage yank, he tore the fragile bodice of the frock and came down atop her.

Uri cried, fighting to save his sister regardless of how bad his injuries were, but weak from lack of blood and the savage beating he'd already received, he couldn't last against Jaken.

The breaking of glass broke through Matheus's lust, and he lunged to his feet, swearing. The girl scrambled over the armrest of the sofa and ran straight to where Uri lay bleeding on the floor.

But Matheus's gaze was on the woman who had burst through the window and was now rolling lithely to her feet. One look at the brown jacket and pants the woman wore and Matheus knew who he was facing. The IPS Security never came alone, and he knew there were more somewhere.

He bolted, leaving Jaken and Meka lunging for the Security Officer.

In another area of the house he heard fighting and he had no doubt that Ceazon was getting the worst of it, especially when he heard his cry of pain.

Diving through the broken window he'd entered through earlier, he scrambled down off the veranda roof and into the bushes, ignoring the clinging branches. The moon was hidden by clouds, and a crack of lightning rent the air. Rain started to fall and he laughed as he pounded down the pathway.

A heavy downpour was just what he needed to aid his escape.

He ran, sliding in the mud, not hearing the sounds of pursuit, so when a body slammed into him from behind, it caught him by surprise. They slid in the mud, he kicking and cursing, his attacker silent and deadly. A dagger blade bit deep into his leg, sweeping sideways, and he knew instinctively what his assailant was after - cutting his hamstring.

Rolling, he kicked savagely, unable to see in the pouring rain but able to hear the grunt of pain. He kicked again, rolled, and sprang to his feet. He hadn't gone a few feet before his attacker hit again, a dagger burying deep in his buttock.

Swinging around with a roar of pain, he swung his fist, missing the attacker as they ducked. He lunged at the assailant and was brought up short by a savage kick to his knee. Managing to dodge it, he nevertheless was caught behind the knee which knocked him off balance, and with a howl of rage he fell backward, but not before grabbing his attacker.

The mud slid, and together they went tumbling down the slope, rolling through bushes and breaking out into the middle of the rain-drenched street. In the light he caught a glimpse of cobalt eyes above him, a flash of blonde hair, and he knew who his attacker was now. The female Security Officer.

Lashing out, he put full force behind the slap across her face, expecting her to roll away. Instead, she punched him square in the jaw, following it with a left hook that crushed his nose.

Blood welled, tears rolled and his fury soared.

Lunging up, he took her with him, using his brute strength to lift her and run with her towards the building behind her. She didn't seem to notice or care, grabbing his hair in one hand and slamming her hand under his chin. He recognized her manoeuvre as soon as he felt the force she exerted on his head.

The bitch was going to break his neck.

With a roar he propelled himself forward, slamming her back into the wooden wall behind her. It succeeded in dislodging her hands, and he slammed her back again.

She retaliated by slamming her hands over his ears, almost shattering his ear drums.

In pain, blood seeping from him, he whirled and threw her through the window, but she took him with her, hanging on so that his momentum had them both smashing through the glass.

People yelled, their jugs and mugs of drink shattering as they scrambled to get out of the way. Tables went down as

Matheus and the woman fought, he furiously, she with a grim intent, a fire burning in her eyes.

Grabbing a broken glass, Matheus slashed at her face, missing her by mere inches. She slammed her elbow into his jaw, then slid her forearm under his chin, pushing his head back and back until he could swear it was going to snap, the tendons stretching.

He slammed his fist into the side of her breast, rewarded by her gasp of pain, but still she didn't shift her arm from his throat.

Desperately now he rolled, seeking to squash her with his bulk, but somehow she kept her arm against him.

Unable to see with his head thrust back, he blindly grabbed for her throat, his nails raking across tender, wet flesh, while his other hand ripped along her ribcage, tearing through cloth to rake down her side as he sought somewhere, anywhere, to rip. He dug his nails in and pulled, trying to rip flesh from bones. Skin tore.

His vision was starting to go black. And then he felt his hand close around her throat, and he squeezed. He'd teach the bitch! He'd choke the life from her!

The arm at his throat vanished and triumphantly he tipped his head forward, ignoring the pain of abused, stretched muscles, only to widen his eyes when he met that piercing, cobalt blue gaze. Instead of panicking as he squeezed, her cheeks reddening, she was bringing the heel of her hand up fast and hard.

It was too late to dodge. The heel of her hand slammed up into his nose, pushing upward, breaking bone and forcing shards of it up into his brain. Agony such as he'd never felt blocked his vision, a red haze, and he lunged upright, one hand cupping his nose, fear filling him as he stumbled back.

He heard the coughing dimly, blackness coming over him, but he felt the cold steel pierce his stomach, the neat slice as the blade jerked upright. Heard the Security Officer's rasping voice as she said, "Burn in hell, you bastard."

He dropped, his thoughts foggy, scattering, a sudden emptiness inside him, and with one hand he reached down, recoiling as he felt the slippery, hot mass of something that should have been inside him spilling out.

The last thing he heard was a female voice complaining, "Damn it, Sabra, you know I hate intestines on my boots!"

Then Hell claimed him.

~ * ~

Standing beside the bed, Marly finished taking the statement from Uri. Pale, bruised, stitches closing the gashes on his face and arms, he was lucky to be alive.

"Well, that's it." Marly stood up and pocketed the handtronic. "The report has been sent to IPS Security and the peacekeepers."

Sabra looked down at the gardens below. Uri's two sisters played happily, their doting parents watching them carefully. It could have ended horribly, but now, hopefully, it would be only bad memories that would fade, but never disappear, with time.

Uri's voice was weak. "Sabra?"

She turned from the window to gaze steadily at him. Uri's eyes held pain, but it was of another kind.

"Nedula wants me to forgive her," he said.

"Will you?" Her own voice was raspy, her throat sore, but she ignored it, just as she ignored the bruises and scratches that marred her skin.

"She betrayed me." He looked at the bent, silver disc with the missing stone that sat on his bedside table, the little disc the only thing left of the necklace he'd given Nedula as a betrothal gift, and the Security had found in the ruined space shuttle.

"She betrayed you and more," Sabra agreed quietly.

He looked at her. "Would you forgive her?"

Not bloody likely. "'Tis not my choice to make. This decision is something only you can know." She touched her chest. "Deep in your heart, Uri, only you know if you can live with her, if you can forgive her."

"If someone betrayed you, Sabra? What would you do?"

She looked at him for a long time, debating what to answer.

"Please." His words were barely audible from between the jaw brace.

"Betrayal is the worse thing anyone can do to you," Sabra finely replied. "My opinion? Dump her arse and don't look back."

"Yes." He blinked the tears from his eyes.

"We have to go." She stepped away from the window and made for the door. "Take care of yourself, Uri."

"Thank you. For everything."

She heard the thickness of tears in his throat and knew he was thinking of Nedula and her betrayal. Pausing at the door, she turned one last time and smiled slightly at him. "You, Uri, are loyal to your family, and they to you. Guard your sisters well. Everything you need, the love and loyalty, you have here. I hope you find a wench worthy of you one day."

And then she left.

Marly strode along quietly beside her until they came to the road. Freeman was waiting beside the small spaceship which he'd docked in an open field beside the road.

"You told him to dump Nedula," Marly stated.

"Hell, aye." Sabra stretched and winced. "Bloody hell, I am so sore."

"I'll rub you all over." Freeman leered.

"Cam'll break every finger on your hands," Marly informed him cheerfully. "Especially when I tell him what you offered."

"You're just jealous. You want my hands on you."

"Not even if I was on fire."

Smiling at the insulting exchange, Sabra strode up the small ramp and into the ship.

Once they were in space, she went to her cabin and lay down, picking up the photo image of Cam and holding it up to study the dangerously handsome, laughing face. Now here was a man who knew loyalty. He'd been more than willing to sacrifice everything, aye, and all for her. His loyalty was unquestionable. Cam would never betray her.

And she would never betray him.

"For you, my love, I'd give my life," she murmured.

Aye, she had done some despicable things in her time. She'd conned friends into situations where they'd been hurt a little, but never would she allow them to be dangerously hurt. To gain knowledge of those who killed, raped, and hunted the innocent, she'd do things others would frown upon, but she knew her limits.

Peace filled her. Aye, Delias had been slapped and roughed up a little, but put a slap to gain knowledge against rape and murder, and it was a small price to pay. Mayhap not many would understand that except her fellow IPS Security Officers, her bounty hunter pack family, and a few friends, but it was all right. The main thing was... she smiled at Cam's image. The main thing was that Cam loved her and he'd never betray her, even if he didn't always understand her decisions and actions.

And she'd never betray him.

~ * ~

Walking home along the flower-lined pathway, Cam fought the urge to run. He knew Sabra was home, he knew she'd been injured. It hadn't taken a genius to know who the female Security Officer was that had been in a vicious fight in a tavern after being thrown through the window first. Stories travelled fast and it very soon hit his ears. So he'd contacted the Chief of the IPS, knowing that Sabra would tell him nothing, and Uleah would at least assure him she was all right.

Since 'twas a well-known fact that a fight had occurred in Ordra between illegal slavers and Security not long after the Daamen trade ship had left the planet, Uleah didn't bother denying that Sabra had been hurt, and he assured Cam she was healing. But he did advise him to be gentle for awhile in his handling of her.

That scared Cam.

He'd seen her on the viscomm since, always with shadows around her face and she'd complained about the lighting, but he knew she hid scratches and bruises from him. Going by the stories doing the rounds, she'd been badly scratched, hit and half throttled, but she'd taken out the bastard who did it, and it was exactly what Cam had hoped would happen.

Now he just wanted to assure himself that she was really all right, that she was safe, which was stupid because he knew she was safe, but until she was face to face with him and he could see for himself, he wouldn't be satisfied.

Turning into the gate that led to what had once been Sabra's childhood home and was now their home, he glanced fleetingly at the gardens that were full of flowers and trees. Bounding up the steps, he passed the pillars with the graceful vines twining around them and opened the screen door. Almost immediately he heard voices and the smell of baking assailed his nostrils. It smelled delicious, but one never knew... he grinned.

"Are you sure this mixture is right?" Sabra queried.

"Of course. Trust me, Cam will love it."

"He better or I'll come looking for you."

"You can't hit me, I'm breastfeeding."

"What's that got to do with it?"

"I'll get milk everywhere."

"'Tis disgusting. Reya, do something about her."

"Huh?" Reya grunted, obviously not paying much attention.

"Besides, if you hurt me, I can't go home and relieve Garrett of baby duty."

"Garrett's fine. He coos over those babes as much as he coos over you."

There was silence for a second and then Dana's disgruntled voice sounded again. "I thought he'd stop hovering over me, but he's bad as ever."

"'Tis because he's been brainwashed by you."

"Nasty tongue you have there, hunter."

"Keep your boobs off my table, warrior. The milk I want in this bowl isn't from you."

Cam peeked into the kitchen. Dana was sitting at the table and she did look bigger breasted than normal. He guessed feeding twin babes would do that to a wench.

Reya was lounging back in a chair and reading, her booted feet up on a corner of the table. It was perfectly obvious she wasn't taking any notice of her cousin and friend.

Sabra was standing at the other end of the table, a mixing bowl in her hands, a frown of concentration on her face as she stirred. He grinned. Dressed in a work tunic, her long legs bare from mid thigh to her sandalled feet, a patch of flour on her flushed cheek, and her hair bundled up into a messy, loose ponytail, she looked adorable. And very domesticated.

Until one saw the fading bruises on her throat and jaw, the thin scratches that had almost vanished. His sweet lass had been in one hell of a fight. His gut clenched. He had to step back into the hall and lean against the wall, closing his eyes and taking a deep breath. Every time he saw her with a new injury, a self adhesive patch, or a bruise, he had to bite his tongue. He wanted to go out, find the bastard who had given her the mark, and beat the living hell out of them. Unfortunately he couldn't and that went against his every Daamen gene.

It was just too damned bad. All he could do was pray for her safety when she left on another job to save the universe, support her, and hold her close and enjoy every minute he had with her.

Taking another deep breath, he straightened up and walked into the kitchen. "Something smells good."

Sabra's eyes lit up immediately, a smile curving her full lips, and she dropped the bowl onto the table. He met her halfway across the room as she launched herself into his arms.

"Time for us to go," Dana observed. "Lecherous session coming up."

He didn't even hear them leave, his attention solely on

Sabra. He kissed her long and deep, savouring having her in his arms again. It had been a long two week trip home.

When he finally lifted his head, Sabra laughed a trifle breathlessly up at him. "Hungry? I have cake in the oven, and biscuits... oops."

"Oops?" He raised one brow.

She drew her hand back from around his neck and showed him the dripping spoon. "I think you'll have to change your vest."

Catching her hand, he licked the spoon. "Mmmmm. Delicious. I was always partial to biscuit batter."

"Really?"

"But I'm more partial to Sabra batter."

"Huh." Leaning back in his arms, she grinned widely. "I quite like the taste of Cam batter myself."

"Then ditch the plain batter, my love, and let's do some intense tasting." Sweeping her up into his arms, Cam started for the door.

"Wait! Wait, wait, wait!"

He stopped, one brow arched inquiringly.

"We have to get the cake out of the oven to cool." She frowned. "I won't have it burning."

He sighed. "Very well." He put her down and she'd barely managed to take the cake from the oven, place it on a cooler and turn the oven off before Cam swooped her up in his arms again.

"My," she said as he carried her up the winding staircase with good speed. "You are in a hurry. Where's the fire?"

"If you really don't know by now…"

Sabra laughed. "Poor baby. Let me tend the fire."

"With you tending it, I'll burn out of control."

"You do have a way with words."

"I have many ways and 'tis all to do with you." He winked as he strode into their bedroom.

She giggled, and the light sound touched him. Sabra never giggled except with him. Instead of placing her feet on the floor, Cam stood her on the big bed in front of him.

"Whoa! No sandals or boots on the bed, not after I had to soak our lace cover after the mud we put on here last time." Sabra kicked her sandals off and curled her neat little toes in the satin cover.

"'Twasn't my fault you made me so hot I couldn't wait to take my boots off before having my wicked way with you." Laughing, Cam looked up at her.

The amusement faded from her eyes, replaced instead with tenderness. "I love you, Cam."

"I love you, Sabra."

A twinkle lit her eyes. "Mayhap you'd better reserve that for after you've tasted my cake."

"Lass, I'd eat mud for you."

"You romantic, you."

Catching her face between his hands, Cam pulled her head down for a gentle kiss. Sliding his lips to her throat, he kissed a fading bruise. She sighed softly and arched her throat for his gentle kisses.

He kissed every bruise before angling up to administer the same to the bruise on her jaw. When he'd finished, he slid his hands to her shoulders and hooked his fingers into the thin straps. He drew them down over her slender shoulders, down further over her lace clad breasts and over her hips, revealing the fading bruises on her sides, the scratches now almost invisible to the eye.

Before she could lift her feet one at a time so the tunic could come off, Cam wrapped one arm around the backs of her thighs and lifted her easily. She grabbed onto his shoulders and her soft breasts nestled against his cheek. He breathed deeply as he discarded her tunic, nuzzling his nose in the valley between her breasts. Her faint floral scent seeped into his senses.

Placing her feet back on the big bed, he pressed his lips to that tempting valley before lifting his head and unsnapping her lacy support garment with deft fingers.

He tossed it aside, his gaze lovingly following his hands as he cupped the fullness of the creamy mounds. And then he saw them, five fading bruises on the side of her right breast, five fading bruises each the perfect fit of the knuckles of a fist.

He stilled, rage beating through him, the urge to go out and kill the bastard all over again if only he could, but he was already dead. May he rot in Hell.

"Cam?" He heard the uncertainty in her voice and forced his rage down before he looked up. Obviously he wasn't that successful because she flinched a little. "Don't be cross."

"I'm not cross, sweet lass," he replied in a low voice. "I'm bloody furious at the bastard who did this to you, and I'm so glad he's dead though I wish to the stars 'twas I who had killed him instead."

"You heard," she whispered.

"Aye." Reaching up, he ran his fingertips along the almost healed scratches on her throat.

"I'm all right." Leaning down, she laid her forehead against his and looked him steadily in the eye. "I'd have told you if I wasn't."

"'Twas why, on the viscomm, you hid these marks from me when they were new?"

Her smile was a little wry. "I was a bit scary looking there for awhile."

Cam closed his eyes.

She kissed him gently on each eyelid. "Don't fret, Cam. I hate seeing you fret."

What could he say? That he wished she'd stay home, safe and sound on Daamen? That he wished he could be by her side every second she was in danger? Nay, 'twould smother her. She'd been through too much in her life to be able to simply sit back and allow others to hunt those she abhorred.

Just as he knew he only had to say the word and she would stay home on Daamen. One word from him, one plea, and she would stop.

And it was because he knew she loved him enough to stay,

that he loved her enough to allow her to fly free. It was a mutual respect, a recognition of each other's life that allowed them to live like this, and he knew, no matter where she was, that the ties between them would never break and they'd always end up back together.

Like now.

Like so many times before, and so many times to come.

He wanted the extra intimacy he craved, the forbidden delights he'd held back from until she was ready. He wanted it now. Wanted to show her how good it would be for them. Opening his eyes, he locked his gaze to hers and said softly, "Let me love you."

Those cobalt eyes, so beautiful and fathomless, so piercing and intent, widened a little, flickered, and he was about to retract what he'd said when she whispered, "Aye."

He didn't think he'd heard right. "What?"

"I love and trust you. I know you won't hurt me. Show me." Her small hands slid across his cheekbones, fingers tangling in his wild, curly black hair, dislodging the tie that held it back at his nape. "Love me the way you want to."

It was almost exactly what she'd said to him the very first time they'd made love, when he'd banished her demons. Tenderness swept through him, love welling up, and he gazed steadily at her. His heart pounded at the love and trust in her eyes. He said the same words he'd said all those months ago. "You're safe in my hands, sweet lass."

And he knew she remembered when she smiled so sweetly at him and pushed the vest back off his shoulders. He slid her lace panties down, and this time she lifted each small foot so he could flip it free.

Toeing off his boots and shoving his pants down, Cam kicked free of them, leaving them in a heap on the floor.

Sliding his arms around her waist, he came onto the bed, lifting her as he went, sliding her back so that she reclined amongst the fat pillows at the head of the bed.

Slowly he kissed his way down her body, lingering over the

bruises, laving them gently with his tongue. His desire for her surged up, and he felt the matching heat in her as her slim legs shifted beneath him, her thighs opening so his weight could settle between them. One of her small feet slid up his calf, leaving a tingling in their wake.

Her breasts were plump offerings, handfuls made perfectly for the size of his palms, and he kissed each small, pink nipple before rubbing the flat of his tongue against the hard little nubs.

"Cam!" She was almost breathless, her fingers digging briefly into his shoulders.

He lifted his head to look at her face. Her eyes, so beautiful and expressive, glowed with an inner heat. Her lips were red, swollen from his kisses, and a flush of need graced her cheeks.

Those soft breasts rose unevenly, the little nipples grazing his chin with each rise, and he cupped his hands carefully around the fullness, mindful of the bruising on her right breast.

Keeping his gaze on her face, he engulfed one nipple into his hot mouth and sucked.

Sabra's head fell back into the pillow, her throat arching, his name a husky moan on her lips.

Cam made his move, using his fingers on her breasts to keep her in the throes of passion while he slid his lips lower, down her flat belly, his tongue dipping into her belly button, and then he watched her as he slid lower. Lower. Lower, the broad width of his shoulders moving her thighs even further apart, opening her to him.

He knew the instant she became aware, for her breathing hitched and she froze for several seconds before slowly lifting her head to look down at him. Down where he hovered above the soft curls guarding her mound.

"Sabra," he said softly, forcing down his carnal desire to simply lick and taste her feminine folds with the hunger that beat inside him.

It was hard to do when she swallowed and nodded. The

trust in her eyes was almost his undoing. One part of him wanted to cuddle her close and soothe her, the other part of him wanted to dive into her feminine secrets and discover them all.

He moved slowly, sliding his muscular arms under her thighs and lifting her legs so that she bent them at the knees, her feet moving further up the mattress, opening her to him. Soothingly he ran his big hands along the outside of her thighs.

Turning his head, he kissed one of the scars high up on the inside of her thigh that she'd been given by a savage pirate when he'd bitten and clawed at her like a rabid hound. Ravished by a monster when she was a tender eleven years of age, her fear of Cam's mouth near her femininity wasn't a fear of him, but of the memories of a young girl being brutalized by a space pirate.

Cam had broken the ties of most of those nightmares and taught her the joys of love making, but this was the last bastion, the last fear he had to break to set her completely free to enjoy all lovemaking.

He bit me in several places, drawing blood. He drank my blood, Cam. Right from the bite wounds.

He'd glimpsed the scars when she'd been asleep, or when he'd had his hands on her thighs, but he'd never gotten this close to them. The scars were healed, mostly flat now, but their raggedness spoke of the brutality of the bites, the savageness.

He kissed them gently, tenderly, moving further down towards the delights he just knew were so close now. So very close.

Sliding his hands down the length of her thighs, he gently framed her hips in his big palms, squeezing gently, rubbing his thumbs on her hip bones. Letting her know he was aware of her, of her every breath, the tension in her. The trust she placed in him to venture where she'd always feared.

The first flick of his tongue at her curls had the muscles of her belly tightening and he placed his palm flat on it, massaging gently.

Inch by excruciating, erotic inch, he ventured further into her femininity. Her open position didn't hide anything from him and he could see the slick lips of her labia, the beckoning of the swollen flesh.

He licked gently along the edge of her labia, rewarded by the ripple that ran through her, and without taking his mouth from her, he lifted his gaze to see the darkening of her cobalt eyes.

He licked a little further in, saw her breath catch, but her fear didn't spiral out of control. Instead, she licked her lips, her soft breasts rising and falling, her nipples little hard buds.

She was still aroused, and if her eyes and breasts hadn't told him, the slick heat of her was a sure indication. Now he had to ensure she didn't forget who lay between her thighs, who was tasting her, loving her. Protecting her.

"Who am I?" He watched her.

Almost instantly he felt her relax just a little. "Cam."

"And what am I to you?" He slid his tongue along the inside lip of her labia. She tasted so damn sweet.

"My lover." The words were a trembling moan as he nudged the little clitoris hiding high in the protective folds of her femininity.

He sought the little nub out, flicked it with his tongue, flattened the surface of his tongue against it and rubbed, mimicking the movement he'd only recently done to her nipples. He blew against the now wet clitoris, felt her strain upward, and quickly he checked her. Aye, her head was back against the pillows, her fingers twisting into the bed cover. Blood surged hotly through his veins at the sight of her heightening heat, and he smiled hedonistically.

"And as your lover, I am sworn to what?" The words rolled as easily from his mouth as they'd done that night months ago when he'd first made love to her.

"Cam…" She twisted her hips, but he held them firm.

"Please!"

The scent of her arousal was heady, her thighs rubbing against his shoulders, but he spoke firmly, though huskily. "As your lover, I am sworn to what?"

Sabra came up on her elbows and he saw the carnal light in her eyes. "Please, Cam, don't make me go through this. Not now. Not when..."

"When?" He deliberately let his breath blow through the curls topping her mound, enjoying watching her shiver.

"Please," she whispered. "Please..."

"Please what?"

"I want your mouth on me." The words were stated boldly. Hotly. Carnally.

His staff, already swollen, throbbed angrily against his belly. Patience. Soon. Soon. But first... "Not yet."

"Cam!" She tried to pull away, agitated sexual desire making her squirm, but he didn't release her.

"Not until you tell me what, as your lover, am I sworn to do?"

"Drive me damned wild!"

Surprised, he almost laughed out loud. It would seem Sabra was fast getting over her fear. "Little wench - "

"You're really going to make me repeat everything we said that night?"

"You're really going to argue?" And in one carnal move, he licked right along the inside of her labia, his tongue scraping across her perineum.

Oh God, she tasted so hot and sweet, like spice and cinnamon and her own unique taste. He wanted to devour her then and there, his blood pounding through his veins, his staff burgeoning, demanding release, but first... he hung on to his plan with grim determination.

"What," he could hear the harshness of his own voice, the sexual hunger scraping through it, "as your lover, am I sworn to do?"

"Protect me!" She fell back against the pillows, and only his firm hold on her hips stopped her from writhing across the bed. "Cam!"

He was losing control, feeling it slip fast through his iron will. "What else, Sabra?"

"Love me."

He sucked the little clitoris between his teeth, careful of the sensitive flesh, holding it gently between his teeth as he laved the tip with his tongue.

Sabra cried out.

Releasing the little nub, he growled, "Aye, and 'tis loving you I'm doing now. Me. Who am I?"

"Cam!"

It was all he waited for. Hands pressed flat against her belly, his forearms holding her hips still, he feasted on her, licking the slick folds, sucking the little nub, rubbing his tongue against her perineum.

He felt her shudder, tasted the wetness, tart and sweet like her own personal spices spilling from her, and he lapped as she fell apart, drinking her essence in with insatiable rapacity.

She was still in the throes of orgasm when he fastened his mouth on her inner thigh and sucked, marking her intimately where only they could see and know.

His ardour flared out of control and he thrust up on his arms, forcing her thighs wider apart, moving up her body while keeping her knees locked around his elbows.

As he came over her, he felt her hips roll, the apex of her snug against him, his scrotum hard against her perineum.

The wet heat of her almost scalded him and as she opened her eyes in dazed wonder, he didn't allow her to think of this new position, of how open she was to him, before he shifted, lifting, flexing his hips so that his staff slid between her folds, hearing her sharp intake of breath and watching her pupils dilate at the sensation of his leaking tip sliding against the seam of her body. He lodged at the entrance to her body.

"You are mine." His voice was harsh with the carnal prurience that filled him. "I am Cam, and I am your one and only lover forever. You are mine to protect and love. 'Tis I who will taste you, who will make love to you in any way that pleases us. Do you understand me, Sabra?"

"Aye. Aye! Please…

"You - " He thrust deep, feeling her sheath instantly clasp him fiercely, and withdrew just as rapidly.

Sabra cried out, her arms coming around his neck.

" - are - " He thrust back in, burying himself to the hilt, loving the way he filled her, knowing she was his. His shaft dragged back through the shivering walls of her vagina.

" - *mine* - !" The third time he shoved in, he kept pushing, pushing and pushing, hearing her cry out his name.

Leaning down, he took her lips, ravished her mouth, kissed her with pure male heat, rutting her fiercely, taking everything she had, and marking her inside as surely as he'd done her thigh on the outside.

Sabra kissed him back just as fiercely, her mouth a hot, sweet cavern, her tongue clashing with his as she sought to take his essence.

The sex was pure hedonistic heat, a ravenous hunger to possess and mark, her teeth nipping at the pulse on the side of his neck before she sealed around it and sucked, marking him, while he tangled his fingers in her silken tresses, holding her head to him as she marked him, revelling in the eroticism of her possessive streak.

The hunger ate at them, pushing them higher, their carnal fire blazing out of control as their rapacity forged hotter, more desperate, a complete furnace of sexual need.

They teetered on the edge of the cliff, the fires consuming them, and with one last hard shove of his hips, Cam flung them both out into a sea of pure eroticism. It sucked them down, crashed them high, shattered their souls, and hurled them out into a million prisms of prurience as one orgasm followed another.

~ * ~

When Sabra opened her eyes, she found her arms trembling,

her fingers buried deep in the wild black curls that covered half her face and spilled over her shoulders to mingle with her own hair on the pillows.

"Oh my God," she whispered, turning her head to bury her face deeper into the thick curls, sucking Cam's scent deep into her lungs as she tried to steady her ragged breathing.

Slumped over her, his complete weight resting on her for the first time she could ever remember, Cam snuggled closer into her, his massive chest flattening her breasts, his strong, muscular legs entwined with her own slender ones.

The last she remembered, her knees had been locked in the crook of his elbows keeping her open for him. Stars knew when he'd let her go.

His curls slid across her face and realizing he was turning his head on the pillow beside her, she reached up with one trembling hand and brushed his curls back over his broad shoulders. Dark eyes, hot and heavy and slumberous, met hers. The flush of sexual desire still faintly coloured the strong cheekbones, and his lips were slightly swollen from her ravenous kisses.

He looked as thoroughly loved as she felt. Sabra grinned. "Hello."

His dark eyes were suddenly alert, his gaze sweep over her face. "Did I hurt you?"

"Nay." Laying her hand against his chin, she ran her thumb along his lower lip. "Did I hurt you?"

His smile was slow and filled with complete, masculine satisfaction. "Nay."

"Oh my God, Cam, what did you do to me?" She shook her head. "I never thought it could be so good when..." He arched one brow, and she knew full well he knew what she meant. Grabbing a silken curl, she gave it a sharp tug, not enough to hurt, but enough to give him warning.

He laughed again. Coming up on one elbow, he slid one big hand behind her head. "You taste like sugar and spice."

Sabra's cheeks crimsoned.

"Down below," he whispered huskily, "You taste like spice. I could eat you all day, wench."

Stars above! Not expecting those words, Sabra stared up at him.

"And above here..." He licked across her lips, avoiding her mouth teasingly when she opened on a sigh. "You taste like sugar."

"You're a sweet talker."

"I but speak the truth." Lifting his head, he shifted over her, resting his forearms either side of her so that he took most of his upper weight on his arms, causing his massive biceps to bulge. His expression grew serious. "Do you still fear the intimacy of oral sex?"

Her cheeks crimsoned but she kept her gaze steady. "Nay."

Framing her cheeks with his hands, he rubbed his thumbs tenderly along her cheekbones. "Thank you for trusting me, Sabra."

"Thank you for being so patient." She slid her hands up his sides, her fingertips caressing over hard muscles. "I think I'm ready for anything with you now."

"You think?" His dark eyes started to twinkle. "Do I have to persuade you some more?"

"I know I'm ready for anything with you now," she corrected.

"My good, obedient little wench."

"At least," she amended, "I'm ready for anything with you."

His brows lowered in a mock frown. "'Twill only ever be with me."

"Now, now, lover boy, don't start getting cranky."

"Besides," he said, "once we're out of the house, everyone will know you belong to me."

Her hand went to her throat. "You marked me again, didn't you?"

"Just a little love bite."

Sabra rolled her eyes.

Cam's eyes gleamed wickedly. "It matches the one you gave

me."

"You wish!"

"Don't believe me, wench?" He tossed the cascading, wild curls over one shoulder and turned his head. "Take a good look at the love bite you gave me in the throes of our little encounter."

Sabra didn't know whether to be mortified or laugh when she saw the mark on his throat. It was there, undeniable, a love bite on the smooth skin of his throat. Now she remembered tasting him, the pulse beneath her tongue, her lips fastening on his skin... "Oops."

"Oops?" Cam tuned his head back to gaze down at her. "'Tis all you have to say?"

"Um..."

"You do know what everyone is going to say when they see this love bite on my neck?"

"You'll just have to wear your hair loose until it fades."

"Not bloody likely. I'm tying my hair back and showing the world what a ferocious little wench you are."

She grinned up at him. "Come on, you don't want everyone to know that 'tis not only you marking me!"

"I never guessed how wild you could be."

"You were mostly to blame for that."

"Oh, aye." His grin was supremely male. "I am."

She smacked him on his massive triceps.

"And now the whole of Daamen will see how wild I make you. Wild enough to mark me."

"And what about when they see your love bite on my neck?"

"They'll know we had a hell of a wild sex session."

"Oh, shit."

Cam started to laugh.

Sabra couldn't control her own amusement, even though she was a little mortified that anyone seeing their necks would know, and boy, Dana and Delias were going to make sure she didn't live that down.

Leaning down, Cam kissed the tip of her nose. "So, little

sugar and spice, shall we go and sample that cake?"

Sabra's cheeks flushed. "Sugar and spice?"

"Oh aye." His eyes gleamed. "And I'll be wanting another sample of that sugar and spice later."

Just the thought had her all hot and flustered.

Laughing, Cam rolled off her, pushing to his feet and stretching leisurely. As she came up on her knees, Sabra ran her gaze appreciatively over him. The muscles in his tall, strong body bunched and stretched, his long, wild curls reaching halfway down his back. Even the muscles in his backside were toned and hard.

Turning, he caught her look and grinned. "Like what you see?"

"The scenery is rather interesting."

"Cheeky wench." Catching her hand, Cam pulled her to the edge of the big bed.

Laughing, Sabra swung her legs over, felt a twinge and glanced down. Well, what else could she expect? She'd been in a position previously untried before, and - "What is that?"

"Hmmm?" Cam's face was innocent.

Standing up, Sabra placed one foot up on the mattress and looked at her inner thigh. What she saw made her gasp. "Cam!"

His grin was hedonistically wicked.

She dropped her foot back to the floor and frowned up at him. "What is that all about?"

"That, little sugar and spice, is the mark I'm going to be giving you right before you go off to work, the mark I'll be giving you if our paths cross while we're both working, and the mark I'll be giving you when we return home here. By the way, when we return home here, you'll still be getting my love bite on your neck as well."

Hands on her hips, she frowned at him, but inside her heart leaped. "'Tis so?"

"Aye." Moving fast, he bent forward, slinging one arm behind her thighs and his shoulder into her stomach.

She shrieked, tried to back away, but it was too late. He straightened and she found herself slung over his shoulder. "You big oaf! What are you doing?"

His hand patted her bare bottom. "'Tis time to feed your lord and master."

"Naked?"

"Why bother getting dressed?" He strode from their room and she admired the play of muscle in his tight buttocks from her upside down position.

"You have a nice arse," she commented.

"Why, thank you, lass. So do you." He rubbed her bottom, his fingers deliberately slipping to rub against her exposed femininity.

Heat immediately flooded through her and she gave him a sharp pinch on one hard, muscled buttock.

Cam nearly dropped her, which started her laughing. Regaining his equilibrium, he gave her bottom a harder pat. "Behave yourself, wench."

"Ooohhh, my lord and master."

"I do like hearing that." He strode down the stairs. "Say it again."

"Once a day is your limit, lover."

"I have a limit?"

"'Tis either that or we'll not get your huge ego through the door."

"I'm hurt."

She patted his buttock, deliberately letting her finger trace down the crease separating the hard globes.

"Shit, Sabra!" Cam exclaimed as he nearly dropped her again.

Sabra laughed.

Cam hurried down the last few steps and swung into the kitchen. Bending, he placed Sabra on her feet and straightened, ensuring he had his arm around her waist to hold her close while she regained her balance.

"Wow," Sabra remarked with a huge grin. "You make my head swim, lover boy."

"You make me hot and bothered."

"So I can feel against my belly."

"You, wench, are incorrigible."

"Only around you."

His gaze softened, the amusement fading to be replaced with tenderness. His fingers trailed beneath her chin, tipping her head back so he could kiss her lightly on the lips. Warmth flooded her and she nestled closer.

Leaning his forehead against hers, he looked deeply into her eyes. "I love you, Sabra."

"I love you, Cam."

Their kiss was loving, gentle, and when he drew his lips from hers, she looked up at him with a small smile on her lips.

"About that cake," he whispered.

"Aye?"

"I've changed my mind."

She raised her brows. "I assure you, 'tis good cake."

"I think I'll be having some sugar and spice first."

"Well, now that you've tasted sugar and spice, as you call it," she rubbed against him, feeling his staff press hard against her belly, "Having your fantasy, so to say, I think 'tis my turn."

One dark brow arched. "Oh?"

"Aye. I think I want to taste some cream."

For several seconds he was stunned, then her meaning dawned on him and he gaped down at her.

"Fair turn about, lover boy," she cooed. "After all, 'twas you who said we'll do anything we wish in our love making and -" She shrieked as he bent and slung her back over his shoulder.

The trip up the stairs was the fastest she'd ever had in her life.

####

OUTLAW	**MERCENARY**	**BETRAYED**	**ASSASSIN**
ANGELA VERDENIUS	ANGELA VERDENIUS	ANGELA VERDENIUS	ANGELA VERDENIUS
HUNTER	**THIEF**	**FORSAKEN**	**WITCH**
ANGELA VERDENIUS	ANGELA VERDENIUS	ANGELA VERDENIUS	ANGELA VERDENIUS
TRAITOR	**FORGOTTEN**	**HEALER**	**PEACEKEEPER**
ANGELA VERDENIUS	ANGELA VERDENIUS	ANGELA VERDENIUS	ANGELA VERDENIUS
PREDATOR	**WARRIOR**	**SMUGGLER**	**GUARDIAN**
ANGELA VERDENIUS	ANGELA VERDENIUS	ANGELA VERDENIUS	ANGELA VERDENIUS

MOMENTS

ANGELA VERDENIUS

Read on for all books available now in ebook and print.

BIO

*

Angela lives in Australia, where she is happily ruled by her cats. When not reading, at work as a nurse, or watching horror movies, she can usually be found at her trusty computer…procrastinating by cruising the internet looking for funny cat clips and upcoming spooky movies.

Angela has written sci-fi romances, BBW contemporary romances, 2 novellas, and several short stories, one of which is a zombie story she had great fun writing (because zombies rule and are the coolest of the monsters).

Newsletter for updates & new releases:
http://www.angelaverdenius.com/

Connect with her on:

Goodreads:
https://www.goodreads.com/author/show/34381.Angela_Verdenius

Amazon:
https://www.amazon.com/Angela-Verdenius/e/B003GHWB9C

Book Bub: https://www.bookbub.com/authors/angela-verdenius

Keep reading for a list of all available books in both ebook and print

Other Books by this Author
*

Contemporary Romances

Big Girls Lovin' trilogy
Doctor's Delight
Cop's Passion
Vet's Desire

The Lawson Boys duet
The Lawson Boys: Alex
The Lawson Boys: Marty

The Virgin Sex Queen

The Mackay Sisters duet
Call on Me
Lean on Me

Seducing Sam
Adam's Thorn
The Goodbye Girl

The Gully's Fall series
Burn for You
Fall for You
Lie to Me
Fly with Me
You're the One
Second Chance

Promises

The Wells Brothers trilogy
The Wells Brothers: Luke

The Wells Brothers: Aaron
The Wells Brothers: Blue

Echoes

Hope Bay series
Secrets

<u>Novellas Contemporary Holiday Romance</u>

Christmas Blue at Flynn's

<u>Heart & Soul sci-fi romance series</u>

Outlaw
Mercenary
Betrayed
Assassin
Hunter
Thief
Forsaken
Witch
Traitor
Forgotten
Healer
Peacekeeper
Predator
Warrior
Smuggler
Guardian
Moments

<u>Novellas sci-fi</u>
Operation Seduction (BBW)
Blast from the Past

<u>*Free Short Stories*</u>
Zombie Hospital
Perceptions

www.ingramcontent.com/pod-product-compliance
Lightning Source LLC
Chambersburg PA
CBHW061507120726
48001CB00004B/1249